We hope you enjoy this book. Please return or renew it by the due date.

You can renew it at www.norfolk.gov.uk/libraries or by using our free library app.

Otherwise you can phone 0344 800 8020 - please have your library card and PIN ready.

You can sign up for email reminders too.

NORFOLK ITEM

30129 083 035 106

NORFOLK COUNTY COUNCIL
LIBRARY AND INFORMATION SERVICE

D1424554

ALSO BY SIBEL HODGE

Fiction

Beneath the Surface
Duplicity (DS Carter Book 1)
Untouchable (Mitchell and Maya Book 1)
Where the Memories Lie
Look Behind You
Butterfly
Trafficked: The Diary of a Sex Slave
Fashion, Lies, and Murder (Amber Fox Mystery No 1)
Money, Lies, and Murder (Amber Fox Mystery No 2)
Voodoo, Lies, and Murder (Amber Fox Mystery No 3)
Chocolate, Lies, and Murder (Amber Fox Mystery No 4)
Santa Claus, Lies, and Murder (Amber Fox Mystery No 4.5)
Vegas, Lies, and Murder (Amber Fox Mystery No 5)
Murder and Mai Tais (Danger Cove Cocktail Mystery No 1)
Killer Colada (Danger Cove Cocktail Mystery No 2)
The See-Through Leopard
Fourteen Days Later
My Perfect Wedding
The Baby Trap
It's a Catastrophe

Non-Fiction

A Gluten Free Taste of Turkey
A Gluten Free Soup Opera
Healing Meditations for Surviving Grief and Loss

INTO THE THE DARKNESS

SIBEL HODGE

Text copyright © 2018 by Sibel Hodge
All rights reserved.

Published by Thomas & Mercer, Seattle

www.apub.com

Amazon, the Amazon logo, and Thomas & Mercer are trademarks of Amazon.com, Inc., or its affiliates.

ISBN-13: 9781503905504
ISBN-10: 1503905500

Cover design by @blacksheep-uk.com

Printed in the United States of America

INTO
THE
DARKNESS

PART ONE

Hell is empty and all the devils are here

William Shakespeare

THE MISSING

Chapter 1

It was a mistake, that's all. A stupid, stupid mistake. We all make them – it doesn't matter if it's a calculated risk or à split-second decision, but sometimes we're only one step away from disaster.

I *had* to see if what she'd said was real, though. I thought she was winding me up. Messing around. Trying to scare me. Like those stupid ghost stories we'd told each other on sleepovers when we were little kids; a torch held under our chins in the darkness, pulling creepy faces at each other. But she was right. It was all real. Everything she warned me about and more. Much more. I knew a lot, but this stuff was beyond any gruesome nightmare.

I don't know why I've always been interested in the evil things people do. I'm not alone, I know that. People who devour true crime stories. People who watch the horrors on the news every day or read about them in the paper. People who rubberneck at accidents. They want to see it, hear it, talk about it. The dark side of human nature is fascinating to people. We're so obsessed with all the bad things that happen in the world and not with the good. But what factors trigger vicious acts of violence? That question was always at the forefront of my mind. Could you ever get a proper answer? And if you did, would it be the same answer for every inhumane person out there? Why did some people do those things? Because there have always been *doers*. Right back to the beginning of time, evil has existed in human form. But the *followers* interested me, too. Why did some people watch and do nothing? What made some watchers join the doers?

I wasn't just researching it for sick, twisted reasons, though. I was obsessed with it all, yes, but I wanted to use it to do something good. For me, the main reason for trying to understand those kinds of people was that if we didn't know *why* they did what they did, we couldn't try to fix it. We couldn't stop it happening again and again. And to understand why, you had to get inside their minds and find the reason.

I know a lot of my co-students call me weird. What eighteen-year-old has hardly any friends and isn't interested in clubbing and getting drunk, and make-up and guys? That stuff bores me. It isn't important. It's just candy floss: materialistic, superfluous. When there are so many real horrors and crimes going on in the world, how can I obsess and fawn over celebrities or whether my hair looks trendy or pout for a selfie? I don't care about any of that.

Mum always said I was ahead of my years, and she's right. From an early age I felt like I had a life purpose. I wanted to help heal people who had been hurt. In the beginning I didn't know why. It was just how I was; something I felt in my heart. Until I learned about empaths and how they literally experience and feel the pain of others as if it's their own. That's when I got it and everything kind of clicked into place. Ever since I was a kid, I've felt the pain of others. And I want to leave behind a legacy of doing something really useful with my life.

But now I'm stuck in the nightmare of my own questions. I don't think I'm going to get out alive. Not after what I've seen.

I shouldn't have gone down there.

I shouldn't have gone into the darkness.

THE DETECTIVE
Chapter 2

I had two weeks left. Two weeks as a Detective Sergeant in CID before I left and started a new job in a new unit in a new city. This meant masses of paperwork and tying up loose ends. In my twenty-five years as a detective, the paperwork had increased to ridiculous proportions. You couldn't even get a paperclip these days without the proper paperwork. Then there were the stupid training days. Diversity training was the latest trend. Thank God I'd be missing out on that. The force had become one long chain of bureaucracy, meetings about meetings, and general time-wasting that actually prevented us from doing our jobs at a time when we were so short-staffed.

DI Ellie Nash had headhunted me for my forthcoming job at the newly formed National Wildlife Crime Enforcement Unit in London. I never thought I'd say 'headhunted' and 'me' in the same sentence. I mean, I was good at my job: tenacious, focused, determined. But I knew I was a maverick. Old school. I hated the political crap and the brown-nosing that went with the job and I'd needed a change for a long time. So when Ellie had asked me to join her, I'd jumped at the chance. Ever since the death of my wife, Denise, I'd been depressed, feeling like I was swimming underwater, and CID had been doing my head in. But now, as the time to move crept closer, the excitement about the prospect of a new start was wearing off and I was seriously thinking I'd made the wrong decision. At my age, change was scary. Plus, my last case had affected me more than I wanted to admit to anyone. It had resulted in my colleague, DS Richard Wilmott, being killed in the line of duty. No one blamed me, but I felt the guilt deep in my gut, twisting every now and then. The world was becoming more dangerous and disturbed, and I was also getting to that age when I'd started realising I wasn't invincible. I'd been questioning my own mortality. How long did I have left? And did I really want to spend it putting in paperwork requests for bloody pencils with a side order of possible death on duty?

On top of all that, I'd worked on some cases recently where the offender had walked away scot-free. I loved my job, but I didn't think justice was actually served much these days. And spending painstakingly long hours conducting enquiries and interviews to build a case, putting heart and soul into it all, only for the guilty to walk, free to commit another violent crime, was as heartbreaking as it was infuriating. The trouble was, no one thought about the victims any more. It was all about human rights for the criminal. *In*justice was the name of the game now.

So I'd been thinking, again, about retiring. Giving it all up and walking away. Taking up golf or something. It was better than getting stabbed to death. I'd even been looking up completely different jobs in the classifieds. I could work part-time for one of those big companies who have car parking security, sitting in a booth all day checking vehicles in and out. And the only danger or stress I'd have to worry about was dropping the barrier on my foot or getting a paper cut from reading a magazine to while away the hours.

Who are you kidding, Carter? You'd be bored out of your head.

I shuffled the paperwork on my desk into a neat pile, looked at the clock, which read 7.16 p.m., and stuck it all back in my in-tray to finish off tomorrow. The office was empty. Both DC Becky Harris and DC Ronnie Pickering had gone home an hour ago.

I stood up, arched my back to work out the kinks embedded deep in the muscles from hunching over the desk and glanced around. Would I really miss this place or not? I was becoming more indecisive with age.

My mobile rang as I was contemplating that question.

'DS Carter,' I answered.

'Hi, sarge, it's Kim in the control room. You're the on-call CID, aren't you?'

'Yeah. What have you got for me?' I perched on the edge of my desk.

'A double shooting of a couple at Beech Lodge in Turpinfield. Mr and Mrs Jameson were found by their daughter, who called it in. Uniform were despatched and they found a deceased male and female victim with gunshot wounds. The daughter, Mrs Eagan, is still at the house. SOCO are en route.'

I sighed. A shooting? What the hell was wrong with everyone in the world? Why couldn't people just get along with each other? 'OK, give me the address.'

She rattled it off and I scribbled it down. Then I hurried from the building and got in my car.

Turpinfield was en route to nowhere in particular so I'd only ever driven through it a few times. A small hamlet with a handful of houses and farms separated by acres and acres of agricultural fields and woods.

I headed down a country lane, past Simms Livery Stables, and the next property I came to was Beech Lodge. I turned into a long driveway, the car bumping over ruts in the old concrete, my headlights sweeping over waist-high fields of rapeseed either side. At the end I found an old, traditional-style farmhouse made of red brick with several outbuildings and barns off to the sides.

A scene-of-crime van was already parked up next to a police car. There was also an old Land Rover Defender and a Mini. I pulled to a stop, then called the control room to log my arrival. After retrieving a white forensic jumpsuit from my boot, I pulled it on, along with some latex gloves, and entered the house.

I logged my arrival with the male uniformed officer standing on the front step and walked through the front door. The property opened up into a hallway with flagstone floors worn smooth over the years. To my right was an open doorway. A lounge with one duck-egg blue sofa, one armchair, two dead bodies, a lot of blood, and one SOCO crouching down over the male victim, taking photos.

The SOCO was a replica of me, suited in white, with a mask covering her face. I saw a flash of brilliant red hair poking out of the hood and felt relieved it was Emma Bolton, a senior SOCO, dealing with the job in hand. She was meticulous, conscientious and down-to-earth.

'All right, sarge?' She glanced over at me before taking another photo.

'I would be if people didn't keep getting murdered all the time.'

'Then you'd be out of a job.' She winked.

'Yeah. But maybe that would be a good thing.' I stepped into the room and surveyed the scene. No matter how many times I'd seen a violent death, I never got used to the anger and hopelessness it ignited in me.

The couple were probably in their early seventies, both dressed casually in jeans and shirts. The male victim was lying closer to the door I'd just walked through, near the armchair, flat on his back. His arms were thrown out wide either side of him. He'd been shot in the chest, leg and forehead. The female was half lying, half sitting against the far wall next to the end of the sofa, her legs splayed out in front of her, her chin resting on her chest, eyes wide open. A moccasin slipper had fallen off her right foot. There was a lot of blood spatter around her and against the wall behind her and I could see a gunshot wound on the side of her neck. On the sofa was a paperback book face down next to a bookmark. In front of the sofa was a coffee table with spatters of blood on it and a cordless landline handset. At the side of the coffee table was a black handbag. There were more blood droplets on the carpet. 'Anything helpful you can tell me yet?' I asked.

Emma stood. 'It's a bit early for that; I just got here. I can tell you they've been dead a while. I'd hazard a guess and say about thirty-six hours. No sign of a weapon so far, though.'

I looked at the open patio door that led to the rear garden. A security light was blazing, illuminating the large, grassy area. At the end of the grass the shadows of trees loomed where their property bordered some woodland. Another white-suited figure held a powerful torch as they took slow, methodical steps up the grass towards the woods.

'Was the patio door open or closed when you got here?' I asked.

'Open. The daughter said she knocked on the front door, and when her parents didn't answer she got worried and used her key. She found them like this, and then went back outside the front door to call uniform. No signs of forced entry anywhere.'

'So did they open the front door to their killer, or did the gunman come in through here?' I said, thinking out loud, stepping closer to the patio doors. I took another step and my foot hovered in the air as I spotted something embedded in the carpet, near some blood droplets and what looked like soil ingrained in the green pile weave.

I crouched down, my knees cracking in response, and stared at the item. 'Got something here you need to bag.'

Emma made her way towards me, took a photo of what I was pointing at and then pulled out a plastic evidence bag from her case on the floor.

She picked up the small, pink stone with a pair of long tweezers, eyeing it carefully. It had what looked like yellow glue on the underside.

'Looks like it's come from clothing or some kind of costume jewellery. Not a real gem.' She bagged it.

I glanced at Mrs Jameson. She wore a gold wedding band, a gold bangle and a gold necklace. No sign of any pink jewellery or clothing the stone could've fallen from.

I stood up, my knees groaning again, and turned to survey both bodies.

Emma walked towards the wall behind Mrs Jameson, staring at it. 'There's a bullet lodged in the brickwork. I'll collect it after I've finished photographing everything, but it looks like that's where the female victim was standing when she was shot. The bullet hit her carotid artery, which resulted in the blood being sprayed in huge spurts initially. You can see from the spatter that it gradually diminished as she collapsed to the floor and died. But the pattern of blood spatter around her is interesting.'

I walked to where she was pointing at the wall behind and to the right of where Mrs Jameson's body now lay slumped against it. To the right of the bullet hole, in amongst the arterial spray, was a circular shape, roughly five feet up the wall.

'If there's an object in the way when the blood begins to spurt out, it will block it from striking a nearby surface – in this case the wall. The object leaves a void. A kind of reverse mark, if you like.' She paused, her latex-covered fingertip tracing around the shape without touching it. 'I think this is the shape of someone's head, which blocked some of the victim's blood from hitting the wall. Someone was standing next to her when she was shot.'

I glanced at Mr Jameson. 'There's no spatter covering him or his clothes. And anyway, he's probably over six foot tall.'

'If it was him, you'd expect to see a different pattern in that spot, the shape of his shoulder or chest.'

'Could it have been the shooter?'

'No, the gunshot wounds aren't that close range.'

'So either two offenders or a witness who hasn't come forward yet.'

'Yes. Someone about . . .' She tilted her head and stared at the wall. 'About five foot tall.'

THE VIGILANTE

Chapter 3

Pure evil. I'd it seen it too many times in my life, and there were three things I'd learned about it. The first was that it could be disguised as many things. Monsters weren't just for fairy tales and horror stories. They weren't just the Jeffrey Dahmers or the Myra Hindleys. We brushed shoulders with them every day as they walked amongst us, unseen for what they truly were. Your friend, your work colleague, your neighbour, your brother.

Secondly, if you knew about evil and did nothing, it made you complicit – maybe an unwilling pawn in a game played by others for a higher purpose, but just as dangerous nevertheless. Inaction was still an action.

I drew my gaze away from the paperback I was trying to read and watched Maya. She sat in a chair, doing leg-extension exercises with ankle weights that the physio had given her to help strengthen the muscles that had atrophied and weakened while she'd been wearing a cast. From the look in her eyes I knew she was thinking about the night she'd nearly died. She was still in pain from her injuries, but she was lucky she'd escaped without any brain damage. Lucky she was alive. The men who'd hurt her were evil personified. They'd tried to shut Maya up for good so they could keep their barbaric secrets hidden, and she'd been in a coma for six weeks. When she woke up she'd had intensive physiotherapy to help heal her battered body – a broken leg, arm, ribs, and several fingers and toes. The internal and external bruising had now gone, but the scars inside would last forever. I understood completely. The same scars ravaged me.

Maya bit the corner of her lower lip, her forehead scrunched slightly with the exertion, sweat beading on her upper lip. She glanced towards the sofa where I sat, and pulled a face. 'Stop watching me, Mitchell. You're putting me off.'

I held my hands up in mock surrender. 'Sorry.' I grinned to myself. If she was getting fussy, hopefully it meant she was getting better.

'No, *I'm* sorry. I'm just finding it really hard to move on.' Maya's voice was small and laced with all the emotions I knew so well: heart-shattering grief, longing, rage; fear of what her life would be like now. She unstrapped the weights, threw them to the carpet, and swung around to face me, her eyes filled with unshed tears. 'Jamie's gone.' Her voice cracked. 'I have no home. I have no job any more. I have no future.' She wiped at the tears spilling down her cheeks with her fingertips. 'I don't know what to do with my life.'

'Hey, hey, hey.' I put the paperback on to the sofa cushion beside me, then kneeled down in front of her. I took her hand and clutched it in mine. 'You've got a home.' I gestured around my living room with a hand. She'd sold her own house – Jamie's house – to get away from the memories of her boyfriend's murder and was living with me until she worked out the next stage of her life. But Maya was stuck now, in limbo, waiting for the pain of losing Jamie to get less raw and visceral. Waiting to find a new direction in life. To redirect the anger somewhere else. Waiting to find some meaning to existing. It was Maya who'd given *me* meaning again. I owed her a debt I couldn't repay. She said she owed me for keeping her alive. Those men wouldn't trouble her again – I took care of that. Through the hell of it all, she'd slowly become like a daughter to me, and I wanted to help her get through this but I didn't know what else I could do.

'I can't keep taking your charity by staying here.'

'It's not charity.' When I'd left the SAS I'd worked for a private military company and made more money than I knew what to do with. Until I woke up to all the lies and bullshit we were being force-fed. Until I realised that psychopaths and monsters actually ruled the world and were the ones dishing out orders with hidden agendas. The politicians, corporations and banksters who watched the wars and devastation and destruction they wreaked upon every single one of us unfold as planned. Who proved time and time again that ordinary, innocent people were dispensable.

'I feel like I need to stand on my own two feet. I used to be independent. Before . . .' Her voice hitched. 'Before they took Jamie away from me. I can't rely on you all the time. Or Ava. She's got Jackson to look after.'

'Ava loves you. You're her sister, of course she wants to help you. And your future can be anything you want it to be.' I knew how she felt, though. Knew putting one foot in front of the other every second of every day could be torture. I wrapped my arm around her. 'You're still young. And Jamie would want you to live your life again. You're so strong, you can do anything.' Even when she'd almost been killed trying to expose those men and what they'd done, she'd found a strength from somewhere to carry on and not give in.

'But I don't know *what* to do now.' She rested her head on my shoulder.

'So don't think about it. Just see what happens and the answer will come. You're still recuperating. Don't be so hard on yourself.'

'I can't stay here forever. It's not fair on you.'

I put my hands on her shoulders and looked into her eyes. 'Like I said before, you can stay as long as you like. And you're doing me a favour being here, believe me.' I was about to say more but my mobile phone rang from the arm of the sofa. I glanced at it – it wasn't a number I recognised. I looked back to Maya.

'It's OK. Take it.' She wiped her eyes and rubbed at her right thigh, where her femur had been broken, wincing slightly at the pain and trying to hide it.

I hit the answer button and a desperate voice catapulted me back to the past.

You see the third thing about evil is, even if you eliminate one manifestation of it, there will always be more.

THE DETECTIVE
Chapter 4

I walked into the kitchen and found the Jamesons' daughter, Paula Eagan, sitting at a pine table next to a female uniformed officer. Paula was maybe early forties and dressed in a crisp, white shirt and pale-blue skirt. She wore a lot of dark eye make-up which had run around her lids and down the side of her cheeks from her tears. She stared into space, lips pressed tightly together, a balled-up tissue clutched in one hand.

The officer gave me a relieved smile, stood up and introduced Paula to me.

'Thanks,' I said to her.

She nodded and slipped out of the room.

'I'm DS Warren Carter.' I sat down in the seat the officer had just vacated, the wooden chair retaining her heat.

Paula fixed her watery eyes on me. 'I just can't believe this.' She shook her head and squeezed the tissue in her fist.

'I'm very sorry for your loss.'

She mumbled, 'Thanks. I can't take this in. I just don't understand. Who could've done something so . . . so awful?'

'Well, that's what I'm here to find out,' I said gently. 'Can you tell me what happened when you arrived and found your parents?'

She sucked in a deep breath and blew it out again. 'I got here about six and . . . I knocked on the door. There was no reply, so I knocked a few more times and then I thought something was wrong. Their Land Rover was outside so I knew they were in. It's miles to anywhere from here, you need a car, and they normally eat dinner at this time so I knew they wouldn't be out walking. I looked through the lounge window and . . .' She took a deep breath. Held it. Exhaled and closed her eyes. 'I saw them lying there. I used my key to get in and . . .' She pressed her lips together and blinked rapidly.

'It's OK. Take your time.'

'I . . . um . . . I found them in the lounge like that. Were they shot?' She looked at me wild-eyed. 'I saw this . . .' She pointed to her forehead. 'A hole. On Dad. It was a bullet hole, wasn't it?'

'Yes. I'm sorry.'

'Oh, God!' She brought the shaking hand that was clutching the tissue to her lips and pressed it against her mouth so hard her lips distorted.

'Did you touch them or move anything when you saw them?'

'No, I just . . .' She looked blank. 'Um . . . I . . . kneeled down beside them and looked and I called their names, but I knew . . . I mean, I could tell they were dead and . . . they weren't breathing. I screamed, I think. And then I went outside and called you and they told me to wait, so I did.'

'You didn't open the patio doors in the lounge?'

'No, they were like that when I got here. I definitely didn't touch anything.'

'Did your parents normally leave the doors open like that? Or were they usually locked?'

She shrugged. 'Well, it depends on the weather. They might've had it open. It's been quite mild lately, and they liked to get a bit of fresh air in.'

'Was it a prearranged visit? Did they know you were coming?'

'No. It was . . .' She hesitated a moment. 'Kind of a surprise. They weren't expecting me.'

'When did you last speak to your parents?'

'Um . . . a few days ago, on the phone. Monday night. Well, I spoke to Mum.'

'So you didn't visit them yesterday?'

'No. I was . . . at work.' She stumbled over the words slightly.

Statistically speaking, most murders were committed by people who knew the victims. And I was pretty sure she'd just told me a lie. 'Where do you work?'

'Um . . . Eagan's Scaffolding. It's my husband's company. I do admin and the books there.'

'Do you know if your husband spoke to or saw your parents recently?'

A flush crept up her neck. 'No. He's always busy working.'

I observed her for a moment, detecting a hint of defensiveness. 'Can you think of anyone who'd want to hurt your parents?'

'Not at all.'

'Did your mum mention anything about any problems they were having when you spoke to her last? Anyone suspicious hanging around here? Or any worries they might've had?'

She shook her head.

'Are your parents farmers? I noticed the rapeseed at the front of their property as I came in.'

'Not any more. They retired five years ago. They rent out the fields now to a neighbour who still farms.'

'And his name is?'

'Bill Graves. His property is the next one along the lane – Turpinfield Farm.' She jerked her thumb to the left, indicating the direction.

I wrote that down in my pocketbook. 'Did your parents keep any valuables in the house?'

'No. They don't own anything really valuable. Mum had some gold jewellery that's been in her family for years. A couple of rings, a brooch, and a gold watch. I doubt it was worth much, more sentimental value. They didn't keep much money in the house.'

'What can you tell me about your parents?'

'Well . . . they're just retired farmers.' She shrugged.

'Can you think of any reason why someone would want to hurt them?'

'Of course not!' She gasped. 'They're an old couple. They like gardening and reading and walking.'

'Did they have any access to firearms?' The control room had already told me there were no firearms licences listed at this address, but I had to ask. A lot of rural farmers had shotguns or rifles for protecting livestock, or protecting crops from game birds and other animals.

'God, no.'

'Do you have any idea what their movements would've been? Did your mum mention what they'd be doing when you spoke to her?'

'She didn't say. But Dad has had this flu bug that's going round. For the last couple of weeks he's been pretty poorly. He's only just started getting over it so he was taking it easy and Mum was just looking after him. She didn't mention they were going out or doing anything.'

'What would their usual routines be?'

Paula shrugged. 'They both get up early, about five a.m. Dad's usually pottering around the house, fixing something, or doing gardening with Mum. Mum likes to read. They both like walking in the fields. They're homebodies, really. Sometimes Mum meets up with her friends for a bit of shopping or a coffee, but other than that they don't really go anywhere much.'

'Can you think of any problems your parents were having? Did they mention any disputes with anyone?'

'No.'

'How about the neighbours? Did they get on with them?'

'Yes. Well, like I mentioned, they rent out their fields now to Bill Graves. The neighbour on the other side was an old lady called Emily Simms, but she's got dementia now and is in a home. Her son has power of attorney so he's selling the house and stables. The house is empty at the moment. The girl who runs the stables used to rent them off Emily and she's still there. For the time being, anyway, until it's sold.' She wiped her red nose on the tissue. 'The only other neighbour is behind.' She pointed out of the kitchen window towards the woods at the end of the long garden. 'Parker Farm. Mum and Dad used to be friendly with them but they died and left the place to their son, Connor, and they don't really see him any more.'

'What about any other issues? Financial problems? Marital problems? Was there anything else going on in their lives?'

'No, nothing I can think of. There were no problems.'

'OK. Is there anyone I can call for you? Any brothers or sisters?'

'It's just me. There are no other relatives left now.'

I nodded solemnly. 'Can you think of any other information that might be useful?'

'No.' She sat upright and wiped her eyes. 'My parents didn't have any enemies. They were good people. They grafted all their life. They were supposed to be enjoying their retirement.'

A brief thought flashed into my head that maybe I shouldn't retire after all. This couple had obviously worked hard and now look what had happened. At the time when they should've been able to finally relax and take it easy, their lives had been cruelly snatched away from them in a vicious irony. 'Right. Well, I think that's it for the moment, thank you.' I stood up. 'Our forensic team will be here for quite a while so I'm afraid you'll have to leave. Are you OK to drive? I take it that's your Mini out there?'

She nodded.

'Or would you like an officer to take you home?'

'I'm OK. I can drive.'

'Before you go, I'll just get one of the SOCOs to take your prints and DNA so we can use them for elimination.'

'Yes, of course.' She nodded quickly and stood.

And I couldn't help but notice that Paula was about five feet tall.

THE VIGILANTE
Chapter 5

I knew who it was as soon as she said, 'Is that Mitchell?'

Her voice had always been distinctive – hoarse, deep and with a faint trace of a Scottish accent from her parents.

'Corinne? Is that you?' I frowned, staring out through the patio doors into my garden.

'Yes. It's me.'

My mind wandered briefly back to the last time I'd seen her at Tony's funeral. And then she'd left Hereford. Left the support group of friends from the Regiment. Left everything and disappeared. It had been almost two decades since I'd last spoken to her.

'Wow! How are you? Where've you been? What have you been doing for the last eighteen years?'

'I'm sorry. I couldn't handle all the memories after . . . after Tony died. I had to get away,' she said. But she left the real words unspoken. *I blamed you. It was your fault.*

'You don't have to explain anything to me. But you know I was worried about you.'

Maya sloped out of the room, wanting to give me some privacy.

'Look, I'm calling about my daughter. She—'

'You have a daughter now? Congratulations.' I thought about how she and Tony had been trying for a baby before he was killed. I still missed him, my good mate, but I couldn't hold it against Corinne for finding happiness with another guy and starting a family. Happiness was something precious to hold on to in this world, and Tony would've wanted her to move on.

'Oh, God!' she wailed. 'I called her Toni, after him. He didn't leave me completely alone after all. But I didn't call you to reminisce about the past, Mitchell. You said something to me when I saw you that last time. You said—'

'If you ever need me, for anything, all you have to do is call and I'll be there.' I repeated the words I'd said the day they put Tony in the ground, even though Corinne had already turned and was walking away, not prepared to listen to me.

'Did you mean it? Because I need your help. I *really* need your help.' Fear and worry were obvious in her shuddering voice.

'Of course I meant it. What's happened?'

'Toni's gone missing. I reported it to the police but they believe she's just run away so I don't think they're taking it seriously. But she wouldn't do that. I know my daughter. She's not an angel but I know she'd never just run off and not tell me. The police said she's an adult now and has probably just gone off somewhere for a few days for a bit of space. They said thousands of youngsters run away from home every year. But I'm really scared. Something's happened to her, I know it. And I need your help to find her. You can do things the police can't.'

'Jesus, I'm sorry to hear she's disappeared. Of course I'll help you.'

'Thank you!' She breathed out a relieved sigh.

I walked into the kitchen, grabbed a pen and a pad and sat at the table. 'Where are you?'

'Bournewood. It's a small town in Buckinghamshire.'

'Where did Toni go missing from?'

'I . . . I don't know. The last time I saw her was at the house.'

22

'When did she disappear?'

'Yesterday.'

'All right. Look, you stay where you are and I'll get there as soon as I can. It will probably take me an hour or so from London, OK?'

She let out another wail and told me her address, which I scribbled down on the pad.

I hung up, tore off the sheet of paper and stuffed it in my pocket.

Maya entered the kitchen, her eyes still a little red from crying.

'I've got to go away,' I said, resting a hand on her arm and explaining how an old friend needed me to help find her missing daughter.

'God, how awful. She must be out of her mind with worry,' she replied.

'I'm leaving as soon as I can.' I made my way up the stairs to my bedroom and grabbed my daysack hidden in a secure location. I had no clue as to what I'd need but it was already filled with the things I'd used to dispose of the men who had hunted Maya. I pulled the items out, checking they were still in situ and in working order: wire-cutters, a camouflage net, binoculars, night-vision goggles, a Maglite torch with IR filter, an expanding ASP baton in a small pouch that could attach to my belt, a small but punchy taser, and a few other items. I packed some clothes in another daysack, and lastly grabbed my Glock 19 pistol, pancake holster, and double-mag carrier which I'd secrete into a hiding place I had constructed inside my pick-up truck.

'I'm coming with you.' Maya watched me from the doorway, bending and straightening her right hand where several fingers had been broken – more exercises she'd been given to help with mobility. 'I can help you try to find her.'

'Are you sure you're up to that? Why don't you stay here and rest?' I looked down at the gear, wondering what else I might need.

'I'm sick of resting! I've been doing nothing but resting since I got out of the hospital. Please, I want to help. I *need* to help. I need to do *something* useful.'

The tone of her voice stopped me. I looked up at her. Her eyes were steely dark, her jaw rigid. I'd seen that look before when she'd been trying to find out what had happened to Jamie. When she'd stopped at nothing trying to expose his killers. There was no question Maya would be an asset. She was strong, focused and determined. And she had a big heart. Besides, Maya was right. Maybe she needed to do this as much as I wanted her with me. It could give her life a sense of purpose again. Or at least stop her worrying about her own situation for a while. 'OK. Pack a few essentials and we'll leave in ten minutes.'

'I'll be ready.' She disappeared to her bedroom down the hall.

I replayed Corinne's words in my head.

If someone had harmed Tony and Corinne's daughter, I *would* kill again.

THE DETECTIVE
Chapter 6

I spent the next three hours at the Jamesons' property, checking out the house and outbuildings. Forensically, it was going to be a nightmare because there were three large barns, plus fields of rapeseed to the south, woods to the north and acres of land all around.

The Home Office pathologist, Professor Elizabeth Hanley, came and went. Her estimated time of death was between 8 a.m. and 11 a.m. the previous morning, but she hoped to narrow it down further during the post-mortem, which would be conducted early the next morning.

I left SOCO there at just gone midnight and headed back to the office to do a little research and call my boss to update him on the crime scene.

'Damn,' Detective Superintendent Greene said when I explained the situation. 'That's all we need. You're off in two weeks. I've still got no replacement for Richard Wilmott *or* a new DI since Ellie Nash left.'

'Yes, how inconvenient, having a couple of murders when we're so short-staffed. Maybe if we could cut down on paperwork we could free up a whole department,' I suggested.

Greene huffed down the phone. 'I'll have less of your sarcasm, Carter. You'll have to be SIO on this. You're all I've got. For the rest of the time you're with us, you can be acting DI.'

There was a time when that would've been music to my ears. But I'd always been too unorthodox and outspoken, too independent-minded to toe the party line, which had hampered my advancement up the promotion ladder. After Richard Wilmott had been killed in the line of duty, though, Greene had offered me the acting DI position. I'd handed my notice in instead and accepted DI Nash's offer to work with her on the new department being set up. Now, I was just confused. I didn't know what the hell I wanted any more. I was tired of it all. All the bullshit that went with the job. All the people getting away with offences. One thing was sure, though: even if I only had two weeks left, I'd do what I did best – solve crimes.

Greene didn't give me time to respond; he carried on by saying, 'Call a briefing for eight a.m.'

'Yes, sir.'

'And keep the forensics contained to just the house and very immediate grounds around it at this stage. We don't have the budget for searching twelve bloody acres of land!'

'Unfortunately, criminals aren't predisposed to conveniently leave evidence in only the immediate area of a crime scene.'

'Are you questioning an order from a superior officer?'

'Look, to restrict SOCO's sweep of the scene is dangerous. We have no direction of travel for the killer. They could've left through the open patio doors at the rear of the property, gone through the garden and into the woods. They could've disappeared through the field of rapeseed. They could've left to the east, through the livery stables, or gone west through Bill Graves's land. And there could be evidence in any of those places. Evidence that might never be found if we're hampered by budget constraints from the outset.' This was just one example of the bullshit I was sick of.

'When you control the budget, you can make those decisions. But until then, you'll follow my orders to the letter. I'll see you in the morning,' Greene said and hung up.

I grabbed a coffee from the vending machine in the hall. I looked at the murky, grey offering and wondered, not for the first time, if the canteen recycled their dirty dishwater in it. I sniffed it and pulled a face as I spotted a green blob of something I didn't want to analyse floating on the surface. I chucked it down the sink in the toilets and went back to the office, where I headed to the fridge in the corner of the room, on top of which sat the kettle that DC Ronnie Pickering was so protective over. No one else was allowed to touch the shiny chrome in case they got dirty fingerprints on it. Bless him. He definitely had a touch of OCD. Still, it meant no one else had to make the teas and coffees, which was always a bonus.

I measured out instant coffee granules, opened the fridge, and discovered some bugger had nicked our full, unopened pint of milk, along with a custard eclair that I'd put in there earlier that day. There were more thieves in a police station than anywhere else.

My stomach rumbled. I'd missed dinner earlier and was starving. So, the first job as acting DI would be to put a padlock on the fridge.

I sat at my desk and searched our various databases. Jan and Mike Jameson had reported no crimes in the past, and there'd been no previous incidents at the address. Neither of them had a criminal record. Their daughter, Paula, also wasn't known to police. Her husband, Grant, was a different story. He was forty-five years old with a string of arrests for drunk and disorderly, possession of cannabis, drink-driving. Last year, he'd been arrested after he'd ploughed into a roundabout while drunk, writing off his car. He'd been banned from driving for eighteen months.

I sat back and tapped my biro against my lips, thinking about Paula faltering with her words. The defensive note when I asked her about Grant. Maybe the Jamesons disapproved of their daughter's marriage to him, but was that enough for Paula or Grant to shoot them? Plenty of murders had occurred for less.

THE VIGILANTE
Chapter 7

I reversed my pick-up truck out of my driveway and on to the quiet North London street where I lived.

'So how do you know Corinne?' Maya asked, clutching the seatbelt across her chest for reassurance.

I glanced in the truck's mirrors after we pulled out on to the busier main road and caught Maya doing the same. The counter-surveillance techniques I'd taught her in the past were second nature to her now. And two pairs of eyes were always better than one. Not that I thought anyone was after her now, but it always paid to be vigilant. I was silent for a while but I wasn't concentrating on the road any more. I was seeing memories of another time. Another life. Another tragedy.

Maya's voice cut into the images. 'If this was eighteen years ago, I'm guessing you knew her from the SAS?'

I glanced over at her inquisitive face. Maya was the only person outside the Regiment I'd spoken to about some of the things I'd done. Things that still haunted me. In the weeks and months we'd spent together since Maya came out of the hospital, she'd wanted to talk about her own situation, and slowly I'd found myself opening up to her in a way I'd never done before. She was the one who'd made me admit to myself that the flashbacks and nightmares I'd been suffering from weren't healthy. That I shouldn't cling on to them because of the guilt that tore me up. She'd finally made me start to deal with the post-traumatic stress I was suffering from. And since she'd been living with me, things had been improving. The nightmares were getting less frequent. The flashbacks less intense. And because of what we'd been through together, we had a bond now that no one else could ever understand. I'd thought I'd been saving her, but she was really rescuing me.

'I was mates with Tony, her husband. We met during SAS selection.' A picture formed in my head – two younger guys passing each other in the freezing mist during the gruelling daily slogs over the Beacons, finishing Endurance together. To Brunei, in the trees, the same patrol during the jungle phase, and on the run and in the bag together during combat survival. 'After selection we both went to the same squadron.' I tried to blink away Tony's face from my mind and concentrate on the road ahead but it was no use. I could still remember the last time I saw him. It was emblazoned in my skull as clearly as if it was yesterday. 'He died in 1999, in West Africa. There was a civil war going on at the time, and the British Army was assisting in a multi-national stabilisation force in the country. But it was a nightmare. They weren't only trying to deal with the rebel groups and armed gangsters, the country's own army were corrupt, too.'

'So what happened?'

'There were many NGOs on the ground, trying to provide humanitarian assistance to the people, and they were suffering badly because of the violence going on – murder, mutilations, rapes, kidnapping, tit-for-tat assassinations. The country was practically lawless. There was an International Development team out there, trying to improve living conditions. One of their projects was a well-drilling programme to provide safe drinking water in a remote village. So the team went out to check on the project, escorted by a small British Army protective detail. But . . .' I trailed off, a rock-sized lump forming in my throat.

Maya waited.

I ground my teeth together. I hadn't told this story in a long time. And the person who should've heard it from me didn't want to listen.

'But what?' Maya pressed gently.

'But the team never came back. The last heard from them was an excited message from one of the soldiers in the call sign saying they'd driven into an illegal vehicle checkpoint and were surrounded by armed men. Then there was the sound of shouting and gunfire and communication was lost. A Quick Reaction Force was deployed and found there were signs of a fight. One British soldier was found dead at the scene.'

Maya gasped. 'And that was Tony?'

'No. That came later.' I gripped the steering wheel tight.

'What happened?'

'I killed him.'

'What?'

'I didn't pull the trigger, but he's dead because of me. Because I fucked up.'

Maya reached out and touched my arm. 'I'm so sorry.'

'Yeah. Me, too. It was my fault.' I hit the steering wheel hard, making Maya flinch.

'It wasn't your fault. There was a war going on. It was your job. It was the rebels that—'

I glanced over at her. 'Don't say it. You can't justify what happened. *I* can't justify it. It *was* my fault. And now Corinne needs me to find her daughter, I've got to do everything I can to make amends.' I shook my head to try and push away the past, took some breaths to slow the adrenaline pumping through me. Blinked a few times. Clutching the steering wheel even tighter, I explained, 'In Stirling Lines, we have a large clock with the names of all the guys who were killed in the line of duty. If your name's on it, it's because you "didn't beat the clock". Tony's name's there. He didn't beat the clock because of me. We buried him with full military honours in St Martin's Church. After the funeral

Corinne left Hereford. She didn't want to stay with all the reminders of the life they'd had together there. I didn't even know she was pregnant.'

'I can relate to Corinne wanting to move away after Tony's death,' Maya said, a thoughtful expression on her face. It was the same reason she'd sold her house after Jamie's death. It was too painful to stay.

'If Toni has run away, I'm going to find her. And if she's been taken by someone, then I won't stop until I catch who's responsible and get her back.'

We drove the rest of the way in silence as memories of Tony and Corinne wormed their way to the surface of my brain. Memories that had been dimmed over the years but not forgotten. Memories that I grasped on to again now and clutched tightly.

THE DETECTIVE

Chapter 8

I stifled a yawn as I stood in front of the whiteboard in the CID office, where I'd added the few details of the Jamesons' murder that I knew so far. I tacked up a satellite map of the Jamesons' property and surrounding houses and land and stepped back, studying the image.

By the time I'd finished up in the early hours of the morning, there had been barely enough time to go home, take a shower and change into a fresh set of clothes before heading back in to prepare for the briefing. I'd had no sleep, but then I was used to that. I'd turned into an insomniac in the year since Denise had died of breast cancer. There were too many questions rolling around in my head these days, and I didn't really like the answers.

I sipped a can of Coke and called the SOCO, Emma Bolton. 'How're you getting on?'

'I'm just heading back to the nick, going off duty. I've handed the scene over to the day shift. I was going to come up, anyway, and update you on what we've found so far.'

'Great, thanks. I'll see you soon.'

DC Ronnie Pickering bounded into the room, his permanently ruddy cheeks glowing, his hair still damp from the shower. He was like an excitable toddler who'd just discovered everything for the first time. Full of energy, which meant you could rely on him to do all the head-bangingly boring jobs and research that a lot of detective work involved without complaining, but his initiative and common sense were some-times lacking. And although he was an intelligent guy, his reasoning and logic teetered between being baffling and downright odd sometimes. I'd wondered on more than one occasion if he had a touch of autism.

'Morning, Ronnie,' I said.

'Morning, sarge.' He beamed a smile at me, then turned to the ket-tle and saw it had been moved out of its usual 45-degree angle against the wall that he rigidly lined it up to. He stared at it for a moment, horrified, then adjusted the kettle back into its required position. He moved the box of tea bags an inch over to the left and, satisfied, headed to his desk to dump his manbag.

I suppressed a smile and shook my head, wondering how he'd noticed the misalignment of the kettle but not that the massive white-board had a new case written on it. But our personal little quirks were a good thing when it came to a murder inquiry. Sometimes you couldn't see the wood for the trees, and it took an unusual or different perspec-tive to click something into place. Three people could look at the same thing and interpret it in three different ways.

'All right, all?' DC Becky Harris wandered in, stuffing a cereal bar in her mouth. 'Oh. You got a job after we'd gone?' She noticed the whiteboard immediately.

'Yes. A double murder. Greene will be here for the briefing in . . .' I glanced at the clock. 'Five minutes. So I'll explain all then.'

'Oh, God. Who are they bringing in to be SIO? Is there actually anyone left? It's like the *Mary Celeste* in here.' Becky shoved the last of the bar in her mouth, draped her coat on the back of her chair, and came to join me at the board, reading with interest.

'Me.'

She grinned. 'Really? That's great.'

'But you're going in two weeks,' Ronnie said as he joined us.

'Well, we'd better be quick then, eh?'

Detective Superintendent Greene stalked into the office behind us and got straight down to it. 'Right, what do we have? I've got an acute strategic budget-centric breakfast meeting in twenty minutes so please be quick.'

I wondered what that even meant in real-speak instead of corporate buzzword bollocks. 'What's that in English?'

'More central cost-cutting proposals,' he said, although he didn't sound quite sure, either.

'Are we actually police or accountants?' I asked.

He frowned at me as he perched on the end of a desk and put his briefcase down. We'd had our spats in the past. He'd suspended me before, and although in the aftermath of Wilmott's murder he'd offered me an acting DI position, that was only because there was no one left to promote, and I was the booby prize. There was definitely no love lost between us. He was too busy with office politics and budgets to be a hands-on copper. From his ivory tower of an office he'd forgotten what life was really like on the streets.

Becky and Ronnie sat at their desks as I stood next to Greene and addressed my team. If you could call it that. Three people investigating a crime like this was woefully inadequate.

'Last night I was called out to the scene of a double murder in Turpinfield,' I began. 'Jan and Mike Jameson were a couple in their mid-seventies, retired farmers. The standard background checks have revealed nothing of interest. It doesn't look like a burglary. Nothing appeared ransacked or disturbed. A flat-screen TV, laptop and smart-phone were all still in the house. The gold jewellery Jan Jameson had been wearing was still on her when she was found, and other jewel-lery she owned was in a wooden box on her dressing table. A wallet containing a debit card and two hundred pounds in cash was found in Mr Jameson's pocket, and Mrs Jameson's handbag with a hundred quid and a credit card was still in the lounge near her body. So I'm confident at this stage that we can rule that out for a motive.' I paused for Ronnie to catch up while he took eager notes. 'When I arrived at the scene, both of them were lying in the lounge approximately four metres from each other. The Home Office pathologist examined them, and although the post-mortems will be carried out this morning, she did estimate a time of death as between eight a.m. and eleven a.m. two days ago. Jan Jameson was shot in the neck. Mike Jameson had three bullet wounds. One in the chest, leg and also in the centre of his forehead.'

'Blimey,' Ronnie said. 'You mean, like an assassination?'

'I don't know what it means yet until we get more information. But his wounds seem a bit like overkill to me – pun not intended.'

'Maybe they were bad shots,' Becky said.

'Or maybe the offender was just making sure he was dead?' Ronnie offered.

'The couple were found by their daughter, Paula Eagan, following a spontaneous visit to see them. She says she arrived at Beech Lodge at six p.m. and found them in the lounge. The front door was closed when she arrived at the property, but the patio doors in the lounge which back on to the rear garden were open. No signs of forced entry.'

'Maybe they opened the door to their killer?' Becky asked.

'There are several possibilities. They knew their killer and let them in the front, or they felt unthreatened at the time of opening the door and thus let them in, or the killer threatened them with a gun on the doorstep and then they retreated to the lounge. The shooter could have also come in through the patio doors, which may have already been unlocked.' I stood and walked towards the satellite map I'd tacked up. 'If you look at the whiteboard you'll—'

'Um, guv, you can't say "whiteboard" any more,' Ronnie interjected.

'What?' I frowned.

'Haven't you had the new Standards of Conduct diversity training yet?' Ronnie looked nervously between me and Greene.

'Why can't I say whiteboard?'

'It could be a potentially racial slur,' Ronnie said.

Becky rolled her eyes at the ridiculousness of it.

I snorted and looked at Greene, who nodded and said, 'That's right.'

'That's bloody ridiculous! I've been calling it a whiteboard for thirty-odd years. I don't think a bit of plastic is going to get pissed off with me for calling it what it is.'

'Nevertheless, DC Pickering is correct. You can't use that term any more,' Greene snapped with a serious face.

Was this what the top brass did all day? Dreamed up ways to waste time and money with ridiculous new training ideas?

I threw my hands in the air. 'What am I supposed to call it now?'

'A notice board,' Greene said.

I bit my lip and blew out a frustrated breath. 'Right. If you look at the map on the *notice* board, you'll see that the Jamesons' farm is in the middle of a rural area with only four properties. After the briefing I'm going to speak to the people at the neighbouring houses. Maybe one of them saw a suspicious vehicle or person passing through their land or on the lane that runs outside Beech Lodge or heard the shots. Only these two properties are apparently occupied.' I pointed to Bill Graves's land to the west and Parker Farm to the north. 'This one, on the east side, is owned by an elderly lady in a care home. The property is up for sale, but there are stables there which are rented out.

'Apparently, the Jamesons had no enemies. I've found no possible criminal connections. Paula said she wasn't aware of any financial problems, or any other reason they could've been targeted. There were no bank statements at the house but a lot of people have gone paperless now so, Becky, I want you to get hold of the standard financial records, along with phone records, and see if you can dig anything up.'

'Yes, guv,' Becky said.

'Was there anything else of note found at the house?' Greene asked.

'Some paperwork that needs going through. A laptop that I've taken to be analysed along with a mobile phone found in Mrs Jameson's handbag. Emma Bolton will be here soon to brief us on forensics.'

Ronnie shot his hand up in the air, a habit he had when wanting to ask a question, no matter how many times he'd been told it was unnecessary. Wilmott had ridiculed him for it but that was just Ronnie being Ronnie. 'What if it *was* an assassination? It seems a bit random, doesn't it? Or maybe so random that it's *not* actually random.'

Greene scowled with impatience. 'What does that even mean, DC Pickering?'

Ronnie's cheeks flushed, embarrassed. 'Well, what I mean is, if it's not a burglary, they had no connection to any criminal activity, and no enemies, why would someone target a retired couple in the middle of nowhere?'

'Good point, Ronnie,' I said. 'Which is why I want you to look more closely at the Eagans. Dig into their background and see what you can come up with.' I went on to explain what had happened when I'd questioned Paula Eagan and told them about Grant Eagan's past criminal record.

Ronnie nodded vigorously and wrote something in his notebook. 'Will do.'

'Last night I checked for any similar patterns of gun crime in the county but found nothing like this,' I carried on. 'There have also been no recent burglaries in the area with anything that matches this MO. According to wills I retrieved from the house, Paula Eagan is the sole heir of Mr and Mrs Jameson. They both had life insurance policies totalling two hundred thousand pounds. So at the moment the Eagans are our prime persons of interest.' I nodded at Ronnie and said, 'I also want you to talk to the Jamesons' friends and see if they can shed any light on their relationship with their daughter and son-in-law. Something struck me as odd when Paula was talking about them. I'm going to check her alibi that she was at work on Wednesday and find out what

Grant Eagan was doing. They both work at Eagan's Scaffolding, which is Grant's company.'

'Righty ho.' Ronnie made a note of that.

'There's something else, too,' I said. 'We don't know which victim was shot first, or how the scene played out yet. We'll wait to hear from SOCO when they've done a crime scene reconstruction and the results of the post-mortems, *but* what they can tell us at this stage is that when Mrs Jameson was shot, someone was standing next to her, in front of the lounge wall.'

Ronnie put up his hand to say something. I looked at him to go ahead, but he shook his head and said, 'Never mind. Sorry.'

'The spatter is in the shape of a head, basically. About five feet up the wall.'

'So there were two offenders?' Greene asked.

'No witnesses have come forward to report being there so it looks that way, yes,' I said.

'Why would the offender stand so close to Mrs Jameson if the other one was going to shoot?' Ronnie asked.

'Maybe they were restraining her,' I said.

'Maybe the gun went off by accident,' Becky said. 'One of them could've been involved in a struggle with Mr Jameson and the gun went off and hit his wife. Then they had to shoot Mr Jameson because he was a witness.'

Emma Bolton entered the room then, dressed in civvies, with dark circles under her eyes, clutching a coffee in one hand and a couple of clear plastic evidence bags in the other with her laptop tucked under her arm. 'Morning, guv.' She nodded to Greene. 'Sarge.' She smiled at me, then aimed a general smile in the direction of Ronnie and Becky.

'Morning, Emma.' I smiled back. 'I'll let you take over now as you're about to go off shift. What can you tell us?'

Emma put her laptop on the desk and held up one of the bags. 'OK, this is the bullet recovered from the crime scene that killed Mrs Jameson.

It's a nine-millimetre, most likely from a handgun, and will be passed on for firearms analysis to see if it can be matched to any previous crimes and hopefully determine the type and manufacturer of the weapon that fired it, but that's going to take some time.'

'Did you recover any other bullets from the scene?' I asked.

'No. Mr Jameson's wounds weren't through and through shots. All the bullets are still lodged inside him and the Home Office pathologist will recover them during the PM.' She placed the evidence bag on the desk and held up the other one. 'This is a pink stone. One of six we found lodged in the carpet of the lounge. All appear to be identical. They're the kind of cheap stones commonly used in costume jewellery and applied to clothing. There are traces of what looks like glue on the underside, which is how they would've been stuck to whatever surface they were on.'

'Those things are a bugger for falling off,' Becky said. 'I've got a black top with green stones on just like those and they come off all over the place.'

Emma nodded. 'According to the daughter, she never saw her mum wearing anything remotely like it. Paula said Mrs Jameson never wore costume jewellery or anything fancy or sparkly. We didn't find any clothing in Mrs Jameson's wardrobe, or anything in her jewellery box, that it could've come from, and Mrs Jameson wasn't wearing anything of a similar nature when she was found. It's a possibility it could've come from the offender.'

'So we're looking for a woman?' Ronnie asked.

'I just give you the evidence. Do with it what you will.' Emma raised her eyebrows.

'Could be a cross-dressing man,' Becky said.

Greene tutted under his breath. 'Have you had the diversity training yet?'

'No, guv,' she said.

'Well, I'm fast-tracking you for it.'

I stifled a smile. Becky was a girl after my own heart. 'Actually, it's a good point. We should never make assumptions. Of course, it's also possible these stones were dropped some time before the murder by an unknown person, a friend of the Jamesons perhaps, and are totally unrelated to the events of yesterday. Although, judging by the state of the rest of the house, Jan Jameson seemed very house proud. And there were fresh vacuum marks in the lounge carpet, so I'm guessing whoever came in and shot them entered after she'd cleaned in there.' I tilted my head to Emma, indicating for her to carry on.

'Also, on top of the fresh vacuum marks, we found a few blood droplets which may have transferred from the clothes of the person who was standing next to Jan Jameson when she was shot. They head towards the patio doors but there are none outside. We also found some smudges of soil on the carpet, most likely transferred by the offenders' shoes. Their pattern indicates that the point of entry and exit was the patio doors. They only went a few metres into the lounge, as far as the coffee table, then retreated back the same way. I'll get them analysed, see if we can come up with a useful tread pattern, but I don't think that's likely from the poor quality of them. Soil samples will go to the lab.'

'Can you determine the height of the shooter from the evidence at the scene?' Greene asked.

'No. From the blood spatter and bullet hole in the wall near Mrs Jameson's body, I'd estimate the relative position of the weapon when fired at her to be in this area.' She opened her laptop and brought up a simulated computer image of the Jamesons' lounge, complete with furniture, doors and their bodies. She pointed to a spot in front of the coffee table, where the killer would most likely have been facing Jan Jameson when she was killed and at a slight diagonal angle to Mike Jameson. 'The pathologist will be able to determine the angles of the wounds, but we'd need forensic firearms experts to analyse everything. Even then, it's most likely all they'd be able to tell is the height that the gun was fired from, which doesn't necessarily translate to the height of the attacker since it would depend whether they held it at wrist, shoulder, waist height, or anything in between.'

'I can't authorise spending part of the budget on that, especially if there's nothing to be gained from it,' Greene said to me.

Emma clicked a few buttons on her laptop and pulled up a photograph on screen. It was a close-up shot of the patio doors. 'We're still taking fingerprints, but we found three palm prints on the outside of the patio door, which are recent. All three were overlaid on top of each other.' She traced her forefinger around the prints on the glass. 'Mixed in with the prints was a fine dusting of grey powder. We don't know what it is yet. Neither of the Jamesons had any similar dust on their hands at the scene, and we found no traces of it in the house, the barns, or immediate area.'

'So the prints could belong to one of the offenders?' Greene asked hopefully.

'Possibly. I've handed them over to the fingerprint department but they're backed up so I don't know when you'll get a result if they find a match.' She slapped her laptop closed.

'Did you find any tyre tracks?' Becky asked.

'Nothing so far but the SOCO team will let you know if that changes.' She stood up. 'That's all I've got for now. The day shift is still at the house. Good luck!' She left us with a tired smile.

'OK,' I said. 'I'm going to speak with the neighbours first and see if they can shed any light on things.'

Greene stood up and glanced at his watch as Becky reached for her phone and Ronnie started typing. They were a good team, hardworking, but they were only two people.

I followed Greene into the corridor. 'Guv, is there any chance of getting more bodies on this?'

'I'll see what I can do but everyone's in the same boat. We're shortstaffed and overworked, and I have a dwindling budget that won't allow me to authorise extra people power.'

'This is a brutal double murder of an elderly couple! How am I expected to solve it when I have no staff?' I slapped the wall with the palm of my hand.

Greene glared at me briefly after my outburst. 'I'm not promising anything.' He walked off down the corridor towards his office, where he could push paperclips around and never come into contact with the real people whose lives were negatively affected by the 'dwindling budget'.

'Do you ever wonder why we slog our guts out to catch criminals?' I said to his retreating back. 'All the man-hours searching for evidence to put them away and then they just get away with it?'

Greene stopped, turned around. 'I suppose you're referring to the Jeremy Wellham case?'

'Yes, as a matter of fact.'

'Our job is to apply the law. What happens afterwards is not our concern. The CPS declined to prosecute Wellham so it's out of our hands.'

'Yeah? Well, tell that to Mandy Bowyer.' I snorted. 'He raped her – we all know it. And so what if she'd invited him to her house because she wanted to get back together with him. So what if they'd been drinking wine beforehand? It doesn't mean she wanted that! I *saw* the bruises on her wrists and throat. I *saw* the girl who'd once been confident and lively break into desolate pieces. I witnessed how her life fell apart in just a few tragic minutes because of his jealous rage. She didn't fake her pain. It was real. It wasn't a case of consensual rough sex, even if the CPS thinks that's how it would be seen. Wellham is a callous rapist and he's got away with it.' I knew my mouth was running away with me. Knew I should shut up, but I was on a roll now. 'And what about Lord Mackenzie? That never even *got* to the CPS. The law most definitely wasn't applied there.' Mackenzie had been involved in a fake theft of his classic car collection, which turned into a multi-million-pound insurance fraud. As soon as I'd started discovering Mackenzie's involvement in it, Greene had told me the investigation had been quashed on orders from the top brass and I'd been threatened with suspension unless I stopped digging. 'It doesn't matter whether you're scum masquerading as a pillar of society with friends in high places or you're a lowlife scrote, what's the point of it all if we can't get these people off the streets and protect the innocent?'

'You're not still going on about that case, are you?' He gave me an exasperated sigh. 'And it's *person*-hours. You can't say *man*-hours any more. It's sexist.'

'Oh, for fuck's sake!' I rolled my eyes. 'Is that political correctness rubbish all that matters to you?'

He narrowed his eyes. 'It's a good job you're only here for two more weeks or you'd be in my office now for insubordination.'

'What, again?' I muttered.

'Don't forget you are speaking to a superior officer!' His cheeks had turned a mottled, angry red. I always seemed to have that effect on him. He was probably counting down the days until my departure by the second. 'You're getting way too personally involved in all these cases. I've had it up to here with your attitude and—' He broke off and glared at me, shaking his head. 'And stop swearing! The force is undergoing a change, and you have to change with it. It's not like the old days any more. You'd better get used to it.'

But maybe I didn't want to.

THE VIGILANTE
Chapter 9

The satnav announced our destination as we pulled up in a sleepy suburb on a street lined with small, terraced cottages. They were quaint and obviously old. I had no idea how old, but knew that Bournewood had sprung up as a market town in the seventeenth century. I turned the engine off and stared at number 15, a cacophony of sounds penetrating the silence. Kids. Lots and lots of kids, shouting and screaming. There was a school somewhere very nearby.

I glanced at the clock on the dashboard. Twelve thirty p.m.

'Looks a nice area,' Maya said, stepping out of the car and slinging her handbag diagonally across her body.

I swung around in the front seat, reaching for my equipment daysack in the rear footwell. My pistol, mags and taser were secured and hidden in my covert compartment in the pick-up. The other daysack and Maya's rucksack filled with clothes could stay in the car until I knew what I was dealing with.

I got out of the car, locked it, and looked up and down the street. The houses were well maintained but small. The properties had no driveways so vehicles were parked on the road. Average cars. Not a rich and affluent area but comfortable and cosy.

As we walked up the pathway of Corinne's house the door swung open, stopping me short as I saw her again. She wore the last eighteen years well. Her once-blonde hair was darker now, pulled back into a loose ponytail. Her forehead was a bunch of tight wrinkles, but that was due to stress and anxiety. Her eyes were swollen and red. She had no make-up on, but in better circumstances, she could easily pass for someone in her late thirties, instead of a decade older.

Tears filled her eyes and her knees seemed to sag. Her voice cracked as she said, 'Thank you for coming.'

I strode towards her and wrapped her in a hug. She clung on tight to me as I breathed in her perfume. The years melted away between us and a picture formed in my head – me hugging her on her and Tony's wedding day, inhaling the same perfume, just before I'd given my best man's speech.

I cleared my throat so the emotion in my voice wouldn't give me away and released her. 'Come on. Let's go inside and you can tell me everything.'

Corinne looked at Maya uncertainly. Back to me.

'This is Maya. A good friend of mine.'

Corinne blinked and nodded and turned around, leading us into a kitchen that overlooked the small patch of paved front garden and the rest of the street. She went to the window above the sink and stared out through the net curtains, her neck turning right and left as if scanning the road for any signs of Toni. 'I didn't know who else to call.' She whipped around to face me, her trembling fingers touching her lips. 'I'm sorry. I know after . . . Well, it's been a long time. I got your number from one of the other Regiment wives. I kept in touch with a few people, but I . . . I had to get away from that environment, from the memories, and start afresh.'

'You did the right thing contacting me.' I sat at the kitchen table. 'I'm going to do everything I can to get Toni back, but I need as much detail as you can give me about her.'

She clutched her arms around her waist. 'I know she wouldn't have just run away. There was absolutely no reason to. She was fine.'

'You hadn't argued about anything?' Maya asked.

'No. We . . . I mean, we did have arguments, naturally. But nothing lately. It's completely out of character for her to disappear.'

'OK. Tell me the facts first,' I said. 'What happened when she disappeared? When was the last time you saw her?'

Maya sat quietly next to me as Corinne started to speak.

'She went missing yesterday. She's due to start her uni course next week so she's still on summer holidays and was at home when I left for work.'

'Where do you work?' I asked.

'At Jones and Co, a local accounting firm. I'm a bookkeeper there. Toni had made breakfast but she wasn't eating it. She seemed distracted. She'd been acting weird for a few days, actually – moody and jumpy and just . . . I don't know, out of sorts. I put it down to worrying about starting her uni course even though she was excited about it.' Corinne rocked herself slightly as she spoke. 'But now she's disappeared, I keep thinking maybe something was troubling her that was more than just her being nervous about uni.' Corinne sniffed. 'Anyway, the last time I saw her, she was standing in front of the window, just watching the street.' Corinne pointed outside. 'Like she was thinking, or looking for someone. I asked her if her friend Laura was coming round – I thought maybe that's who she was waiting for – but she just snapped at me and said no and then told me to stop suffocating her and hassling her all the time and stormed off up to her bedroom and slammed the door. She's not usually a sulker or a door-slammer. But . . .' She blew out a breath. 'She's an adult now. I have to give her space. So I didn't push it.' Corinne picked at the skin around the edge of her thumbnail. 'Anyway, when I got back from work about half five she wasn't here. I didn't think too much about it at first. I thought maybe she'd gone to see Laura. I texted her but she didn't reply, which is unlike her. She knows I worry. We're really close, you know. It's always been just us two, really.'

The knife of guilt twisted deeper in my chest. If it wasn't for me it would've been three of them.

'I left it a bit, then called her, but her phone was turned off. It went to voicemail straight away so I left a message. I thought at first she was still in a mood. But then I called Laura who said she hadn't seen Toni for a few days. About quarter to seven, and with no contact from her, I started getting a bit concerned.' Corinne chewed on her lower lip, her eyes filling with tears. 'I didn't know where else to try because Toni doesn't really have any other friends. She's a bit of an introvert, really. A loner. I suppose Toni's what people would call a geek. Ever since she was a kid she's always had her head buried in a book – mostly true crime, or stuff about profiling or psychology. She's going to be studying criminology with psychology for her degree. She's mad about delving into people's heads. Or if she wasn't reading, she'd be on her laptop.'

'She doesn't have a boyfriend?' Maya asked.

Corinne shook her head. 'No, like I said, all she's interested in are books and psychology. She's not a typical young woman, wanting to go to parties and go clubbing.' She walked to the corner of the room, extracted her phone from her bag on the worktop and sat down, tapping at the screen. She scrolled through the phone then handed it to me. On screen was a picture of a beautiful girl with long, dark, wavy hair, brown eyes, and a thin nose, fresh-faced and looking younger than eighteen. She was so much like Tony that I had to take a breath to hold the emotion in check.

I handed the phone to Maya.

'And what about you? Is there a boyfriend in the picture?' I asked. If something had happened to Toni, the threat could've been close to home.

'No. I mean, there have been people in the past but . . .' She shrugged. 'It's never worked out. My last relationship ended about two years ago.'

'Was it an amicable split?' I asked.

'Yes, although he was the one who ended things. He was moving to Saudi to work. He asked if Toni and I wanted to go but, well' – she raised her eyebrows – 'it's not the kind of place I wanted either myself or Toni to live. He's still out there, met another ex-pat and got married. There's been no one since then.'

'Has anyone that you know taken an unhealthy interest in Toni?'

'No.'

'You mentioned Toni being on her laptop,' Maya said. 'Was she going on teenage chat rooms or social media or . . .' Maya glanced at me, her mouth twisted with worry.

I knew what she was thinking. An alarm bell was ringing in my head, too. A stunning young girl online was a prime target for grooming by sick men. Maya and I both had devastating, first-hand knowledge of that. I didn't want to tell Corinne that yet, though. Didn't want her to imagine a parent's worst nightmare unless I was sure. I knew how it could rip someone into shreds. And falling apart wouldn't get her daughter back.

But Corinne must've guessed from our expressions what we were thinking. 'No.' She shook her head. 'Toni's an intelligent girl. She's streetwise, too. Not naïve. After studying killers and criminals for so long, she knows what people are capable of. She'd never fall for some online grooming. She's not the sort of girl to get herself into trouble like that.'

There was obviously trouble now, though. But what kind? 'So, Toni didn't mention any problems she was having? Or anything that was worrying her?'

'No. But . . .' Corinne's face crumpled, as if she was about to cry again. She blinked a few times to hold the tears at bay. 'Like I said, she was acting a bit . . . I don't know, tense, I suppose. She kept staring into space, chewing her fingernails. Then when I'd come into the room and find her like that and ask her if something was bothering her, she'd jump a mile. It was as if she was scared about something.'

'Did she mention anyone strange hanging around or following her? Anyone hassling her?' I took another look at Toni's image on the phone which Maya had put in the centre of the table. 'Or did you see anyone or anything suspicious recently?'

'No.'

'OK. So what did you do next? After you couldn't get hold of her by phone?'

'I drove around town, seeing if I could spot her, but there was no sign of her. When I got back an hour later she still wasn't here so I asked my immediate neighbours if they'd seen her at all. The couple next door are at work all day anyway so they weren't here.' She pointed to the left wall of the kitchen, indicating which neighbour. 'And the other side are on holiday. I asked the old guy who lives across the street, too. He's like the equivalent of a one-man neighbourhood-watch committee. He's in a wheelchair and doesn't get out much, and he's always at the window or in his front garden, watching the street. He said he saw Toni leave the house at one o'clock but he never saw her return.'

I looked out of the kitchen window to the house directly opposite. There was an elderly man with short grey hair and glasses in his front garden, sitting in his wheelchair, reading a newspaper. 'Is that the guy you asked?' I pointed to him.

Corinne twisted around. 'Yes. Bert Williamson. The police spoke to him, too. He said Toni was carrying her rucksack when she left.'

'What do you know about Bert?' Maya asked.

'He's a sweet old guy. I often get him food at the shops when I go to the supermarket. He was a lorry driver who was involved in a terrible accident about five years ago that left him paralysed from the waist down. Why? You don't think he could be involved, do you? He's just a harmless old man.' She frowned at Maya.

'At this stage we can't assume anything,' I said. 'Anyone could be suspicious.' Malevolence could live in the most innocuous of people. But again, I didn't convey the thought to Corinne. 'Until we know more, we can't discount anything.' I leaned forward and rested my hands on the table. 'So what happened when you called the police? Why did they just assume she'd run away, especially as it was out of character?'

She clenched her hands together and glanced down at them. 'It got to about nine o'clock and I called them. But they've got it in their heads she's a runaway. They said she's eighteen so she's an adult, and since she's not vulnerable, they only seemed to do the bare minimum.'

'Not vulnerable?' Maya said. 'She's an eighteen-year-old girl!'

'That's exactly what I said.' Corinne's nostrils flared with anger. 'They meant because she wasn't physically disabled or didn't have mental health issues.' She shook her head. 'They said hundreds of thousands of youngsters run away each year and she'd probably come back in a few days. They checked there'd been no accidents involving anyone of Toni's description, so I know she's not lying in a hospital somewhere. They had a quick check of Toni's bedroom. They asked a few of the neighbours if they'd seen anything. And after Bert told them he saw her leaving the house, they said she'd probably just gone to stay with a friend for a few days. They spoke to Laura briefly, who said she had no idea where Toni was.' Corinne paused for a breath. 'I explained to them there's no way Toni would've run away but they said it was the most likely explanation because her rucksack was missing, along with her laptop and phone. They said if I hadn't heard from her in a few days to get back in touch with them. It's like they're not even interested.' She shook her head vehemently. 'She wouldn't just . . .' Corinne swiped at her eyes. 'I know my daughter. Something's happened to her. She's been taken by someone or . . . she's been attacked or something.' She glanced up at me, all the fear evident in her eyes.

I reached out and took her hand in mine. 'Is there any reason why someone would want to target Toni to get at you? What about your bookkeeping job?'

'No. We do work for small businesses mostly. We're not dealing with huge corporations or anything dodgy.'

My gaze strayed to a silver laptop on the worktop. 'Is that your laptop, then?'

'Yes. Toni's is black.'

'Did she usually take her laptop out of the house?'

'Only to college sometimes, if she needed it for her work. But apart from that, no.'

'Did she take anything else?' I asked. 'Clothes? Her passport?'

'I looked in her wardrobe and drawers and don't think any of her clothes are missing, but I can't be sure. Her passport's still here with mine. And I keep trying her phone all the time, just in case, but it's still switched off.'

'Did she take any money from the house?' I asked.

'I only keep a few hundred quid in the house for emergencies but that's still here. She's got a bank account, but since she's not working, she doesn't have much in it. I give her a small allowance and she does jobs round the house but I give it to her in cash. It's only thirty pounds a week. She wouldn't get far on that.'

'What about your parents? Or Tony's? They haven't heard from her?'

'Tony's parents are both dead now.'

'I'm sorry. I didn't know.' I stared at my hands on the table.

'And my parents are up in Scotland, as you know. They haven't heard a word from Toni.'

'Were there any signs someone else had been in the house when you got back from work that day?' I wondered if Toni had returned at some point and been abducted from inside. It was unlikely, with Bert as a neighbour, and in broad daylight, but not impossible, especially if someone had come in via the rear.

'No. The house was all locked up. There were no signs of a disturbance or anyone else being inside.'

'How tall was Toni?' I asked.

'Five foot.'

'Weight?'

'About seven stone.'

I sat there for a moment and thought, my gaze wandering back to Bert in his garden. The newspaper rested on his knee now and he was watching the house. He seemed to be looking straight at me.

Corinne clutching my hand drew my attention back to her. 'I know something bad has happened to her. That's why I called you.'

I stared into her desperate eyes. A missing teenage girl sounded pretty bad to me.

Where the hell was Toni?

THE MISSING

Chapter 10

I'm cold. Freezing. And scared. Terrified of what's going to happen. I've seen some of the things they've done and it's worse than any imaginable horror story.

I touch my face with hands that won't stop shaking and feel the caked snot and dried tears. The blood, too, where he punched me in the face before he dragged me into the van.

It happened so quickly I didn't even hear the footsteps before someone grabbed me from behind. Never saw the punch coming that knocked me off my feet. No time to cry out or make a sound. I remember falling to the ground. Dazed. Disorientated. Then the sound of an engine. Being picked up in his strong grip. Struggling. Kicking. The hand over my mouth keeping my scream silent. A pinprick of pain in my neck. Something stabbing into my skin. And then I was thrown into a van, the doors slamming shut. A loud click in my ears. Then . . . the edges of my vision fading to darkness.

They'd drugged me with something. My head still feels woozy, my stomach lurching up and down. They left two soggy sandwiches wrapped in a paper bag on the floor, along with three cartons of orange juice. I still can't face eating with my stomach like this, but I'm down to one carton of OJ now.

My nose has only just stopped bleeding. My whole face throbs in time with my racing heartbeat. I flinch from the pain of my fingertips on my skin and drop my hands to the concrete floor, the hard coldness of this prison engulfing me, swallowing me whole.

I thought he was going to kill me right there and then. And maybe that would've been better. If he'd just strangled me or snapped my neck in two, it would've been quick. I know whatever they're going to do to me will be worse. So much worse.

My throat is scratchy and raw. I've tried screaming. Tried begging. But I don't think anyone can hear me in here. My voice just echoes in my ears, and I've said the words *please help me* so many times they don't even sound like real words any more. *Pleasehelpmepleasehelpme.* Just one long, mashed-up sentence. A blur of letters.

And I'm certain they won't help me, but I don't know what else to do. I wish that I'll die of dehydration and starvation long before they come back and then I won't know anything any more. Maybe I shouldn't drink the last carton of juice, after all.

I don't know what to call this place, but I know I have to take notes in my head. Remember every little detail so that when someone finds me – *if* someone finds me – I'll be able to tell the police everything.

I glance around. It's dark but there's a sliver of light coming from underneath the door. My eyes have adjusted to the blackness and I can see it's a small room. A cell.

Oh, God! A cell!

My heartbeat rages beneath my ribs. Sweat oozes through my pores. I glance down at myself. At least I'm still fully clothed. I don't think they've raped me. Yet.

Back to the notes, Toni. Concentrate on that.

OK. Right. Don't fall apart. Breathe. Being strong is the only way you can survive.

THE DETECTIVE

Chapter 11

I drove along the country lane, past Simms Livery Stables and house, past the Jamesons' farm, until I came to the neighbouring property belonging to Bill Graves. More tall fields of rapeseed welcomed me to the right of the long driveway before it opened up on to a whitewashed farm building.

As I got out of the car, I spied a couple of large barns, one open-ended and one with sliding metal doors that housed some kind of agricultural beast of a machine. A man with short grey hair, wearing blue overalls, leaned over the bonnet of a van parked in front of it, inspecting something in the engine bay as the motor idled.

'Mr Graves?' I shouted over the engine noise.

The man jumped and spun around.

'Sorry, I didn't mean to frighten you.' I smiled. 'I'm DS Carter. I'm investigating the murder of your neighbours, Mr and Mrs Jameson.' I flashed my warrant card at him.

'I didn't hear you pull up.' He patted the area where his heart was and gave me a grave smile. He was stocky, with the kind of physique that would've been muscly in his youth but was now turning to fat, late fifties, maybe, with a face that reflected a lifetime of working outdoors – red cheeks and skin like old leather. 'I heard the terrible news. I'm still in shock about it all. Awful business.' He shook his head and wiped his hands on a rag tucked in his pocket. 'What's the world coming to? Let's go into the house and talk.' He reached inside the van, turned off the engine, then pocketed the keys.

I followed him to his back door which led into a spacious, airy kitchen.

'Want a cuppa?' Bill reached for an old-style kettle before I had a chance to say yes. He filled it with water, lifted the lid of an ancient-looking Aga and placed the kettle on it. 'Have a seat.' He nodded towards a pine table not dissimilar to the one in the Jamesons' kitchen.

'Were you at home the day before yesterday?' I asked.

'Well, I was here in the afternoon.' He ran his hands under the tap at the kitchen sink and washed them, his back to me. 'I was pottering around out in the yard, doing a few odd jobs. But in the morning, I had some errands to run and went into town. I left about eight and got back about midday.' He dried his hands on a tea towel and swung around to face me. 'What time did it happen?'

'We're not a hundred per cent sure yet. Sometime between eight a.m. and eleven a.m.'

'Terrible,' he muttered as the kettle started a slow whistle. He grabbed some mugs from a wooden holder on the worktop and filled them with teabags. 'Sugar?'

'No, thanks. Did you happen to see or hear anything suspicious? Anyone hanging around? Or maybe a vehicle?'

'No, I didn't see or hear anything, I'm afraid. I didn't pass any vehicles in the lane, either.'

'Is there a Mrs Graves?'

'No. Never been married.' He poured the now boiling water into mugs and let the teabags stew.

'What can you tell me about Mr and Mrs Jameson?'

'They were a lovely couple. Salt of the earth, really. Good neighbours. I've lived here since my parents bought the place when I was eighteen, and Mike was born on that farm. They're the kind of people you can always rely on if there's a problem. We've helped each other out over the years with farming issues or if one of us needed help of some kind. I can't understand how anyone could want to hurt them.' He brought the mugs to the table and set one in front of me.

'Thanks. Is there anything you can think of that would make them a target?'

'A target? You mean it wasn't some kind of robbery that went wrong?'

'We don't think so, no.'

'Blimey.' He rubbed at the back of his neck with a hand and stared down at the table. 'I can't see why anyone would target them.' He shrugged helplessly.

'Do you know what the Jamesons' relationship with Paula and her husband Grant was like? Did they get on?'

He looked up, opened his mouth to speak, then shut it again. He took a sip of tea. 'Look . . . I don't want to speak out of turn, but . . .' He stopped, scratched his head, looking uncomfortable.

'We have to ask these things, Mr Graves. They're routine questions.'

'I'm sure you do.' He nodded and took a deep breath. 'Paula had a falling out with her parents when she began going out with Grant. She met him when she started working at Grant's scaffolding firm about three years ago. Jan and Mike didn't like him. Grant was always getting in trouble. Getting drunk all the time, smoking drugs, drink-driving, gambling. That kind of thing. They didn't think he was good enough for her. They were worried he'd end up getting her into trouble, and they didn't want him at their house. So Paula's relationship with Jan and Mike has been a bit strained for the last few years. I was . . .' He trailed off and chewed on his lower lip.

I waited.

'I was at Jan and Mike's house about a week ago. Mike had the flu and Jan didn't want to leave him too long so I'd popped over with some bits and bobs of food as I was doing a supermarket run. Mike was in bed, but I was chatting with Jan in the kitchen. Then Paula phoned up. I could hear part of the conversation, and then later, Jan told me about it. Anyway, Paula was asking her parents for money. Apparently, they had some big debts that they couldn't pay back. Construction had taken a downturn since the recession so the scaffolding business was suffering. Paula said if they couldn't pay the money back they were in danger of losing their house and the business.'

Interesting. Desperate times bred desperate measures. 'How much money are we talking about?'

'Thirty grand.'

Not exactly small change, then. And now her parents were out of the picture, as their sole heir, I guessed Paula would get her money, and more, after all. 'And I take it that Jan and Mike refused to give Paula the money.'

'Yes. Jan felt awful about not helping Paula out, especially as their relationship was precarious anyway, but Mike flat out refused to give her any money. Jan said they'd got into trouble because Grant had a gambling problem and she and Mike were worried if they gave them the money, Grant would just do it all over again and they'd never repay it.'

'How did Paula react to Jan refusing her request?'

'Jan was trying to explain to Paula that Grant needed some help for his addiction, but Paula kept shouting down the phone at her. Jan kept telling her to calm down and stop swearing. Paula was ranting and raving at her so much that in the end Jan hung up. She was really upset by it all.' He paused. 'Do you think . . . Do you think Paula or Grant is involved in what happened?'

'I'm not sure of anything right now. It's early days.' But Paula and Grant now had a motive, and I was pretty certain Paula had lied to me when she'd said she was at work all day.

'If it's not them, do you think whoever did this will come back? Could they target me next? Not that I've got anything much worth stealing, but that doesn't seem to matter these days, does it? I mean, I've got a shotgun licence. And an air rifle licence, too, for rabbiting – the buggers eat the crops – and I'll damn well use them if someone breaks in with a gun. But you know what happens these days. You remember Alan Connolly? He got put away for shooting a burglar.'

I, like many thousands of others, had been absolutely disgusted by what had happened. Alan Connolly was a farmer who'd been the repeated target of a gang of youths who'd burgled him on several occasions. A rural farmer in a remote location, which were often hardest hit by police cuts, by the time the police arrived on scene after his emergency calls, the bastards had always disappeared. After the fifth time, Connolly had had enough and ended up shooting one of the burglars in the foot, but instead of the burglar being convicted, Connolly found himself on trial for GBH and was sentenced to two years in prison. It was yet another prime example of the law no longer protecting the victims.

'The Jamesons never reported any incidents of burglary in the past, but did they ever mention to you that something like that had happened? Had they ever caught anyone on their land?' I asked.

'No, they never said anything of the sort, and they would've told me if that was the case so I could keep an eye out.'

'Can you think of any other reasons someone would murder the Jamesons? Was there anything in their private life you knew about that could attract the wrong kind of attention?'

'God, no. They were both as straight as a die.'

I took a sip of tea. 'I believe the Simms property is empty, is that right?'

He nodded. 'Yes, poor old Emily is in a home now. Her son, Roger, has put it on the market.'

'Do you have a contact number for Roger?'

'Hang on a sec, I'll get it.' He pulled his mobile phone from his pocket and tapped a few buttons. 'Here it is.' He relayed it to me.

I wrote it down before taking a final mouthful of tea and standing up to leave. 'OK, thanks for your help. If you think of anything else that might be useful, can you give me a call?' I handed him a business card.

'Of course I will.'

I headed back to my car and called Roger Simms. He told me he was in Hong Kong, where he'd been working for the last two weeks, so he had no information to share, but told me to head over to the livery stables behind the house as there was usually someone on site during the daytime.

Next, I called Becky to check on the firearms licence status of Bill Graves. As he'd told me, he held both a shotgun and air rifle certificate. There were several incident logs attached to his address when he'd informed police he would be shooting rabbits at night. Another background check revealed he had no criminal history.

I hung up and tapped my phone against my lips. Although Graves had access to firearms, the Jamesons hadn't been killed by a shotgun blast; the damage would've been far worse if they had. And the 9 mm bullet recovered from the wall obviously wasn't a match to an air rifle pellet. I couldn't see a potential motive there, either, but I tucked the thought away for later as I started the car.

THE VIGILANTE

Chapter 12

I wrote down Toni's mobile phone number, her email address and bank account details. Ideally, I wanted to get hold of Toni's laptop, but since that was gone, too, I asked to borrow Corinne's laptop and found her IP address given by the broadband company she used. Both laptops were working off a router, so Toni's IP address would be the same.

'Do you remember Lee?' I asked Corinne. 'He was in the Signal Squadron?'

She shook her head, looking confused and pale, her head most certainly filled with a jumble of horrifying scenarios.

'When he got out of the Regiment he did a stint with some of the UK security agencies. He's got his own cyber intelligence and security company now, and he can help us track down Toni's digital communications. If we can find out what she was doing or who she was talking to before she disappeared, it might help us locate her. And if anyone can find out, it'll be Lee.' I pulled my phone from my pocket and left the room while Maya carried on talking to Corinne in a gentle, soothing voice.

I made my way down the corridor to the back of the house and entered a square-shaped lounge with French doors that looked out on to the rear garden. At the end of the garden was a five-foot wooden fence. Behind that was a large area consisting of playing fields, a tennis and basketball court, and finally a large two-storey building with a mish-mash of smaller buildings that appeared to have been added as an after-thought. The school where I'd heard children playing earlier. There were kids in the grounds, whiling away their lunch break in various ways.

I dialled Lee's number and placed the phone to my ear, revisiting in my mind the previous question I'd had about someone entering the house from the rear. I leaned closer to the French doors and checked out the neighbours' fences, looking for further possible entry points. The house on the left had a three-foot wooden fence with hedging growing another couple of feet above it. The house on the right had a six-foot fence. One set of neighbours were on holiday, and the other at work all day, so it was possible someone could've slipped over the fence from either side unnoticed. But there would be kids and teachers in all those school buildings – hundreds of potential witnesses with eyes on the rear of the house. And there were no signs of forced entry or a struggle. So if Toni had left through the front door at 1 p.m., I thought it was unlikely she'd ever returned. Whatever had happened to her had occurred somewhere else.

Lee picked up on the fifth ring. 'Mate! How are you? Everything still sorted with that thing?'

I knew Lee's phone would be secure and encrypted. I was using a pay-as-you-go phone. Not quite 100 per cent anonymous, but as close as I needed it to be these days. No one knew what 'thing' Lee was refer-ring to, apart from Maya, so I wouldn't be on anyone's watch list. 'Yeah, it's all good. But I have another problem and need your help.' I relayed all I knew about Corinne and Toni.

'Shit. I still think about Tony now. He was a cracking guy. I didn't know Corinne was pregnant when he was killed.'

'Neither did I.'

'Of course I can help. What've you got for me?'

I gave him all the details I'd got from Corinne. 'I need phone and text records, any websites accessed by their IP address, the content of her emails and social media accounts, anything suspicious she kept on cloud storage. She might've arranged to meet someone that day or been in contact with someone who took her.' Lee was my equivalent of the NSA. If it left a digital trace, he'd find it. He could hack or spy his way into anything. 'I'll email you some photos of Toni when I get off the phone.'

'I'll check CCTVs, too. I can do facial recognition for the surrounding areas.'

'Great stuff.'

'OK. I'll call when I have news. But I hope to God she turns up safe and well before then.'

'Me, too.' I hung up and was walking down the hallway when some post clattered through the door, landing on the mat.

I picked it up, just in case it was relevant. I doubted Toni had been kidnapped for ransom – Corinne seemed comfortable but not wealthy – but if she had there would be a demand in some shape or form arriving soon.

I flicked through two leaflets, flyers touting wares, and a menu for an Indian takeaway. Then I walked into the kitchen and put them on the worktop.

Maya had made a brew and Corinne was clutching her mug to her chest, staring down into it.

'That's yours.' Maya jerked her head towards a mug containing dark, strong builders' tea.

'Thanks.' I took a swig and set the mug back down. 'First thing. I'd like to search Toni's bedroom. Is that OK?'

'Of course.'

'Second, we speak to the neighbours ourselves and her friend Laura. By then, hopefully Lee might have something we can work with.'

'After the police just did a cursory look in her room, I searched it, too. But I didn't find anything that might help.'

'There are plenty of places to hide things where people won't look,' I said.

Corinne stood. 'I'll show it to you.' She led us upstairs, past the bathroom, to the end of the hallway, where there were two doors opposite each other. She entered the room on the left, and Maya and I followed her inside. It was painted pale lilac. A window overlooked the street in front. The dark-purple curtains were wide open so I had a direct view of Bert's house opposite. He'd moved inside from his front garden now and was sitting at his window, looking out at the street. His features weren't clear from this angle, but I could see the sunlight glinting off his glasses.

I turned away and took in Toni's bedroom. There was a poster on the wall opposite the window with a quote from Albert Einstein in script writing: 'The important thing is not to stop questioning. Curiosity has its own reason for existing.' There was a bedside table with an iPhone docking station on top, a dressing table under the window, and a small wardrobe in the corner next to it. The bed was made up neatly with a black duvet set with a gold design of a huge lotus flower in the centre. Above the bed were several shelves, jam-packed full of books: *Profiles of a Serial Killer*, *The Jigsaw Man*, *Helping Victims of Violent Crime*, *Rose and Fred West: The Full Story*, *A Study in the Psychology of Violence*, *Inside the Minds of Psychopaths*, *Horrifying Cases of True Evil*, *Criminal Profiling: The Science of Behaviour*. All the true crime topics and psychology books you could think of were there.

I scanned the room, taking an inventory. It was tidy for a teenager's lair. Nothing seemed disturbed. 'OK. Maya, can you check the drawers?' I walked around the room as Corinne moved to the doorway to give us space to work, chewing on her thumbnail, anxiously watching. 'Did anything look out of place when you came in here?' I asked Corinne.

'No. She's normally tidy like this, organised.'

'So this was exactly how you found the room, or have you moved anything?'

'I made the bed. Apart from that, it's as I found it. When I looked through it, I put everything back the way it was.'

I leafed through the books, shaking them to see if anything was hidden between the pages. Nothing. I inspected the original wooden floorboards and tested them for loose ones, seeing if any had been lifted.

'You think she might have hidden something?' Corinne asked.

'I don't know what to think yet. You know your daughter best and believe she wouldn't run away. But everyone keeps things hidden. She may have had a secret boyfriend. She may have been involved in something she didn't want to tell you about.'

I found no loose floorboards, nothing tucked away underneath them. I looked behind the radiator and under the wooden bed frame, then pulled back the duvet cover and inspected the bed. I removed the bedding and turned it inside out but there was nothing hidden. While Maya pulled out the bedside drawers one by one and checked underneath and behind them for something that could've been taped to the outside, I lifted up the mattress and found an A4 notepad with a picture of Supergirl on the front.

'That's her notebook,' Corinne said. 'She was always writing down bits and pieces in there relating to her coursework.'

'Did you look through it when she went missing?' I asked.

'No.' She blushed. 'I guess I didn't think to look under her mattress for something. I thought she'd just taken it with her.'

I sat on the now stripped bed and Corinne sat next to me as I flicked through the notepad. On the inside of the rigid cover Toni had written:

SuperGurrrl991
psychos101
IHatePasswords991
chunkybuttons0809
MissingYou1118

'They're her passwords for things. She always wrote them down so she didn't forget,' Corinne said.

In neat handwriting on the pages were written what looked like ideas and questions and notes.

Psychopath/Sociopath or Psychology of a psychopath? Which one?
Personal moral dilemma?
Emotional centre – amygdala
Master manipulators
Narcissist
Charm?
Never accepts responsibility
Controlling!
I'LL COME BACK TO THIS LATER ☺

I turned a page:

Female killers
Rose West (No 1?)
Tracey Connelly – Baby P
Carole Fishburn
Marie Black

Interspersed throughout the notes were what looked like random thoughts:

Or should I do serial killers?
Picking up the Pieces – Paul Britton. Want that one!
Documentary or book?
Nature or nurture? How much does a psychological disorder
play a part?
School shooting massacres? Were drugs involved?
Oh, shit! How did I miss that bit? :O
TheMindUnleashed: 30 Traits of an Empath – OMG, I get
it now! That's totally me. Everything's just clicked into place!

I paused on certain parts as Corinne read over my shoulder. The note-book was half full. The last pages contained notes about her forthcom-ing criminology and psychology degree course:

Dissertation (I know, I'm soooo ahead of myself here when I
haven't even started the course, but you know me!)
CYBERCRIME – sub genre – sexual offences against children
Sub chapters:
Intro
Sexual exploitation/legislation?
Typical ways to commit online sex offences. Or maybe Internet-
facilitated sexual offending – chat rooms and what else?
Law enforcement – combating online sexual abuse for inter-
national and multi-jurisdictional cases?
Subjects of sex offences – offender/victim
Interviews?
Media's role in uncovering sex offences
Sexual exploitation of children
Disturbing trends in commercial online child sexual abuse.
Summary?

'After her course, she wants to get a job in some kind of child-protection capacity, working with kids who've been abused,' Corinne said.

At the bottom of the last filled-in page, a date had been scrawled and underlined – two days before Toni had gone missing. Beneath that was the note:

I've got it! Into the darkness . . .

An uneasy feeling crept up my spine.

The following page had been torn out of the notebook, leaving a thin margin of paper along the spine.

I stared at it, picturing Toni sitting on her bed, scribbling the notes down. Why had the page been torn out? Was it significant to her sudden disappearance or not?

I looked at Corinne. 'Any idea what this means? Into the darkness?'

She shook her head, forehead pinched with worry. 'No. Maybe it means the darkness of human minds? What makes psychopaths tick? Looks like she was working on ideas for her dissertation already. Toni was always obsessed with psychology and criminology. It was her life. She wanted to do something that made a difference to people after they'd gone through traumatic experiences.'

The doorbell rang then and Corinne jumped up. 'Toni?' She rushed out of the room.

I opened the window and looked down to the front door below, but it wasn't Toni standing on the doorstep. It was a middle-aged woman.

I stepped away from the window. 'Anything?' I asked Maya, who was still searching the bedside drawers.

'Nothing of interest.' She picked up balls of socks and underwear, shaking them out.

I stood up and opened the wardrobe, which was full of clothes – jeans, combat trousers, leggings, blouses, jumpers, Converse. I checked pockets and shoes and came up empty.

On the floor was a cardboard box with *Memory Box* written in black marker pen on the lid. I pulled it out and placed it on the floor before climbing inside the wardrobe. I turned on the torch app on my phone and closed the doors behind me, looking for something attached to the interior side of the doors. I ran my hands over the wood to see if any panels were loose. Nothing. I stepped out, kneeled on the carpet and opened the memory box.

Inside were photos of Corinne and Toni, ranging from when Toni was a baby, through the years to her blossoming into a young woman. There were some photos of a girl with Toni, her friend Laura, perhaps. Cinema ticket stubs, airline boarding passes, an aging packet of sweets, a pressed flower. A girl's collection of mementos. At the bottom were some photos of Tony that Corinne must've given her.

I picked up the first one, staring at Tony and me when we were both much younger men, both fresh and keen. We had longer hair. Tony had a Pancho Villa moustache. We were working on the UK Counterterrorist Team back then and were dressed in black Nomex coveralls with body armour, gas masks on our heads. We carried sub-machine guns, pistols on leg holsters.

The breath was snatched from my lungs. A surge of familiar anger and guilt ricocheted through me. Something inside my head tugged me down into a flashback . . .

Me and Tony in the Chinook, sitting next to each other. The rotor blades chopping through the air, vibrating through our skin. Tony staring straight ahead, jaw clamped tight, eyes focused, getting in the zone so he could deal with what was to come. And then the signal to go, go, go. Our guys fast-roping down to the ground . . .

Sweat beaded on my forehead, my upper lip. My heartbeat cranked up. Shots boomed in my ears, explosions, lights, frantic footsteps, and—

'Mitchell! Mitchell!' Maya's voice pulled me back to the present as she repeated my name over and over again. 'You're OK. You're here with me.' I blinked up at her, the blurry edges of her face slowly coming into focus as her words penetrated my head. She touched my shoulder. 'I thought the flashbacks were getting better.'

I closed my eyes. Forced all the darkness down and felt the photo slipping from my fingers. When I opened my eyes, it was in Maya's hand.

'This is Tony?'

I nodded, swallowing down the hard lump in my throat. From the look Maya was giving me it was obvious she wanted me to talk about it but there was no time for that.

Corinne appeared in the doorway again, her eyes glistening with tears. 'It was just my neighbour. The one who's been on holiday. She heard the news and wanted to find out what was happening.'

The distraction was enough for me to get myself together again. I stood up abruptly, not meeting Maya's gaze as I asked Corinne to give me a hand with the wardrobe. 'I'm going to lean it over and I need you to check underneath it.'

'Yeah. Sure,' Corinne said.

I could feel Maya's eyes on me. Knew there'd be a look in them asking *are you OK?*

I stood at the side of the wardrobe, reached up to the top, my toes tight against the wood to brace it, then tilted it towards me as Corinne crouched down by the base until the underside was revealed.

'No. Nothing.'

I pushed the wardrobe back into position and picked up the Supergirl notepad again. 'I need to speak to her friend, Laura. Can you ring her? Ask her to come here to talk to me? Toni may have confided something in her best friend.'

'Of course. Her number's in my phone downstairs.' Corinne rushed along the hallway.

Maya put the drawers back in the unit and said, 'I haven't found anything.'

We headed back downstairs. I put Toni's notebook on the kitchen table and took a swig of what was left of the now cold tea.

While Corinne was calling Laura, my phone rang. It was Lee. He didn't need to announce himself as the caller, and time was too short to waste on pleasantries. It was straight down to business.

'I've been looking at Toni's mobile phone provider's data, going through texts and calls. They're all between Toni and Corinne and a girl called Laura Hammond.'

'Laura's her best mate.'

'I can email you details if you like but they all seem innocent, everyday teenage chatter. There's nothing sinister about them, and there are no messages arranging to meet anyone. Her iCloud has only innocuous photos and some coursework essays on it. Also, her phone's been switched off since 1.12 p.m. on the day she went missing. I've pinpointed the area where the last GPS signal was transmitting from. It's a place locally known as the cutting – a pathway that leads over a disused railway track between some woods a couple of streets away from Toni's house. From the satellite maps, it looks as if it could be used as a shortcut into town. There's no CCTV in that area I can tap into, though. The only CCTV in Bournewood is in the High Street.'

'Thanks. I'll check it out.' I knew military-grade GPS systems could be spot on, but I had no idea how good a smartphone GPS was. 'How accurate is that GPS data?'

'It's getting better all the time. It could be anywhere between one to eight metres, depending on the conditions.'

'OK. Good work. Thanks, mate.'

Lee hung up and Corinne stared at me, her phone in her hand.

'Any news?' she asked urgently.

I told her what Lee had said. 'Do you know of this cutting?'

'Yes. Toni did use it as a shortcut to get to the High Street. Otherwise you have to go the long way round on the main road. I told her not to. It's in the middle of the woods, and I didn't like the idea of people lurking around in there.' She cupped her hands to her mouth, terror in her eyes.

'I'm going to have a look at the place.'

'Do you think she's still there? Injured somewhere? Maybe she fell and hit her head.'

Injury was the best we could hope for. The other alternative – that she'd been abducted or raped and left for dead was far worse. 'How much does the cutting get used by people?'

'Dog walkers use it to get into the woods. Businessmen use it as a shortcut to the station. People going into town.'

'Has anyone ever been attacked there before?' Maya asked.

'No, not that I've heard of.'

If it had a reasonable amount of foot traffic, it was unlikely Toni hadn't been discovered already. *If* she was still there.

I called up a satellite map on my phone, zoomed into Corinne's street, found the cutting a couple of streets away, which looked like a tarmac road, wide enough for a single vehicle. Either side of it were the woods that abutted the old railway track, branching off left and right. 'I'm going to have a look. Maybe it's best if you stay here.' I looked at Corinne. 'Just in case.'

'In case what?' She swallowed nervously, fearing the very worst.

'In case Toni comes back when we're gone.' I put a reassuring hand on her shoulder. 'There's still the possibility she *has* just gone to stay with someone for a few days.'

Corinne gulped and nodded.

'What did Laura say?' I asked her.

'She was going to come round now, but I'll call her back and tell her to come later.'

I nodded in acknowledgement, then Maya and I got into my pick-up and headed down Corinne's quiet street. At the end of the road we could either turn right to reach the main road or left, towards a large close that fed into a further cul-de-sac. At one side of the cul-de-sac, the houses backed on to the woods and the old railway line. The properties were maybe a hundred years old, detached, huge. It was a well-to-do location. An affluent area. Professional people. There was a big gap in the woods at the edge of the cul-de-sac where the tarmac path of the cutting began.

I parked up outside the entrance and glanced around. The street was quiet. The houses nearby were set back from the road. Mature plants and tall walls or fencing edged their properties. From here I couldn't see into their windows so it was unlikely they'd get a clear view of the comings and goings of people using the cutting.

We walked beneath the canopy of trees and up an incline, the dense woods either side of us. We looked left, right and straight ahead, eyes scanning for signs of Toni or her rucksack and its contents.

Maya shuddered. 'This place gives me the creeps. Someone could've been lurking in here, behind the trees, waiting for an opportunity.'

They could indeed. And I wondered if this was some kind of random attack on a young woman – an opportunist waiting here to rape Toni possibly, or mug her. Or was there another reason for her disappearance?

At the top of the small hill the old railway line appeared, branching out to our left and right, exactly like the map showed. We stepped off the path on to the track, Maya searching left, me checking right, eyes poring over the debris of leaves and foliage, looking under bushes, kicking the decaying leaves away. But there was no sign of Toni, her mobile phone or her rucksack and laptop.

Fifteen minutes later we met in the centre again on the tarmac. All we'd found was rubbish – plastic bags, discarded food wrappers, a broken umbrella, a dead fox carcass, golf balls. Nothing that helped us work out what had happened to Toni.

We took a slow walk down the incline to the other side of the cutting, still searching for signs of Toni or something she'd left behind.

We emerged beside an old church that had been converted into a house in another well-to-do street. I consulted the satellite map again. If Toni had been going into town she would've walked to the end of this road and taken a left turn, then carried on going straight towards the High Street.

I blew out a frustrated breath.

'We need to check with the owners of the surrounding houses,' Maya said, glancing around. 'See if they saw Toni that day. I can do it while you go back and speak to the neighbours in Toni's street.'

'Thanks.' I pulled out my phone and emailed Maya a copy of Toni's photo that Corinne had forwarded from her own phone. Maya's phone beeped in receipt. 'I doubt any of them would have a clear view, but it's worth a try. Even if they didn't see something, they might have heard something – a shout or a scream. Maybe they didn't report it to the police. They could've thought it was just kids messing around.'

Maya delved into her bag and pulled out her mobile phone.

'I'll start with Bert. If he saw Toni leave the house at one p.m., he may have seen something he doesn't realise is significant.'

But I wasn't holding out much hope of that. If Toni's phone had last transmitted positioning data from the cutting, it was likely that whatever fate had befallen her had happened right here.

THE DETECTIVE
Chapter 13

After I left Bill Graves, I drove along his front field of rapeseed, swung a left on to the road, passed the Jamesons' farm and carried on until I spotted the turn-off for Simms Livery Stables with a FOR SALE board up outside. I turned into another long, rambling driveway, but this time there were no yellow flowers and long stalks to greet me, just flat fields with tufts of velvety green grass either side.

I parked in front of the main, uninhabited house, which was an old brick building covered with patches of moss and trails of ivy. The outside looked run-down and neglected, hardly surprising if the owner had been suffering from dementia.

I cupped my hands to several windows for a look-see inside and spotted some furniture covered in dust cloths. One had slipped a little revealing an antique desk and an ornate chair that must've been worth a few quid. Denise and I had been partial to antique furniture. After we'd got married and bought our first house we'd scoured the shops for nice pieces, a few items at a time as and when we could afford them. Over the years we'd built up a good collection. They didn't make them like that any more. All this cheap superstore rubbish was flimsy and didn't last long. When I'd decided to take DI Nash's job in London, I'd accepted an offer on the house I'd shared with my wife. The sale would most likely be completed in a few months and I was going to downsize – maybe find a small flat to rent nearer to where I'd be working. But I hadn't stopped to think what to do with all the furniture we'd accumulated. I'd been too busy thinking about a new start. A new opportunity to move on with my life, away from the memories of Denise that had held me captive in grief. An opportunity to start living again. Now the doubts were creeping in. What if I was wrong, leaving those memories behind? What if I was making a mistake leaving CID? What if I was useless at the new job in the wildlife unit? Was I too old to start over? Should I just give it all up and enjoy the time I had left before I popped my clogs? I was starting to think *I* was the antique.

I wandered down a track wide enough for a vehicle that led round to the back of the house and looked to the west, towards the Jamesons' property, but their house wasn't visible in the distance, obscured by their fields of rapeseed. To the north, across more fields with six horses grazing on grass, I spotted a wooden post-and-rail fence in the far distance, separating the Simms's land from the dense wooded area. Behind that, unseen from this viewpoint, was Parker Farm. In the distance to the right of me was a large stable block.

I looked at the horses again and shuddered. It was probably unmanly to admit that they scared the crap out of me. I'd been bitten by one when I was a kid and I always gave them a wide berth now. Those things were *huge*. One kick to the head from their powerful hind legs and hard hooves and you'd be a goner. I'd never understood the fascination with horse riding.

There was a dusty track leading from the house towards the stable block, but I didn't fancy walking it with the horses let loose, even though there was another post-and-rail fence separating me from their field. It didn't look that high, and I was pretty sure they'd be able to jump it if they really wanted to. Yes, I was a wimp.

So I got back in the car and drove down the track, nervously keeping one eye glued to the horses. Luckily, they were at the far end of the field now, munching on grass, and weren't interested in my arrival.

I parked next to a muddy old Ford Fiesta, and as I exited the car, I heard a radio playing in one of the stables and someone talking.

I walked towards the noise and called out a 'Hello?'

Stepping inside the doorway, I found a young woman, mid-twenties, dressed in jodhpurs and a T-shirt, drinking from a mug and talking to a young man who was busy fiddling with his phone. There were bales of hay stacked up and some riding equipment hanging on the walls.

'Hello,' I said again.

The girl jumped and dropped her mug. It bounced over a pile of hay and splattered tea up her riding boots. The guy jerked his head up and then stood, his hand reaching for a pitchfork propped up next to one of the hay bales.

'Who are you?' the guy said, pitchfork now in hand, ready to use as a weapon.

I held my hands up in a placatory gesture, then slowly retrieved my warrant card from my pocket and held it up to him. 'I'm Detective Sergeant Carter. It's not surprising what happened to the Jamesons has made you both jumpy but you can put that down. I just want a chat with you.'

The girl exhaled a relieved breath and fanned her face. 'I didn't want to come up here today. Usually, I come on my own but after what's happened next door I made my brother come with me.' She glanced nervously at him.

'What's your name?' I asked her.

'Jenny. Jenny Fullerton. This is Adam.'

Adam put the pitchfork on a hook along the back wall and said, 'Sorry about that.'

I shrugged. 'It's understandable, under the circumstances.'

'I heard they were shot!' Adam said. 'Is that right?'

'Unfortunately, that's correct. Were either of you here the day before yesterday?'

'I was here,' Jenny said.

'And what time was that?'

'Um . . . I came in the morning. It would've been about seven until ten. I was mucking out and stuff. Then I came again about two. I stayed until about four.'

'Did you pass any vehicles when you came and went? Or see or hear anything suspicious? Notice anyone hanging around?'

'No. I didn't see anyone at all. I was out riding a couple of the horses in the afternoon so I was up and down the lanes. Never saw another car or person at all, actually.'

'Did you hear any gunshots?'

'No, nothing. In the morning when I was here, I had the radio on, though.'

I glanced around. You couldn't see the lane from here, so even if a car had been to and from the Jamesons' house, if Jenny was in or around the stable block at the time she wouldn't have seen a thing.

'How long have you been renting the stables?'

'A few years. Emily Simms is in a home now and her son's got it up for sale but he said I could carry on renting it off him until he sells it. I've been looking at other places, but they're a lot more expensive. I'm hoping whoever buys it will let me stay.'

I looked at the horses in the field. Still at the far end. Good. 'Are they all yours?'

'No, only one's mine. I just look after them for other people.' She bit her lip and said, 'Do you think they'll come back? The people who did it? I'm here on my own most of the time and I'm scared now.'

'I doubt it, but it would pay to be cautious at the moment.'

'You can pay me to be your bodyguard.' Adam grinned at Jenny.

'Did you know the Jamesons?' I asked her.

'No. Only to wave to when I saw their Land Rover.'

'So you can't think of any reason someone would want to kill them?'

'God, no!'

'They must be crazy, the people who did it,' Adam said, pulling a disgusted face. 'Shooting a poor old couple.' He shook his head. 'It's just wrong.'

'OK, thanks for your help.' I handed Jenny a business card. 'If you think of anything else, then just give me a call.'

'Sure.' She pocketed the card. 'I hope you catch them.'

'Me, too,' I muttered. It wasn't just wrong. It was barbaric.

THE VIGILANTE
Chapter 14

I phoned Corinne on the short drive back to her street to update her. Disappointment flooded her voice, but then it was replaced by hope. Because if we hadn't found a body, then there was a possibility Toni was still alive and OK. She told me Laura was coming to the house at 5 p.m. so I had a couple of hours to carry out enquiries with the neighbours.

Parking outside Corinne's house, I looked up and down the street, searching for any signs of CCTV cameras that the residents might have, but saw nothing obvious.

I walked across to Bert's house and spotted him inside, still sitting at the front window, watching my approach.

I waved as I headed up his path and waited for him to open the door.

It swung open slowly as he manoeuvred his wheelchair back. He had short grey hair, alert blue eyes, and was unshaven. He wore a T-shirt that showed off arms toned from pushing himself around. The lower half of his body betrayed the damage to his legs, wasted and stick-thin in black jogging bottoms. 'Can I help you?'

'Hi. I'm a friend of Corinne's. I'm helping her find out what's happened to Toni. She said you told her you'd seen Toni leave the house at one p.m. on the day she disappeared.'

He pressed his lips together in a solemn smile. 'Yes, that's right. I take it there's still no news?'

'Unfortunately not. Can I ask you exactly what you saw?'

'I already told the police,' he said. There was something in his voice – defensive, perhaps?

'It would help if you could tell me, too. They're not doing much to find her. And as I'm sure you can appreciate, every second counts when a young girl goes missing.'

'Well, yes. Of course.' He coughed into his fist, and I wondered if he was stalling for time to think. 'Corinne's been lovely to me. She gets me shopping and whatnot. I'm happy to help any way I can. Toni was a lovely girl, too. She used to come over and help do some cleaning for me and check I was OK. And she didn't want any payment, either. Not like a lot of youngsters. She was sweet. I liked her.'

'Was?' Past tense. Was that significant?

He shook his head slightly, eyes watering. '*Is*. Slip of the tongue.'

'So, what exactly did you see?' I prompted him.

'Well . . . I just saw Toni leave the house. That's what I told everyone. I don't know what else I can say.'

'And it was definitely one p.m.?'

'Yes.'

'Dead on? Not five past or ten past?'

'Exactly one p.m.'

'That's very specific. How can you be so sure?'

'Because the news starts at one p.m., and it was playing the opening music when I saw her.' He scratched his forehead with one hand and then clenched it in his lap, but not before I'd noticed a slight trembling in his fingers. An effect of his disability, or nervousness?

'And then what? Which direction did she go in?'

He leaned his torso forward and pointed around the door frame, up the road to his right. 'That way.'

Which was the direction Toni would've gone to reach the cutting. 'Did you see anyone else hanging around? Anyone watching her? Following her? Or anything else suspicious?'

He thought for a minute. 'No, I don't think so.'

'What about before that day? Did you ever notice anything strange?'

'No. Just the usual comings and goings of the street.' He rubbed a hand up and down the armrest of the wheelchair.

'Do you know what Toni was wearing?'

'Jeans and a black T-shirt with a butterfly on the front. She had the red rucksack she always carries to college. And she had black trainers on.'

Again, it was very specific. The kind of specific from someone who spent his life watching out of his window because his accident had left him without much of a life of his own? Or for another reason entirely? Something about him was making my senses alert. Just because he was in a wheelchair didn't mean he was harmless. I scanned the hallway behind him, searching for any possible sign Toni had been there, her backpack perhaps. There was a small table topped with a couple of letters, an envelope and a set of keys, an umbrella propped up next to it, but nothing else. I looked at his hands and arms for scratch marks but there were none. 'And what happened when she left the house? Did she seem scared or nervous at all?'

He shrugged. 'I don't know. She shut the door behind her and just kind of hurried up the road.'

'Do you have any CCTV cameras?' I asked.

He shook his head.

'OK, thanks for your help.'

'You're welcome. I hope you find her,' he called out to my retreating back.

I visited the other houses in the street but no one had seen Toni and none of them had any security cameras that might've caught something useful.

As I arrived back at Corinne's doorstep and knocked on the door, Lee rang.

'I've got one of my guys checking facial recognition on local CCTV cameras and we've found something interesting.'

My heartbeat quickened. 'What?'

Corinne opened the door, saw I was on the phone and ushered me inside. She hovered beside me, chewing again on the skin around her thumbnail, which was already red raw with dots of blood seeping to the surface.

'There's nothing from the day she went missing, but the day *before*, Toni was caught on a camera in the High Street. She went into the library at 14.52 p.m. Left at 15.45 p.m. I took a look at the library's CCTV cameras and she used one of the computer terminals.'

I wondered why Toni had gone there to use the Internet when she had her own laptop with access at home. It was possible Toni's laptop had stopped working for some reason, but why not use Corinne's in that case? And if it wasn't working, why take it with her when she left the house two days ago? Or was she taking it to be repaired? Unlikely, since she hadn't mentioned to her mum it wasn't operational, and Toni didn't have her own income to pay to get it fixed, so surely she'd have asked Corinne for some money. Toni also had a smartphone with Internet, which, according to what Lee had found, had been working perfectly at that point, so there was only one possible reason that was front and centre in my head: Toni had been doing something secret she didn't want Corinne to know about. That could also explain why the page from the notebook had been torn out – because she didn't want her mum to find it. 'I don't suppose you know what she looked at?'

'I got into their servers, checked the usage for the time period, and I've got Toni's browser history for you.'

I sat down at the kitchen table. 'Go ahead.'

'Toni was using Google. First of all she entered the following search: *missing girl, long hair, cat tattoo*. I'm guessing she didn't get any kind of hits she wanted because a few minutes later she searched: *missing woman, leopard tattoo*, which took her to some more links. A Facebook page titled "Missing and Tattooed", dedicated to trying to trace missing people from their distinguishing tattoos. She browsed the page for a while but I don't think she found what she was looking for.' He paused for a moment, and I detected something worse coming. 'Then she typed in: *are red rooms real?*'

Unease prickled at the base of my spine because I'd heard the term before. It was the modern-day version of a snuff movie. A live-stream video of the torture and murder of someone for the entertainment of all the sadistic people out there in the world who wanted to watch. Some people said they were a myth, but I knew that wasn't true. A year ago, police had caught an infamous paedophile and murderer who'd live-streamed pay-per-view videos of torture and murder from his house in the Philippines. Investigators had said his crimes were so horrific, they wanted to bring back the death penalty. John Crimper had run a website called 'Child Fun' and carried out sexual abuse, torture and murder on young children, including babies – filming and selling it to paedophiles around the world. He'd finally been arrested following a five-year manhunt. I'd also heard rumours over the years of other red rooms that involved adult victims.

'Shit.' I sat back in my chair as if someone had punched me in the chest. My mind raced, working out possible scenarios as to why a teenager would suddenly be looking up missing girls and red rooms. 'Did her search bring up anything she clicked on?'

'Yeah. Plenty of hits. Mostly community discussion pages. Some people saying they're all staged or fakes. Some about a hoax that was going round a few years ago of a terrorist being tortured and killed in a red room. Some from people claiming they've seen a real one. Another about the investigation into John Crimper and his arrest. A *lot* of people asking where they can find one.'

'Toni was going to study criminology and psychology. She wanted to get a job helping child victims of abuse. I found a notebook with a lot of notes relating to that kind of stuff. It could be she was doing some personal research for her upcoming degree coursework, but the Internet search for a missing woman with a tattoo seems pretty specific to me.'

'Yeah, me too. Which made me think that somehow Toni had heard about an actual red room that involved a girl with a tattoo, so I tried searching everything I can get access to, including international law enforcement agencies. So far, I've found nothing relating to a girl or woman with any kind of animal tattoo who was reported missing, nor any kind of significant crime involving a female with a tattoo like that.'

The cogs of my brain turned as he spoke. 'She could've stumbled across mention of it on the Internet.'

'True. But I've been searching keywords and can't find anything that matches that scenario. I'm just about to check the IP history for her home address to see what her browsing was like. I have a hunch I want to check out, but I wanted to give you a sitrep first. I also did a few preliminaries. Toni's bank account hasn't been touched since she left. There's only a hundred quid in there anyway and she made no withdrawals in the days before she disappeared.'

'OK, thanks, Lee. Can you do one more thing for me? There's a neighbour, Bert Williamson, who lives at number 12. Can you check him out? Something seems a bit off with him. His body language is ringing alarm bells.'

'Will do. Speak soon.'

I hung up, wondering what Toni had found that had prompted those Internet searches. Instinct told me that Corinne was right. Toni hadn't run away. It wasn't a random abduction, either. Toni had found out something about a red room and a missing girl and that had made her act scared and jumpy, out of character, in the days before she disappeared. Toni was used to the sickness of dark minds with her interest in criminology – serial killers, rapists, murderers. She wanted to make it her career, so I didn't think she'd scare easily, which meant whatever she'd discovered about a red room wasn't a hoax or staged. She'd seen it for real. Online somewhere. Maybe Toni was worried whoever ran the site could find out what she'd seen and who she was through her digital footprint online, which must've been why she'd used an anonymous library terminal to try to search for a girl with a tattoo reported missing. Because *that's* who she'd seen in a red room. She was double-checking, gathering facts, researching, just like the fastidious notes in her notebook previously, making sure it wasn't a hoax, before she . . . Before she what? What happened next when she left the house?

One thing was certain, though. If Toni had found a red room, the people who did something so inhumane and twisted wouldn't want just anyone finding out about it. And if she had inadvertently divulged her digital identity to them, then they'd stop at nothing to keep her quiet.

THE DETECTIVE

Chapter 15

DI Nash phoned as I got back into my car. I saw 'Ellie' flash up on screen and debated whether to send it to voicemail or not. Would she be able to recognise the self-doubt creeping into my voice? But she hadn't just been my boss for years, she was also a good friend – maybe my only one – and I'd missed her since she'd moved to London.

'Hi, Ellie,' I said, staring out of the windscreen. 'How're things?'

'Yeah, pretty good. Well, better than good, really, all things considered,' she gushed down the phone, which was strange because she wasn't a gushy woman. She was straight-talking and intelligent and strong. Stronger than me. Her husband and fellow police officer, Spencer, had been killed four months ago in a hostage situation that went tragically wrong. She was getting over Spencer's death by throwing herself into setting up a new department. I'd procrastinated and wallowed in grief for a year and still I felt the weight of indecision crushing me, like I was wading through treacle. 'It's been manic, organising everything, but I'm getting there. We've had some amazing applications for the detective constable roles, and I've been interviewing all week. I think you'll be happy with the team I've selected.'

'Right. That sounds . . . good.' My fingertips tapped the steering wheel.

'Two weeks and we'll be up and running, but I've got our first referral already. Some intelligence about a suspected trafficking ring of pangolins.'

'Pangolins? What are they?'

'They're the most trafficked mammal in the world you've never heard of. Worth a fortune, poor things. Used for Chinese medicine.'

'Hmmm. Interesting case.' I tried to muster up some excitement but couldn't seem to get animated about animal trafficking when people were being trafficked in such high numbers, too.

She paused on the other end of the phone for a moment. I heard chattering in the background and a phone ringing. 'You're having second thoughts about the job, aren't you?'

I sighed. She knew me too well. I opened my mouth to speak but nothing came out.

'What is it? Talk to me about it.'

'I don't know.' I sighed again. 'Lots of things, but nothing I can really name. Or maybe it's everything. Maybe I'm just not good at change.'

'Change comes whether you like it or not. You have to go with the flow.'

Greene had said something similar, and I knew they were both right. It was obvious. 'Maybe I'm too much of a dinosaur to change.'

'Well, you know what happened to them when they couldn't adapt?'

'Exactly. I feel like I'm an extinct breed in the force now.'

'Which is precisely why you need to embrace this new challenge.'

'New is scary.'

'Don't be a bloody girl!'

I laughed, despite the worries turning over in my head. 'You're not allowed to call me that. It's sexist.'

'Who says?'

'Greene would. Haven't you had the new diversity training?'

'I escaped before they started it. It's political correctness gone mad.' She was as much a rebel as I was. 'Don't tell me *you've* had it?' She snorted. 'I'd like to have seen that.'

'Greene would have put me at the top of the list if I wasn't leaving.'

'I can just imagine. So . . . anyway, back to the important stuff. Are you thinking of backing out of my team?'

'I . . .' I tried to think what to say but when nothing emerged, Ellie jumped in.

'Look, this is a big thing you're going through right now. Denise is gone. You've sold the house you shared with her for most of your married life. You've finally got rid of her belongings after a year. And you're starting a new job. They're the most stressful things people can go through and you've done them all in quick succession. It's normal to have a bit of self-doubt and fear going on.'

'But you've managed it OK.'

'Because I have to. Because I had to get away from the nick where the memories of Spencer would be too much. Because I had to get away from the house for the same reason. If I stop and let all the grief and bitterness consume me, I'll end up in the nut house.'

'Yeah, well, maybe I am losing the plot.' I rubbed at my forehead. 'I know what you're saying but nothing seems like it makes sense any more. It just feels like I don't really have a clue about my life.'

'Maybe it's my fault. I badgered you into this new job – pun not intended. Maybe it was too soon for you.'

'But you're doing OK. You sound like you're loving it.'

'We're not all the same. And it's not a competition, is it?' Her last words seemed harsh but they were delivered with gentleness. 'What's the alternative, if you don't join me?'

I let my head fall back against the headrest and closed my eyes. 'I don't know. Maybe I'll go on a world cruise or something.'

She didn't reply but I knew what she was thinking. *Your life is policing. What the hell will you do without this job?* I thought I knew the answer, too. I'd probably become a recluse. Or an alcoholic. Or an alcoholic recluse.

'I don't want to let you down,' I said.

'And I don't want to push you. Maybe you just got caught up in my needs because you wanted to help *me* get over Spencer. If you want to back out, I won't stand in your way. I'll be pissed off with you for a while, but I'll get over that.' I heard the smile in her voice. 'And I'll miss you. But we both know life's too short not to at least try to be happy.'

But the trouble was, I didn't even know what would make me happy these days.

'And I've had loads of quality applicants. I'd be able to find a new detective sergeant with no problem.'

'So I'm dispensable?' I quipped.

'Oi! You can't have it both ways.' I heard someone calling Ellie's name and she said, 'Sorry, I've got to go. Why don't you have a serious think about what you really want for your future and let me know. But don't leave it too long, all right?'

'Thanks, Ellie.'

'Take care, mate.'

'You, too.'

I hung up and pushed the swirling confusion to a place in my head where I didn't have to think about it. Didn't have to make a decision. Future? I wasn't sure I even had one.

I started the engine, turned left out of the livery stables and the lane swung around in a circular shape, skirting the edge of the woods on the passenger side of my vehicle. After a short while I arrived at Parker Farm. There was a seven-foot wall around the front of the property with solid metal gates which were closed. I parked in front of the gates and got out of the car. Above the wall I could see the tops of metal spikes every metre or so with shiny new barbed wire strung across them. The same barbed wire was being attached to the top of the gates by a guy in his thirties with his hair tied back in a ponytail, working on a ladder inside the property.

I wondered if he was installing it after hearing what had happened to the Jamesons.

The man on the ladder looked at me over the top of the gates with suspicion and said, 'Can I help you?'

I held up my warrant card and told him who I was and why I was there. 'Are you Connor Parker?'

'Yes.'

'I'm just speaking to the Jamesons' neighbours to see if they heard or saw anything suspicious the day before yesterday.'

'Oh, right. Hang on a sec. I'll come down.' He disappeared from the ladder.

The gates were electric and opened inwards and the man stepped out to meet me. I glimpsed another red-brick house in the distance behind him and a large outbuilding amongst yet more fields.

'Yeah. It sounds pretty nasty, what happened up there.' He frowned, two thick eyebrows drawn up over two dark-brown eyes. 'But, sorry, I can't help you. I was out all day.'

'Right. Can you tell me what time you left and when you got back?'

'I left the house about six thirty in the morning. Got back about ten in the evening.'

'Does anyone else live here who might've seen anything?'

'No. I live alone.'

'Did you know the Jamesons?'

'Quite well, although my parents knew them better. They were friends with them, used to have each other round for drinks and meals, but my parents died several years ago. I'd stop and have a chat with Jan and Mike if I saw them in their Land Rover or out walking, but other than that I've only really seen them in passing in the last few years.'

'You can't think of any reason someone would want to hurt them?'

'Absolutely none.'

'You're not aware of any disputes they had with anyone?'

'Not at all.'

'You've certainly got a lot of security here,' I said. 'Have you had any problems in the past with break-ins or trespassers?'

'No. But you can't be too careful these days, can you? Especially now, after what's happened to Jan and Mike. I thought I'd put up some extra deterrents.' He pointed to the barbed wire.

'I don't blame you. Well, if anything comes to mind that might be helpful, can you give me a ring?' I handed out another business card.

'Uh . . . yeah. Of course.'

THE VIGILANTE
Chapter 16

Corinne's eyes were red with dark smudges underneath. She was pale and looked as if she was on the edge of collapse. 'What?' she asked me desperately. 'What did Lee say?'

'Was Toni's laptop working OK?'

Her forehead bunched up as she thought. 'Um . . . yes. She was using it the day before she went missing. Why?'

I paused for a moment. 'You were always a vodka and Coke drinker. I think you might need a large one before I tell you what I've discovered.'

'What? What is it?' Corinne's jaw fell open as she stared at me.

I told her about Toni's visit to the library. How I suspected what she'd discovered online had been the initiating factor in her disappearance.

'Oh, no!' Corinne wailed, leaning forward at the waist and wrapping her arms around herself. 'I was right. She didn't run away, did she? I knew she wouldn't. But that means . . . someone's taken her.' She reached out and gripped my arm. 'Do you think she's still alive?'

It was a question I'd been thinking constantly since Corinne had first called me, and I didn't have an answer. I wanted to sugarcoat it with a yes, but I also wanted to be honest. 'I don't know.'

'I've never even *heard* of a red room before! How can anyone do something like that? Online snuff films? What's wrong with people?' Corinne's hands shook as she clasped a hand to her mouth, hiccupping back a sob.

I searched the kitchen cupboards for a vodka bottle. Poured a generous slug in a glass and added come Coke from the fridge. Put it on the table in front of her.

'According to Toni's phone data, she hadn't arranged to meet anyone. So why would she take her laptop with her?' I asked.

'I've got no idea,' Corinne said. 'Like I said, she only ever took it to college. Otherwise it was always here.'

'Toni's course wasn't due to start until next week but presumably the uni is open now after the holidays. Could she have been going to the library there to do some more research on true crimes or red rooms?'

'If she was going to uni, she would've caught the bus from the main road. Not gone through the cutting towards town. It's in High Wycombe.'

'There has to be a reason,' I said, more a thought out loud than a question. Toni left the house of her own free will. She must've been intending to go somewhere. Obviously not back to the public library in town, if she was carrying her own laptop.

I pulled my phone from my pocket and called up the satellite map of the area again. I zoomed in, followed the route from Toni's house towards the cutting, swiped down and found the High Street just the other side of it, zoomed in again and searched around. I found the police station at the far end and then it clicked. 'I think Toni didn't want to tell you about what she'd found. She knew you'd be scared and worried for her. But she was convinced what she'd seen was real, and she wanted to tell the police. I think that's where she was heading.'

Corinne picked up her glass and gulped it. 'Why couldn't she just tell me if she'd found something like that, if she was in trouble? I could've been with her. Protected her.' She balled her right hand into a fist, fear and anger at what these people could do to her daughter turning her face a mottled red.

'Because she thought she was protecting you.' I was angry, too, but I had to keep it together. There was no time to fall apart. Falling apart wouldn't help Toni. I was too busy trying to work out why Toni hadn't just written the red room website down and given it to the police. Why take her laptop to show them? I thought about the page torn out of her notebook. Maybe she had written it down on the missing page and taken that with her. But what significance did the laptop itself have that a website address didn't? A threat of some kind that the people who ran the red room had sent her? Or just to show the police what had happened when she'd entered the site so they'd see she'd stumbled upon it accidentally and wasn't involved in any way?

'Do you think I should let the police know what you've found?' Corinne asked. 'The more people looking for her the better.'

'It's your call, of course, but I'd say no. We don't have anything concrete, and besides, they have to follow rules and a load of bureaucracy which will just slow everything down. What Lee's doing isn't legal, but he's doing it quickly and efficiently. It would take them days just to get warrants for access to the same information Lee's found in hours.' I took her hand in mine. 'You trust me, don't you?'

Corinne's eyes, filled with a world of pain, searched mine. Then she nodded her agreement. 'I want her back, Mitchell. *Please.* I don't care what you have to do. Just get her back.'

THE DETECTIVE
Chapter 17

Next stop, Eagan's Scaffolding. I wasn't sure if Paula would be at work the day after her parents' murder, but I wanted to check out her alibi, and establish whether or not Grant had one.

I parked outside their unit on an industrial estate. A sign for reception pointed me to a front door on the right. On the left side of the building was an open-air yard with wrought-iron gates. Several guys were there loading scaffolding equipment on to vehicles but Grant wasn't amongst them.

I walked into the reception and found a young girl behind an old desk with paperwork in a huge pile not dissimilar to the stack waiting for me in the office. She was on the phone but smiled at me and held her finger up to indicate she wouldn't be long. My gaze scanned behind her to a couple of closed office doors. The clanging metal of scaffold poles being thrown into the trucks outside clattered through an open window.

The girl put the phone down and said, 'Hi, how can I help you?'

I showed her my warrant card and introduced myself.

'Are you looking for Paula? It's absolutely awful what's happened. She's not in today, though. She's in a right state. Well, you would be, wouldn't you? I mean, I couldn't imagine anything like it.' She spewed the words out quickly. When she paused for a breath, I jumped in.

'Was Paula here the day before yesterday?' I asked.

'Um . . . no. She had the day off.'

So Paula *had* lied to me. She'd just jumped up from a person of interest to a potential suspect. 'How about Grant Eagan. Was he here then?'

'No. They were both off. Grant's not here today, either. He's probably, you know, looking after Paula.'

'Paula does the admin and accounts, is that right?'

'Yeah. And she looks after the website and sorts out online orders. The only office staff are me and Paula.'

'What about Grant? What does he do here?'

'He goes out on jobs with the lads, even though he's the boss.'

'OK, thanks.'

'Do you need their home address? I can give it to you.'

'That's all right, I have it. Thanks.'

'Sorry I couldn't be more helpful.'

'You've actually been incredibly helpful.'

She gave me a sad smile as her phone started ringing again. 'The phones have been going mad with customers who've heard the news, wanting to give their condolences. It hasn't been this busy with actual jobs for ages.'

I slipped out of reception and called Ronnie to update him on what I'd found. 'Can you give the Eagans a call and get them to come to the nick? It's time to have a proper chat with them both.'

'Yes, guv, will do.'

'Are there any updates for me in the meantime?'

'I've been speaking to the Jamesons' friends. They all said Mike's and Jan's relationship with their daughter was tenuous since Paula got involved with Grant. That they didn't trust him and didn't want him at the house. Jan mentioned to her friend Mavis that Paula was hassling them for money to get Grant out of trouble.'

Which pretty much confirmed what Bill Graves had told me.

'Apart from that, none of their friends know of any recent problems the Jamesons had, and none had seen Mike or Jan in the last couple of weeks. Apparently, Mike had the flu and was struggling to get over it. He wasn't feeling that great still, so he'd been at home with Jan looking after him. Mavis phoned the house at about ten a.m. on the morning before the murder and she said everything seemed fine then. Mavis chatted with Jan for about fifteen minutes about trivial stuff. Jan said Mike was finally on the mend now and they tentatively fixed a day next week for Mavis and her husband to go to their house for dinner. None of the people I spoke to have any clothes or jewellery with small pink stones on it.'

So the stones had jumped up a bit in significance. It seemed very likely now that they had come from whoever else was in the room at the time the Jamesons were murdered. But was that person Paula?

THE VIGILANTE

Chapter 18

Maya returned to Corinne's house with no useful leads. No one had seen Toni at the cutting. No one had heard anything. No one had noticed any suspicious vehicles hanging around. And to make Toni just disappear, they would've needed a vehicle to transport her.

The doorbell rang then, and Corinne rushed to answer it, still expecting – no *hoping* for – it to be Toni coming home, safe and sound. But it was just Toni's friend, Laura.

The contrast between the two young women was obvious from the moment Laura stepped inside the house. Laura was short, overweight, with bad acne, greasy, lifeless hair, and glasses with thick lenses that magnified her eyes.

'Thank you for coming over.' Corinne hugged Laura at the door as Maya and I waited in the hall behind her. 'Come in.' She took Laura's hand and led her into the lounge.

Laura gave Maya and me a fleeting, wobbly smile as Corinne introduced us.

'This is Mitchell. He's Toni's godfather.'

My head swivelled in Corinne's direction. Her eyes met mine with a clear message. *You would've been. If things hadn't gone wrong.*

I ground my teeth to counteract the tightness in my chest from the weight of her words crushing me, and concentrated hard on Laura, trying to stop the images of Tony rushing into my head once more.

'And this is Maya.' Corinne turned back to Laura. 'Please, sit down. We just want to ask you some more questions about Toni.'

Laura sat next to Corinne on the sofa, looking bewildered and nervous. 'I told you everything I knew. I hadn't seen Toni for a couple of days. I don't know what's happened to her, I swear. And I haven't heard from her. I would've told you if I had.' She pulled the cuffs of her long-sleeved T-shirt down and hid her hands inside them, clenching the edges of the material tight with her fingertips.

I sat on an armchair opposite them as Maya perched on the arm beside me.

'We don't think Toni ran away,' I said gently, trying to put her at ease. 'We think someone's taken her. And it's possible you do know something, even without realising it.'

'Oh, no!' Laura gasped. 'Have you told the police?' she asked Corinne.

Corinne glanced at me. 'I don't trust them to find her. Mitchell's helping me.'

Laura followed Corinne's gaze to me, realisation kicking in. 'Oh, you're like one of those special forces guys Toni told me about when she was talking about her dad?'

I nodded.

Laura gulped, as if I might suddenly shoot across the room and deliver a fatal blow to her. 'Seriously, I don't know anything. I would've said, honestly.'

'Did Toni ever mention something she'd discovered on the Internet?' I asked Laura.

'No. Not to me.'

'What about someone threatening her?' I asked.

'No. Definitely not.'

'Toni wrote something in her notebook before she disappeared. It said the words "into the darkness". Do you know what she might've meant by that?'

Laura's wary gaze flicked to Corinne before settling back on me. She swallowed hard. Blinked several times before she said, 'No.'

But I didn't believe her. She knew something. 'Look, I know teenagers keep secrets from their parents. Even secrets that they think might be protecting their parents,' I said. 'But if you know something about what Toni had been looking at, you need to tell us now. No one will be angry with you, but it might help us find her. We need you to be completely honest with us.'

'I am!' She blinked rapidly again behind her lenses. 'I honestly don't know anything.'

'Did she ever tell you anything about a missing girl with a tattoo?'

Laura frowned. 'No.'

'Did she ever talk to you about a red room?'

'Oh, my God.' She bit her lip, eyebrows shooting upwards.

'What is it?' Corinne touched Laura's knee.

Laura's eyes widened. 'A few months back I was telling her about the dark web. Do you know what that is?'

I knew of its existence. A place where any warped person could find anything they wanted at the tip of their fingers – weapons, drugs, child pornography, assassins, cults. The levels of depravity in the world never ceased to amaze me, and all this sick shit and more was readily available on the dark web at the touch of a button.

Corinne shook her head. 'No. What does "dark web" mean?'

Laura licked her lips. 'You've got the surface web, right? Which is anything that can be indexed with a traditional search engine, like Google, that relies on pages containing links so you can find content. Then you've got the deep web, which is stuff that a search engine *can't* find, like a password-protected page or data searches. They say about eighty per cent of what's on the Internet is in the deep web, locked behind passwords and protocols, and is most likely perfectly harmless.' She paused and glanced at us all in turn. 'But then if you go deeper in the net, there's the dark web. It's the bad stuff that's been intentionally hidden, and you can't access it through normal means. You need special software.' She slid her hands out from her cuffs and rubbed them on her jeans. 'Toni was intrigued by the dark web. She wanted to see if the rumours were true. I mean, they say you can get anything on there.' She blushed and pushed her glasses up her nose. 'I've heard all sorts of chatter about what's on it and I didn't want to mess around with it but, you know, Toni was into psychology and crime and stuff. And she'd already decided her dissertation at uni was going to be on cybercrime so she wanted to use the dark web as an example for study material.' She paused, swallowed again, her face pale. 'She was particularly interested in child abuse – paedophiles using the Internet to their advantage through chat rooms and social networks to groom kids. And she knew many popular surface-web chat rooms had been closed down to protect children. But that hadn't stopped them. It had just pushed them further underground. Into the dark web, where what they were doing was much harder to find.' She chewed on her lip.

'Go on,' Corinne said, her face drained of colour.

'Toni . . . um . . . She asked for my help to show her how to get on the dark web because I know about computers. I'm studying computer science,' Laura added for my benefit. 'She thought we should do it together. But I didn't want to go into the darkness. That's what I called it. Those same words. That's what Toni must've meant when she wrote that in her notebook. She must've done it without me and started looking around down there.'

Corinne clenched her hands together in her lap. 'I've never even heard about this dark web. If it exists with all this heinous stuff on it, why haven't the police shut it down?' She asked incredulously. 'How is it possible it even exists?'

'Because the sites are *really* hard to find,' Laura said. 'The dark web is made up of encrypted networks that have been hidden. It's super secure and anonymous. If you use proper OPSEC, it's really hard, if not impossible, for the police to find what's out there or who's using it because IP addresses or the location of devices on a network and servers are obscured.'

'OPSEC?' Maya asked.

'Operational security,' I clarified.

Laura nodded her agreement. 'You have to download special software to go into the darkness, like Tor or Phantom. Phantom is newer than Tor and is supposed to be better and faster. They use what's called "onion routing". What happens when you're using the surface web with a normal browser is that information travels via the net in packets that contain data, which shows the sender and destination. But the Tor network has volunteers who use their computers as nodes, so your packet of info doesn't travel direct to a server. It creates a route through randomly assigned nodes first. Basically, the packets are wrapped in layers of other packets so no node knows the whole pathway.'

I'd had experience with encrypted messages from my time in the military so I was familiar with Tor onion routing. It had become popular with journalists, activists, freedom fighters and whistle-blowers, because it was secure and anonymous, but the same principles that made it a safety net for the innocent to maintain their privacy from the spying eyes of Big Brother had been exploited by criminals and it was a refuge for their ever-growing activity and illicit use.

Laura twisted her lips together, eyes huge behind her glasses. If she'd looked nervous before, she looked terrified now. 'I saw some chatter on an Internet forum on the surface web, rumours about red rooms a while back. A big debate about whether they were real or not. I thought they were trying to wind people up, though. I thought they were just creepy pasta.' She swallowed again.

'Creepy what?' Maya asked.

'Creepy pasta. A horror story spread round the Internet. An urban legend,' Laura added.

'Like you said, you can find all kinds of stuff on the dark web, so why not a red room?' I said. And I knew from John Crimper's pay-per-view site that they existed. I didn't want to mention the details in front of Corinne and Laura, though. Didn't want to put those kinds of images in their heads. I thought Corinne would crumple, knowing Toni was out there somewhere, possibly in the clutches of the same kind of evilness.

Laura threw her head in her hands. 'Is this all my fault? Has something bad happened to her because of me?'

'It's not your fault,' Maya said.

'No, it's mine!' Corinne shouted. 'Why didn't Toni come to me if she was in trouble? Why didn't she say anything if she'd discovered something so . . . so horrific? Why couldn't she talk to me?' Corinne leaped up, a guttural sob exploding from her before she rushed out of the room.

Maya was on her feet instantly, disappearing after her.

'I'm sorry. If I hadn't told Toni about the dark web none of this would've happened, would it?' Tears slid down Laura's cheeks. 'But I don't understand how she could've found a red room. From what I read, if they *did* exist, they'd be well hidden, or you'd have to pay to join the site. They wouldn't let anyone just look at it. Unless . . . Oh, no!' Laura sucked in a breath, wiping her eyes. 'I heard some stuff from a guy in my class. He said he was nosing around to see what kind of content was on the dark web. There's no Google down there so you can't just type in "red rooms" and get a list of hits, but there's something called a Hidden Wiki. It's got a list of dark-web sites on it. They're just addresses made of letters and numbers with the word .onion at the end, so there's no way to find out what's behind them unless you look at them. He said he went on one page and accidentally found a website hidden behind it selling weapons.' She gushed the words out in a long stream, but now she paused to suck in a breath. 'I thought he was just bullshitting, trying to wind everyone up, but maybe there *was* some truth in it. Maybe Toni stumbled across a red-room site down there somehow, and they found out who she was.' She pushed her glasses up again.

I felt panic rising then, my mind churning through everything. There were two scenarios running through my head, both equally disturbing. One: they'd abducted Toni because of what she'd seen and killed her outright to keep her quiet. Two: they'd use her as the next victim in their red room. 'We need to find out exactly what sites she went on right now.'

'But if Toni was using Tor or Phantom, you won't be able to see what she was looking at. The program doesn't store any browsing data like Google does on the surface web. It deletes everything when you close it down.'

'So how can we find out which website she found?' I asked.

'That's what I'm trying to tell you. You can't!' she wailed.

THE MISSING
Chapter 19

My cell is all made of rough concrete. No windows anywhere. There's a wooden door that's solid. I know, I've tried to push it. Tried to shoulder all my weight against it. It won't move. The air smells of stale sweat and dampness and copper and something . . . something else. In the books I've read – the true crimes – many victims said they could smell their own fear. I didn't believe that was possible. Just thought it was something they said. But it's true. I can smell my fear. Taste it. Feel it burning inside me, rippling under my skin.

The man who hit me, he was wearing . . . What was he wearing? I don't know. It was too quick and . . . Well, it doesn't matter what he was wearing. Will I be able to identify him again? *I don't know!* I keep getting flashes of his face but it's all swirly in my head. And if I can't identify them, they'll never be arrested and locked up when I get out of here.

Except I know deep down that I'll never get out of here because no one will find me. How could they?

I don't know how *they* found me. How could they discover I saw it? I don't *understand*. Laura told me it was all anonymous. That was the whole point of it. How could they have known who I was? How did it even let me get that far?

But I saw it. And now I'm going to *be* it.

I rub my hands up and down my arms, my teeth chattering, setting off more pain in my nose and behind my eye sockets. My T-shirt and jeans are damp with sweat and stick to my skin and . . . I've wet myself, too.

I get to my feet, sliding up the wall for support as the room spins around me. *I'm not calling it a cell. I won't.*

I look at the door again. One way out.

Suddenly, a fluorescent tube light on the ceiling turns on. I blink rapidly, the brightness burning my eyes. It's about four metres above my head. If I could jump up and grab it then I could smash it and use the shards of glass as a weapon when they come for me. But there's no way I can get to it. It's too high.

Above the door, way up near the ceiling, there's some kind of small plastic box. There's nothing else in the room. Nothing else I could use as a weapon. Nothing at all.

Except me.

But I refuse to be scared now. *I refuse, I refuse, I refuse!*

I think back to my psychology course. Cognitive behavioural therapy. We did an exercise on thought replacement. Changing negative or fearful thoughts into positive ones. *Thought-stopping. Catching thoughts of fear. Challenge the fearful thought!* People can endure all kinds of things if they do that. So I'm going to do what they don't expect. I'm not going to give them what they want. And I know they want terror and fear and evidence of pain. But fuck them!

FUCK THEM!

Mum always said I was stubborn. That I'd inherited Dad's strength and determination. And even though I never met him, I like to think that's true. It means part of him is inside me. He's always with me, looking over my shoulder, keeping me safe.

Except I'm not safe now and there's no way out. But *I refuse to think that!*

I think instead about the memory box Mum made for me after Dad died. The stories she told me about where he went, what he did. As a child I'd pull out an old jumper of Dad's from the box and smell it, press it to my nose and inhale deeply. It didn't smell of him any more, of course, but when I was little I'd imagine it did. I'd run my fingers over his medals and pull out the photos of him. Stare at them for hours.

I haven't picked up that memory box for years. It's stuffed in the back of my wardrobe now. But I remember one picture vividly – the photo of Dad with Mitchell. I remember Mum telling me that Dad was dead because of Mitchell. She left Hereford after Dad's funeral. Couldn't bear to be reminded of the happy times there with him and their friends, all the guys in the Regiment and their wives. She said she'd never go back.

But Mum will call one of them now, won't she? The old friends Dad knew. She will. Because they know what they're doing. They're used to finding people and getting them back. People in secret locations. Being held by kidnappers who don't want them found.

They'll come. They'll get me out of here.

That's my safety thought. *That's* my fearless thought.

I take a trembling breath and clutch on to it tight.

THE DETECTIVE

Chapter 20

I sat in the interview room at the police station in front of a red-eyed Paula Eagan. Ronnie was in an identical room next door with Grant.

I stated the date and time and who was present for the benefit of the recording equipment, then got straight down to it.

'You told me you were at work the day before yesterday, didn't you?'

Paula glanced down at her lap and bit her lip.

'But that's not true, is it?'

She shook her head.

'So I want to know why you lied to me, Paula.'

She closed her eyes and threw her head in her hands. 'I'm sorry.' Her voice was muffled through her fingers.

'Sorry's not good enough. Where were you? Did you go to your parents' house and ask them for money again to bail Grant out of trouble? Did it escalate into an argument? Did you kill them, Paula?'

'No!' She sat back up.

'Or maybe it was Grant who shot them? We know there were two people there. Did you try to stop him but it all got out of control?'

'God, no! Of course not. But I knew if I told you what was really going on I'd look guilty. My relationship with Mum and Dad had been strained for a long time. I was asking them for money. And then suddenly they're murdered. But I didn't have anything to do with it. I swear!'

I leaned back in the chair and folded my arms. 'Go on, then. Tell me where you were. I'm listening.'

She sucked in a breath and stared at the ceiling for a moment. 'Look, me and Grant are having some financial problems.'

'Because of his gambling debts?'

'Yes. He was using some online casinos. Slots, live games, video poker, anything like that. By the time I realised what was going on, he'd racked up a thirty-grand debt on our credit cards.' She rubbed at her forehead with one hand, grimacing. 'I was paying it off in dribs and drabs, but we never really got far with it because the interest kept making it go up and up. We got behind with the mortgage then, trying to juggle things around, and the bank threatened us with repossession. We made them an offer that we could barely afford to pay – monthly instalments – but they refused. Then they sent us a letter telling us they were going to start court action to recover the debt and would be asking for a repossession order. I was really scared. I thought we'd lose the house. I thought we'd end up on the streets. And the business wasn't doing well, either, so we couldn't get a loan from it to tide us over.' She blinked back some tears. 'I asked Mum and Dad if they could lend us some money.'

'And they refused?'

She bit her lip and nodded. 'I think Mum would've helped us but Dad was adamant that they wouldn't loan us the money. He thought it would just happen again and they'd lose their savings because we wouldn't be able to pay them back.'

'And you were desperate.'

'Yes. But not desperate enough to kill them! I mean, we hadn't got along for a while but there's no way I'd do anything as callous as that.'

'So where were you really on Wednesday, between the hours of eight a.m. and eleven a.m.?'

She lowered her head, a flush creeping up her cheeks. 'We were both at the County Court. Our hearing was due to start at nine and we got there at eight fifteen, just to be on the safe side. But they had a big backlog of repossession orders to get through and were running late. We still hadn't been seen at one and then they broke for lunch for an hour so we went to a sandwich bar just up the road and waited there until we went back at two. We didn't get in to see the judge until just gone three. We got out of there at quarter past four and then went home.'

That would be easy enough to verify. It was a least an hour's drive from Turpinfield to the court. And if what she'd said was true, it was a solid alibi. It didn't mean they hadn't got someone else to carry out the murder for them, though. But who? Neither of them had any known associates who were involved in violent crime or firearms. And if they couldn't afford to pay off their debts, it was highly unlikely they could afford to pay anyone to do it for them.

'What was the outcome of the hearing?' I asked.

She fidgeted with her hands in her lap. 'Well, the night before we were due in court, Grant's uncle agreed to loan us the money so we're able to repay it all in one go. The judge said that if we paid it all off within two weeks, the case would be dismissed and we'd be OK. Grant's going to go to a gambling addiction therapy group as well. I was going round to Mum and Dad's to give them the good news when I . . . when I found them like that.' A tear slipped from her eye and slid down her cheek. 'I was hoping our relationship would get back to normal, but . . . that's not going to happen now.'

Two hours later, Paula and Grant's alibis had been checked out and the court confirmed their attendance times. Grant's uncle also confirmed he'd already done a bank transfer to pay off their debt.

I watched my best two potential suspects go up in smoke. There was no opportunity, and now the motive was flimsy at best if there was no immediate threat of them being turfed out of their house. Yes, Grant and Paula could still have wanted the Jamesons' inheritance money, but thousands of people were in debt and they didn't resort to murder. Although she'd lied in the beginning, I couldn't see Paula as a cold-blooded killer, and I didn't think she was lying about this.

So now I was back to square one.

THE VIGILANTE
Chapter 21

I walked a tearful Laura to her car parked outside on the street and said goodbye as she started the engine.

When she'd driven away I stood, looking up and down the quiet street. Bert was still in place at his window, watching the comings and goings of everyone. The typical nosey neighbour.

I thought about what I'd do if I wanted to find a target and silence them. I'd gather as much intelligence as I could. In this case, I was guessing whoever had taken Toni had discovered her online identity somehow, which in turn revealed her home address. Then I'd spend time observing, following, watching. Waiting for the perfect moment to strike. Someone had to have followed Toni from her house that day and snatched her when she walked through the cutting. If no one else was around, it would've been easy to bundle her in a vehicle and disappear.

But no one had seen anything suspicious and there were no CCTV cameras in the surrounding area, so I had no clue how to find the person or people responsible yet.

I grabbed my daysack full of clothes from my pick-up truck, along with Maya's rucksack. It was obvious we were spending the night at Corinne's.

When I walked back in the house, I found Corinne in the kitchen, crying. Maya had an arm around her shoulder, tears in her own eyes. This must've been bringing back all the horror Maya had recently gone through, too. I regretted bringing her along with me. It wasn't fair on her. But it was too late for that.

Our eyes met over Corinne's head. A silent question in Maya's. *What can we do next?*

I didn't know. I ran my hands over my shaved head and let out a frustrated sigh. I had nothing to go on other than what Laura had said. But I just had to trust Lee could outwit any anonymous online system and find an e-crumb for me to follow.

I picked up the notebook I'd found in Toni's room. From what she'd written down, it was obvious she was meticulous in her research, and if she was studying the chat rooms and people's behaviour, I bet she would've written down the initial webpages she visited in her search of the dark web for future reference or to cite as an example.

I sat at the table, turning the pages until I reached the last one.

I stared at the words *Into the darkness*. The dark web.

I brought the notebook closer to my eyes, studying the page that would have been underneath the one Toni had torn out.

'What are you looking for?' Corinne sat up.

'Hang on.' There were indentations on the paper, captured on the sheet below from where Toni had indeed written something down. I adjusted the book under the light, trying to make out what it said, but it was too hard to read. If I'd had the time and resources, maybe I could've arranged for someone to do some forensic tests on it to enhance the words. But I had no time or resources, so I'd have to make do with the old-fashioned, quick method. 'Do you have a pencil?' I asked Corinne.

'Yes. Somewhere.' She leaped to her feet, eager to be doing something useful, and rummaged around in a kitchen drawer, finally retrieving one and handing it to me.

I placed the notepad flat on the table and rubbed the soft lead over the page, the indentations highlighting in relief as Corinne and Maya crowded round me.

There was one line of writing, comprised of letters and numbers, at the end of which was *.onion*. A Tor network page on the dark web.

There was no point typing it into Google because it was on a hidden page. I needed to get Lee's eyes on this and see what he could find. I took a photo of the page and was just about to email it to him, when he called me.

'OK, first off, Toni's social media consisted of Facebook and Snapchat, but she hasn't been active on them for nine months. There were no personal messages that related to her meeting someone, either. I checked the IP activity from the house and I have some bad news,' Lee said. 'I had a hunch what Toni found might've been on the dark web, and it looks like I was right. Toni was using an anonymous program called Phantom. Do you know what that is?'

'I've just had a crash course from an eighteen-year-old.' I told him what Laura had said.

'Jesus.'

'Toni must've accidentally stumbled upon a red room down there.'

'And they found who she was. The Tor *network* is pretty damn secure from traffic analysis, which makes it a bastard for law enforcement trying to track these sites down. *But* the Phantom or Tor *browsers* are just a modified version of Firefox, which are vulnerable to the same kinds of attacks as Firefox on the surface web. And for people who don't know about Internet security there are plenty of ways to make mistakes and leak your real ID or IP address if you don't protect yourself. Something might've given away Toni's identity to the server or site she was looking at. Or even to other people using the site. Maybe she didn't disable her scripts or plug-ins, like Flash or Java, which operate independently and can transmit data about users. And once they get access to your laptop or PC, they can find anything on it – your email address, bank account details, credit cards, phone numbers. All the data on your computers is vulnerable. They can even remotely turn on your webcam and watch and listen to you.

'When Toni connected to the Internet the day before she went missing, I can tell from her IP provider she connected to the Tor network via Phantom, but whatever she looked at is hidden, so it's impossible to tell *where* she might've found the red-room website on the dark web or who's behind it.'

I stared at the sheet of notebook in my hand. 'I can do one better, though. I've found a hidden website address. I think it's where Toni started from.'

'OK, let me have it.'

I read it to him.

'I'll check it out and see what I can find. But the problem is, it could've led her anywhere.'

I blew out a frustrated breath. 'I know. It's the only thing I have right now, though.'

'I'll call as soon as I discover anything. Oh, and by the way, I checked out the neighbour, Bert Williamson. He worked for a haulage company as a lorry driver for thirty years until an accident damaged his spine five years ago. Never married. No kids. No arrests. He lives off his disability allowance and an early pension. He seems clean so far. I haven't had time to dig deeper but if you want me to, I can, although it seems pointless now in light of what we've found.'

'No, good call. He's not related to this. Thanks, Lee.' I hung up and closed my eyes, feeling useless.

The clock ticking on the kitchen wall reverberated in my head.

THE DETECTIVE

Chapter 22

I was staring at the whiteboard – ooops, *notice* board – at the photos of the Jamesons' dead bodies and the crime scene, scratching my head, both literally and figuratively. Greene had arranged a press conference for 5 p.m. and I had nothing to tell him.

Two questions popped into my head. If it wasn't a burglary, why would the offenders be at the house of a retired couple of farmers who had no known criminal associations and lived in the middle of nowhere? And what was the link between the offenders and the Jamesons, because there had to be *some* kind of connection? Turpinfield wasn't the kind of place you just stumbled upon. It was down a warren of country lanes in the middle of a rural area.

I swung around to Becky, who was on the phone, sounding excited. She hung up and grinned at me.

'Got anything interesting?' I asked hopefully.

'I'm still waiting for the Jamesons' financial and phone records to come through. They're going to be a while, I'm afraid, but all the background checks I've done so far don't throw up any flags. I've been going through the paperwork recovered from the house – bills, mortgage statements and whatnot, and so far, the Jamesons look squeaky clean. *But* I've got something huge and juicy you're going to want.' She winked at me.

'Huge and juicy? That sounds like sexual harassment, young lady. If you're not careful I'll report you to Detective Superintendent Greene and you can be diversified.' I raised an eyebrow.

She laughed. 'That was the fingerprint department. They've got a match to the palm prints found on the outside of the patio door.'

'Really? Who?'

'Tracy Stevens. Aged nineteen. She's got previous for soliciting and drunk and disorderly.'

'A prostitute?'

'I'm not sure you can call them that any more. If Greene hears you . . .' She wagged a finger at me.

'OK, sex worker, then, or . . . pleasure technician? I can't say anything these days. It's like playing that game where you have to describe something without using the actual word.'

'Oh, I love that game.' She chuckled. 'Anyway, yes, she is. She was arrested in August last year for soliciting. Let off with a caution. Then again in January of this year for soliciting and being drunk in a public place.'

'Murder seems a high escalation from those offences. Any idea what patch she works?'

'The arrests were both from London Road in Berrisford. I've spoken to the local intelligence officer down there. Stevens is well known to them as a sex worker. She's also a heroin addict.'

Berrisford was a large town at the other end of the county, fifty-five miles from Turpinfield. 'Any known associates?'

'Only one. Another sex worker called Alice Drew. Alice is the listed tenant at 98 Kings Tower. It's a council flat. That was the last known address for Stevens when she was arrested.'

'Right.' I glanced at my watch. 'Ronnie will be back soon. We'll head up there and see if we can find Stevens. I want you to circulate Tracy's details on PNC and to other forces.'

Half an hour later, armed with a file containing printouts of everything Becky could find on Tracy Stevens, Ronnie and I headed to my car. I wondered why a prostitute from Berrisford was at the Jamesons' house. On the one hand, drug addicts were notoriously unpredictable, and would do anything to feed their habit. But if she'd gone there to rob the place, why was nothing taken? It didn't make sense. Unless there had been an argument, maybe a struggle, and things had got out of hand. Then Tracy and her accomplice had panicked and shot Mike and Jan before doing a runner. But I very much doubted someone callous enough to bring a gun with them to commit a crime and then shoot two elderly people with it would have hesitated to pick up Mrs Jameson's handbag on the lounge floor at the very least before they left.

'You can drive while I read through this intel.' I threw the car keys at Ronnie. 'And I need to stop at a drive-through somewhere and get something to eat.'

Ronnie pulled a face. 'That fast food's too greasy. My intestines are delicate.'

'Well, you can have a gherkin or something.'

I slid in the passenger side and opened the folder as Ronnie started the car. There were several photos of Tracy Stevens, taken at her arrests. In one of them she wore a vest top and jeans. She was skinny to the point of emaciation, her collar and shoulder bones jutting through the skin. Her blue eyes were sunken with dark hollows around them. Her forehead and chin were covered in bright red spots. She had a tattoo of a leopard on her right shoulder. Long black hair.

And she was five foot and one inch tall.

THE VIGILANTE
Chapter 23

It was just gone midnight when Lee rang back. I was sitting at the kitchen table in darkness, watching the silent street through the net curtains, anger and frustration churning inside. Corinne had gone to lie down, although I didn't think she'd spend much time sleeping. Maya was on the sofa in the lounge, trying to rest. Her leg had been playing up, her limp getting more pronounced whenever she was tired or stressed, and I was concerned that I'd asked too much of her.

'That URL led to a chat room in the dark web called Vice Box,' Lee said. 'You have to set up a username and password before you can view anything, which I did. I've had a quick look around in there and it's an unmoderated site where pretty much anything goes. Like the name suggests, the discussion topics cover any vice you can think of, and range from the tame, harmless stuff, to paedophilia, torture, snuff films and red rooms. I don't know if Toni actually posted anything on there or whether she was just lurking, but even to look she must've set up an account. Do you have any idea of what her username and password could've been?'

'Actually, I might.' I switched on the light and turned to the front page of Toni's notebook. 'Try SuperGurrrl991 as the username.' I spelled it out. 'And psychos101 as the password.'

I heard typing on the other end of the line and held my breath.

'No. That's not it.'

I searched down the page. There were four different passwords but Toni's username seemed to always be the same. 'Try SuperGurrrl991 and IHatePasswords991.'

More typing. Another negative hit.

'SuperGurrrl991 and chunkybuttons0809.'

A few seconds later, he said, 'That's it.' I heard frantic clattering. 'I'm checking her chat room account history, but she didn't post anything. She didn't have any personal messages, either. But there's a facility to create a flag on her dashboard so she could watch certain threads.'

'And what were they?'

'There are two. One's titled "Pain4Fun" and the other is "Broken Britney". I'll go through them and see if I can find a reference to any missing girl or a red room. I'll call you back.'

The titles conjured up images that made my stomach clench with fear for Toni. I hung up as Corinne wandered into the room, dressed in the same clothes, which were now rumpled, and wrapped in a blanket. A half-expectant, half-worried look pinched her face. 'I heard you on the phone. Is there any news?'

'Nothing good, I'm afraid.' I told her what I'd found.

'So, these red rooms *are* actually real? It's just unbelievable that . . .' Corinne trailed off, blinking back more tears, and sat opposite me, resting her feet on the edge of the chair and wrapping her arms around her, cocooned in the blanket. 'It's not always been easy, bringing her up on my own.' She stared at a spot on the table. 'When Tony died I was a mess. I was scared and grieving and angry.'

The guilt twisted a knife painfully behind my sternum. 'After Tony, you didn't want to speak to me, and I never got to say how sorry and—'

'No.' She cut me off and shook her head. 'I *did* blame you. Of course I did. For a long time I hated you.'

'I blamed myself. I still do.'

'Tony was going to leave the Regiment.'

'What?' My heart stopped for a second. 'He never said.'

'He'd only just decided. It was because he knew about the baby. I told him just before he left for West Africa. We'd been trying for a long time and she was our precious little miracle. I mean, I knew what he did when I married him, of course. But I didn't like it. Knew that things could go badly wrong. There was always a chance that he might not come back from some deployment. And when I told him . . .' She choked back a sob. 'When I told him about Toni, he agreed it was time to leave. He was going to sort it all out when he got back from the job with you. Put things in motion so we could be a real family together.'

I felt myself choking up, a punch to my heart. A shiver ran over my skin. 'But he never came back.' I rested my head in my hands. 'Jesus, Corinne.'

'You know I mentioned I'd argued with Toni in the past? Well, it was usually about you.'

My head jerked up. 'Me?'

'Yes, it was the only thing we ever really disagreed about. She wanted to meet you. She'd seen all the photos of you and Tony together and she wanted to hear what happened to him that day from you. She said there were always two sides to a story.' She tipped her head to the ceiling, anguish on her face. 'She pleaded with me to let her meet you but I wouldn't let her. I wasn't ready to hear your side of the story then. I couldn't. I heard the official version, of course. And . . .' She looked at me. 'But . . . if Toni was here now . . .' She stopped. Sniffed. 'If she was here, she'd want to ask you about it. She'd want to know. So . . . I'm ready now. I *need* to finally hear it.'

'Are you sure?' I blinked away the moisture filming my eyes.

'Yes.'

I exhaled hard, pushed the wave of sadness down as I fought for the words I'd held in so long. 'After the well-drilling team were kidnapped with the army protective detail, the British high commission in the capital got a call from someone representing a notorious group of armed rebels, the leader of which was a complete psychopath. Proof of life was requested and given, and then they made their demands. They wanted ten million dollars in exchange for everyone held captive.' I paused, my eyes searching hers, a silent question asking if she wanted me to continue.

She nodded.

'We were on standby squadron back in Hereford at the time, kit packed ready to go. By the time we got into the country and set up the Forward Operating Base, the security services had acquired satellite images of the area they thought the hostages were in and had pinpointed their camp. When we were close to the enemy, up the river, we covertly dropped off a recce team, who infiltrated near to the target, set up an observation point and were relaying vital information back to us in the FOB. The usual stuff, how many enemy there were, what weapons and comms equipment they had, any vehicles and escape routes, and of course trying to get further confirmation of life of the hostages and where they were being held in the stronghold.

'Meanwhile, we put together an assault plan, and once we got the green light we were off. Thirty tooled-up SAS guys in the back of an RAF Special Forces Chinook. We flew in low at night up the river then fast-roped down from the heli. We hit the ground and moved forward, quickly fanning out, as we were coming under some serious incoming fire. We immediately engaged the rebels, suppressing them as the designated assault team, hooked up with the recce team and we made for the known hostage location inside the camp. There was a serious firefight going down all around us. It was chaotic, rebels running everywhere but being systematically taken out. The entry to the stronghold was heavily fortified so we blew the door with charges and flash-banged the rebels inside. Once we got through the breach, we engaged the gunmen, clearing the rooms so we could make our way to where we suspected the hostages were.' I stopped and rubbed my hands over my face. Took a deep breath, seeing it play out again in my head.

'Go on. Please.'

'That's when things went wrong. There were dead rebels every-where, hostages screaming and wailing. Trying to control the situation inside that hellhole was practically impossible. Tony and I . . .' I closed my eyes.

Corinne touched my shoulder and squeezed.

I opened my eyes and looked at her. 'Tony and I were working together, covering each other as we checked our sector of the stronghold to make sure the threat had been neutralised. Tony was covering me as I checked the last rebel and declared the room clear. I thought the rebel was dead. He was lying partially underneath another rebel and had blood and brain matter all over his head. But as we got into the re-org phase to extract the hostages, the bastard who was supposed to be dead sat up and let out a burst of AK fire from his rifle. The body fluids covering him weren't actually his. It was the one lying on top of him whose brains were blown out. The rounds hit Tony across his back, into his body armour, but one round got him in the base of his neck. Killed him outright.'

Corinne cupped her hands to her mouth, stifling a gasp.

'I should've fucking put one in him and made sure he was dead, but I didn't!' I shot off the chair and walked to the window, hands clasped to my head. 'I don't know how I could've made such a fatal mistake. Tony died because of me. I'm sorry, Corinne. I'm so sorry.'

She walked towards me, wrapped her arms round my neck and held on tight, her tears wet against my cheek. 'You made a mistake. It was chaos, the adrenaline was pumping, and you had a split second to make a decision. It was a massive error in judgement but it wasn't intentional. I know that now. I know . . .' Her warm breath hit my cheek as she exhaled. 'I don't blame you any more. But even though he was going to leave, the Regiment was his life. And he died doing something he loved. He died *with* someone he loved.' She pulled back and wiped her cheeks. 'I came to realise over the years that Toni was his way of staying with me. She was his legacy and my last link to him. And now . . . what do I do if she doesn't come back?' She broke down then, her shoulders spasming with sobs, a torrent of tears streaming down her cheeks.

I held her tight.

'Toni made a mistake, too, going into this dark web,' Corinne said. 'She's mixed up in something terrible, and she's just an innocent girl. She's *my* little girl. I should've stopped her. She always was obsessed with horrible things because she wanted to use it to help people. Now she needs our help. She needs—'

'I'm going to find Toni. No matter what. I *will* finally get to meet her.' I pulled back and clutched her hands in mine.

Her gaze locked on to me, anguish and pain shimmering in her eyes, her mouth open with the words she wanted to say. The words we both knew were true. *Even if you find her, it doesn't mean she'll still be alive.*

'Just bring her home to me. I can't lose her, too. I just can't. If I do I'll have nothing left.'

I wrapped her in my arms and stroked her hair.

And then my phone rang.

I let her go and picked up Lee's call.

'What've you got?' I asked.

'I think you need to get up here and have a look for yourself,' Lee said, his voice grave.

THE DETECTIVE
Chapter 24

Kings Tower was as far removed from its regal-sounding name as you could possibly get. A posh name for a block of dilapidated high-rise council flats in a concrete jungle that had been built in the sixties.

Alice Drew's flat was on the third floor, which could be reached by a stairwell. As we climbed the steps, Ronnie spotted someone's regurgitated doner kebab on the floor and pinched his nose between his forefinger and thumb, grimacing.

I eyed him with an amused smile.

'What?' He stepped over it carefully. 'Lots of germs are airborne. They can enter your nasal or mouth cavity and then you're in trouble.'

'Let's hope there's no Ebola running rife here, then.'

We walked to the end of the corridor. On Alice's door someone had scratched 'Hor Bittch' into the cracking blue paint. It would've been offensive if they could actually spell.

I banged on the door and peered over the balcony down to the car park while I waited. A teenager was on a bicycle, aimlessly riding in a circle. The whole place smacked of poverty and hopelessness with a side order of desperation.

There was no answer so I banged again. This time the door was opened by a young woman with short, spiky blonde hair. Her skin was so white it was almost transparent. She had the remnants of dark make-up crusted around her eyes and wore a dressing gown with so many stains on it that it would make Ronnie nervous.

'What?' she snapped, rubbing her eyes like we'd just woken her up. 'Who are you?' She glared at us. 'Oh, fuck's sake.' She sniffed the air with exaggeration. 'You're pigs, ain't ya?'

Damn, I obviously needed to change my aftershave. Eau de Porcine was obviously not in vogue these days. 'Are you Alice Drew?'

'Yeah, so? I ain't done nothin'.'

'We're looking for your friend, Tracy Stevens.'

'Why?' She narrowed her eyes at me.

'It's concerning a murder. Is she here?'

'A what?'

'We need to speak to her in connection with a double murder. A shooting in Turpinfield. Is Tracy here?'

'Murder?' Her jaw fell open slightly. 'Nah. I 'aven't seen her for a couple of days.'

'Can we come in and have a look around?'

She rolled her eyes and sighed. 'I s'pose. You'll never piss off otherwise, will ya?'

We stepped inside the cramped living area. There was a small sofa along one wall, an old, boxy TV on a black ash corner unit, next to which was a gas heater with a fraying flex that looked dangerous. Off to one side was a galley kitchen. Alice slumped down on the sofa with a huff of protest as I searched one tiny bedroom, home to a double bed, a single wardrobe and not much else. A second box room had a single blow-up bed in it. Clothes were strewn around in piles or in carrier bags. The bathroom was only big enough for a narrow shower, a sink, and toilet. Unless Tracy was invisible, she wasn't hiding out there.

Alice lit a cigarette as I walked back into the lounge.

'When did you last see Tracy?'

She sucked in a lungful of smoke and blew it in my direction.

Ronnie coughed, waved a hand in front of his face and stepped backwards.

'I don't know. The days blend into one. Was it Monday?' She frowned, picking a stray piece of tobacco from her tongue. 'Or Tuesday? Not sure.'

'I need you to be more specific,' I said. 'Come on, Alice, I really don't want to have to take you down to the station to do this.'

She rolled her eyes. 'Anyway, Tracy wouldn't kill anyone. You've got the wrong person.'

'So what day was it? Monday or Tuesday?'

She took another puff. Blew a smoke ring at me.

Ronnie coughed again. I watched her carefully.

'Tuesday night.'

'Three days ago, then. And what happened on Tuesday?'

'Um . . . well, we was going out, you know?'

'To work London Road?'

She shrugged.

'I'm not interested in the prostitution,' I said. 'This is a double *murder* inquiry. I really don't want to have to nick you for obstruction, so let's make this easier on all of us and just tell me what you know.'

She clicked her tongue against her teeth. 'OK, yeah, we was working London Road. It was probably about eleven when we got there. I had a punter pretty much straight away and got in his car. Tracy was hanging around on her patch at the bottom near Devon Crescent. By the time I got back about a half hour later she weren't there. I didn't see her for the rest of the night but I was back and forth. 'Aven't seen her since.'

'But she was living with you?'

She nodded. 'For 'bout a year.'

'And you weren't worried about her?' Ronnie asked, surprised.

But these girls lived in a different world. A world Ronnie was still learning about.

'Nah. She's always doing it. Pissing off for a few days. One time it was a week. She goes where the good times take her. She's a sma—' She stopped abruptly, but I knew what she'd been about to say. Smackhead.

'She's an addict,' I said it for her.

Alice pursed her lips together. 'I ain't sayin' nothin'.'

'Alice, this is more serious than any drug offences,' I said. 'She's still your friend and we need to find her. So just tell me what you can.'

'Yeah, she's a mate. But I ain't her keeper or nothin'. She's probably off partying with someone who's got some gear, all right?' She scowled at me.

'Any ideas who she could be with?' I asked.

She shrugged and shook her head. Ground her cigarette out in an ashtray overflowing with butts tinged with red lipstick. 'No idea. Could be anywhere.'

'What about her friends? Who did she hang around with?'

'She didn't 'ave any other friends. When she does her disappearing act, it could be with someone she ain't even met before.'

'Did she mention any trouble she was in?'

'No.'

'What's her mobile number?'

Alice glared at me for a moment before rattling off a number that Ronnie wrote down in his pocketbook.

'Did she take any of her belongings?' I asked.

'Don't fink so. All looks the same to me.'

'Her room is the one with the bags of clothes in, I take it?'

'Yeah.'

I wondered how she could tell it all looked the same when it seemed like a crowd of bargain hunters at a car boot sale had rummaged through it all. 'Do you remember what she was wearing that night?'

Alice scratched her nose and thought for a moment. 'Um . . . she 'ad a black mini skirt on and a pink top. High heels. A handbag. And a denim jacket.'

'Jewellery?'

'Don't fink so.'

'Did any of the items have small pink stones on them?'

She frowned. 'Yeah. The top did. It had, like, glittery pink stones in a pattern on the front. They kept coming off. Keep finding 'em all over the flat. It was just cheap shit. Don't fink they stuck 'em on properly.'

I took my phone from my pocket and retrieved a photo of one of the stones found in the Jamesons' lounge. 'Did they look like this?' I passed the phone to her.

'Yeah.' She handed the phone back to me.

'Did you pick up the stones? Have you still got them?' I asked.

'I vacuumed out 'ere so I don't fink there's any left, and I chucked the rubbish out. But there's probably loads of 'em still on the floor in 'er room. I haven't tidied up anyfink in there yet.'

I looked to Ronnie. 'Go and have a look. Bag any of them you find. And look for a laptop or mobile phone.'

Ronnie nodded.

Alice snorted. 'Laptop? You must be joking. How was she goin' to pay for that? And she 'ad her phone with her.'

'Does she have a pimp?' I asked Alice.

'Nah. Neither of us do. We're entrepreneurs, ya know.' She gave me a sneery grin.

'And you can't think of anyone else she hangs around with?'

'Nah. Like I said. She don't 'ave any friends apart from me.'

'What about a dealer?' I asked.

She chewed on her lower lip, looking scared now. 'I ain't a grass. They'll come after me if I tell you.'

'This won't come back on you. I promise.'

She lit another cigarette and this time her hands trembled. She took a long drag. Blew it out, thinking. 'His name's Dex.'

'Dex, what? Is that a first or last name? Or a nickname?'

'I don't know! I never met him. I may be stupid but I ain't stupid enough to get into that shit.'

'You're not stupid, Alice,' I said.

'Whatever.' She shrugged dismissively.

'Any idea where he lives?'

She hesitated for a moment, chewing on her lower lip, before finally answering, 'Over on the Bowes Estate somewhere. Other side of town.'

'How did Tracy seem that night? Did she mention she was going anywhere in particular or meeting anyone?'

'Nah, she didn't say nothin' like that. She was in a good mood when we went out. We'd had a couple of drinks while we was getting togged up. She'd got some stuff from Dex a few days before so I don't fink she would've needed to see him again that night. Why do you fink she killed someone?'

'Her prints were found at the house of the murdered couple. They'd both been shot.'

'Fuck!' She took another lug of smoke with her quivering hand. 'Tracy couldn't do that. She was . . .' Alice trailed off.

'She was what?' I said.

'Look, she had 'er problems. We all 'ave. But she wouldn't hurt no one. I'm sure of it. She weren't like that. She weren't violent or nothin'. No way could she 'ave done it.'

I thought about the void of blood spatter on the wall. Of someone around Tracy's height standing next to Jan Jameson when she was shot. Was Tracy the shooter or accomplice? 'Well, someone did. And Tracy was there.'

She stared at me, chin jutting in the air. 'I can't help you. I don't know anyfink about it.'

'Did Tracy ever talk about knowing a couple called Jan and Mike Jameson?'

'Is that the ones who was murdered?'

'Yes. They were retired farmers.'

'Farmers?' She scrunched her face up. 'No. She never said anyfink about anyone like that. Tracy was a city girl. Doubt she's been anywhere near a farm in her life.'

'How about Paula or Grant Eagan? Do those names sound familiar?'

'Nah.'

'Had Tracy ever been to Turpinfield?'

'Where the fuck's that?' She frowned.

'It's a small, rural hamlet. About fifty-five miles from here. Out in the country.'

'She's bin living with me a year and the furthest she's gone is the other side of town. Anyway, she ain't got no car and she can't drive. How would she get over there?'

'Someone could have driven her.'

'Well, I ain't got a clue who.'

'How did you meet Tracy?' I asked. 'What do you know about her?'

'I met her on the street. 'Bout a year ago. She said she'd run away from home – somewhere in Bristol – and been living rough for a while. Then she moved into a squat in Church Road, near the railway station, and she 'ad no money so she was . . . you know . . . working London Road.'

'Do you know the number in Church Road she stayed at?'

'Nah. Anyway, I offered for 'er to stay here. Thought it would save me on rent and it was nice to 'ave a bit of company. She kind of . . .' Alice trailed off and stared at a spot on the carpet, a desolate look in her eyes.

'Kind of what?'

She shook her head to herself and then the look was gone, replaced with an edge of defiance as she glared back at me. 'She just kind of reminded me of myself, all right?' She stubbed out the cigarette in the ashtray as if it had personally ruined her life.

'What was Tracy like?'

'She was sweet. She was . . . a bit quiet. She . . . She'd had a shit life and she was trying to do the best she could.'

Ronnie entered the room then, carrying several evidence bags with the pink stones inside. His nose twitched from the smoke.

'Do you know why she ran away from Bristol?' I asked.

'Somethin' to do with 'er dad. She never told me. But I guessed, like. He was a fuckin' piss head, weren't he? Liked smacking 'er and 'er mum about a bit when he'd 'ad too much to drink. You know the type, don'tcha?'

Alice blinked then, her eyes watering. The hard exterior finally cracking to reveal the vulnerable young woman behind it. In my job it was easy to judge people, but I hadn't lived in her shoes. Couldn't imagine how she'd ended up at this place she was in now, but I could hazard a good guess. Denise and I had never had kids. We'd tried, but it wasn't meant to be. At the time it had been heartbreaking for both of us, but now I was glad about it. The world was becoming more violent and dangerous every day, with people thinking up new ways to hurt and exploit each other. We lived in a selfish, narcissistic society, where people didn't want to look further than the end of their nose. If it wasn't happening to them they didn't give a shit about it. Most people would walk past Alice and see something dirty, disgusting. A slag, a slapper, a whore – someone who chose to do what she did for a living. I looked at Alice and saw a girl whose life had conspired against her to push her down and keep her there with its foot pressed firmly on her back. Choices were always relative. When you had none, you did what you had to in order to survive.

'So you don't think she would have gone back home to Bristol?'

'No way. She hated him. Sometimes you just can't go back.' She sighed.

'Can you think of anywhere else she could be?' I said.

She shook her head. 'Nah.'

'Well, thanks for your help. If you think of anything else, can you give me a ring? Or if you hear from Tracy, please call.' I took a business card from my pocket and held it out to her.

She stared at it but made no move to take it.

'Or if you just want to talk. If you need some help,' I continued. 'There are women's projects. I can put you in touch with someone. You don't have to be doing this if you don't want to. Support is out there for you. All you have to do is ask.'

She chewed on her lower lip again and looked at the chipped black nail varnish on her hands.

I put the card on the arm of the sofa. 'It's there if you want it.' I nodded to Ronnie and he followed me outside.

'What do you think, guv?' he said as we strode back along the corridor to the stairs.

I let out a sad, deflated sigh. 'I think nothing is ever black and white.'

THE VIGILANTE

Chapter 25

At just gone 1.30 a.m. the roads from Buckinghamshire to London, where Lee's cyber security empire was housed, were quiet.

I pulled up to the closed metal gates of a nondescript industrial unit surrounded by an eight-foot wall topped with barbed wire. There was no company name on the front. Lee still did contract work for the government and anonymity was the name of the game. The last time I'd been here was when I'd asked for his help on behalf of Maya. And I knew that at the rear of the building, completely hidden from view, were satellites and various signal equipment that were too complicated for me to even name.

A security camera positioned on the wall next to the gates faced in my direction. Beneath it was a button, which I pressed. I waved into the camera and the heavy-duty electric gates slid open.

I drove into a car park at the front of the building. There were spaces for fifty vehicles but only seven were in use. I eased into a spot near the reinforced-glass front doors and got out.

By the time I'd jogged up the steps, Lee was tapping an entry-code system on a panel next to the empty reception desk in a lobby that looked more modern than the outside of the building suggested.

The door beeped and I let myself in.

Lee walked towards me, a half-smile on his face. 'Good to see you.' He pulled me into a hug.

'You've dyed your hair grey. Is that a new fashion statement?' I said when I stepped back.

'Cheeky fucker. You'd be grey if you didn't shave it all.' He grinned. 'So, how are you? I mean, apart from this job with Corinne and Toni?'

I shrugged. 'Better.'

'How's Maya?'

'She's recovering, slowly. And you? Keeping busy?'

'Always. I've got more work than I can handle. And this beats sitting under a poncho in a tree at three in the morning trying to send a sitrep by Morse when it's pissing it down with rain.' He clapped me on the back, the grin replaced by a sombre frown. No more time for pleasantries and catching up. We had work to do.

'Let's go to my office.'

We stepped into the lift in the centre of the lobby. Lee typed in a code on a control panel and the doors closed. We emerged three flights up into an open-plan office filled with communications and computer equipment. At the end of one wall was a big bank of computer servers. The aircon was set to a cool temperature. An electronic hum filled the air. Five guys were seated at desks around the room, typing or talking on the phone or with their heads bent over screens. It was an impressive set-up.

He led me to his office at the far end and sat down in front of a huge desk with various monitors, towers and other equipment on it. 'Grab that chair.' He jerked his head in the direction of an office chair on wheels that was parked at a smaller desk flanking the left side of the room, equally as laden with monitors and stuff that I didn't have a clue about.

I pushed the chair next to him and sat down.

He typed on one of his keyboards and then pointed to a screen in the centre of his desk, showing what looked like a regular chat forum layout with a header banner that said 'Vice Box'. There was a main page with various topics and subtopics listed below it.

'OK, so, I checked out the message threads Toni was watching. I went through the most recent pages of chat on the "Pain4Fun" thread and found plenty of hardcore, sick stuff relating to torture and abuse from a large paedophile community.'

I clenched my fists. Felt the rage detonate through me like napalm. Gritted my teeth. 'Mark that for later. When I get Toni back I want to revisit this.'

Lee nodded. 'There are about 500,000 users on the Vice Box site.'

'No matter how many you expose, there's always so many more.'

'And the dark web has just given them even more places to go.' Lee unscrewed the lid from a bottle of water and took a swig. He pointed the tip of the bottle at me. 'Want something to drink, a brew?'

'No, thanks.'

He screwed the top back on. 'OK, I'll spare you the rest of the posts. You know yourself what kind of sick things they do. And nothing relevant jumped out at me on that thread about a red room. The second post on Toni's watch list is a different story.' He clicked on a link entitled 'Broken Britney'.

Dread burned its way up my throat as the original post came up with replies below it.

> *Luvchild: Hey, anyone seen Broken Britney? I heard about it in another chat room and wanted to find a link?*
> *SfK: Never heard of it. Give me more . . .*
> *Luvchild: It's s'posed to be a red room. Some gurl gets some serious HC shit before they do her. I wanna watch some snuff!*
> *DOLSGAME: Where you hear about it?*

Luvchild: HardCandy URL.
TreBleBless: It's a fake!
Luvchild: You seen it?
DOLSGAME: I'm looking for a red room. Been trawling for
ages! Gimme the link.

I read through each post, the dread turning to abhorrence and something I couldn't even name as they debated whether a hardcore snuff film was real and who wanted to see it. When I got to the bottom of the page, I said, 'OK.'

Lee clicked on page two. And that's when things got even worse.

Crusader: Broken Britney doesn't exist. It's creepy pasta. If
you're lookin for a real red room, follow this link: 3l2up4ts-
7fufc9b.onion. Best shit I've seen yet but not cheap!

'I tried the link, which takes you to a blank page.' Lee clicked on the URL *Crusader* had given, and as Lee said, a plain white page filled the screen. 'But there's a page hidden behind it. I would imagine it's supposed to be secure, and you'd have to enter a username and password to see it. But there's a script error on the page. Watch this.' Lee simply hit the 'enter' button and the whiteness disappeared to reveal another webpage behind.

It was similar to a YouTube page in that there was a video box that took up half the left-hand side of the screen. The video box was black, except for a line of white text which said 'Live Stream Coming Soon!'

'I've clicked to play the video but nothing happens.'

Above the video box were two headings: 'Watch Live'. And 'Direct'.

There was a subcategory on the right-hand side of the page which said: 'Previous Red Rooms'. Lee clicked on it and a list appeared:

Baseball bat
Acid
Saw
Disembowelment
Electrocution
Torture
Drowning
Rape

I looked at Lee after I'd got halfway down, my jaw so tight my muscles ached, teeth grinding together.

Lee shook his head sombrely. 'There's some seriously fucked-up shit on here.' He pointed to the video links. 'These are previous murders. Filmed in graphic detail for the pleasure of some messed-up fuckers. The process of watching the videos works like this: you click on the link you want and the site asks for payment in D-coins. I set myself up with a D-coin wallet and paid to check out some of the videos. If they're fakes, then they'd need a million-pound special-effect budget to produce them. You can't fake what's on here.' He sat back and looked at me. 'And people don't just pay to watch them. When they're streaming live, they can pay to direct, too.'

'How does that work?'

'I'm guessing a chat box pops up when the video feed on the front page goes live. You can tell them what you want them to do to whoever's in the red room in return for paying more D-coins.'

I let out a growl. 'I'm guessing D-coins are similar to Bitcoins? A digital currency?'

He nodded. 'They're Bitcoin's biggest rival. They've become almost as popular now.'

'Let me see one of the videos.'

He clicked on the 'Electrocution' link, which brought up a new video box. Underneath it was a price to view the video. Five D-coins.

'How much is five D-coins worth?'

'As of today's price, three thousand dollars.' He pressed 'play'.

A large room appeared on screen with no windows I could see. The walls and floor were tiled in white with a concrete ceiling that had a single strip light attached to it. On the left-hand side of the screen there was a small wooden table, the surface tinged a dark reddy-brown. It held a long prod with a bronze tip and an insulated handle, which was connected to a small black box that would control the voltage. Supplying power to it via leads was a bulky battery unit.

It was a variation of a picana, and I knew that such prods were used for torture on political prisoners and prisoners of war. I'd spent six months working in South America training a branch of the ANP – Anti-narcotic Police – and come into regular contact with the government's Administrative Department for Security. They were mean bastards who hated the freedom-fighting rebels in the country and had no qualms about using commercially made torture equipment to extract the information they wanted.

Adapted from the electric cattle prod, the precursor for what were the modern stun guns, it was designed to deliver a high-voltage electric shock but with a low current. The high voltage meant the shocks were painful, but the low current enabled the torturer to make the session last longer and was less likely to kill the victim until they were good and ready.

But that wasn't the worst bit. In the centre of the room, chained to a long table by leather straps that held his arms above his head and his legs spread, was a young man. He looked to be in his early twenties, but the fear twisting his features made it hard to tell. He screamed, a hoarse, raspy sound, as if he'd been screaming for a long time. His eyes stared wide open, tears spilling on to his cheeks as he tugged repeatedly against the restraints. He was naked, apart from a pair of white boxer shorts ingrained with dirt that couldn't disguise the wet patch at the front of them. He was painfully thin, his ribs showing, the sinews of tendons taut against his skin as he cried out pitifully, trying to move and failing again and again because the straps were too tight. His whole body glistened with sweat.

Then a man appeared from behind the camera. He was tall, thick-set, dressed from head to foot in black – overalls, gloves, a balaclava, boots – so every part of him was covered and undistinguishable in any way. He ignored the noises of whimpering and hoarse cries from the boy, stepped in front of the camera and gave it two thumbs up. Although you could only see his eyes through the two slits in the bala-clava, they creased at the edges, and I knew he was smiling.

The man stepped towards the table. The boy bucked his hips in the air, trying again, uselessly, to free himself. His eyes bulged as he screamed.

The man laughed. A deep, raucous sound.

A black swirling anger mushroomed inside me.

The man turned his back on the camera as he leaned over to the control box on the small table and fiddled with it. Then he stepped back to the boy and pressed the tip of the prod to his thigh.

The boy's heartbreaking scream pierced through my skull. His muscles spasmed rigidly. His head arched back. His mouth opened, tongue lolling out, saliva dribbling down the corners of his lips as the searing firecracker of pain hit his body.

On and on it went, the electrical burns left on every part of his skin growing bigger and bigger. His screams growing hoarser as his whole body was attacked.

And after the boy's final convulsion, his painful death most prob-ably from cardiac arrest, the echo of the man's laughter rang out.

'Fucking hell.' I blew out an enraged breath.

'I told you it was seriously fucked-up. I would imagine the guy with the balaclava has some kind of earpiece in so that whoever is working the website can talk to him throughout and tell him of any special requests from people who have paid to direct.'

'Fucked-up doesn't even cover it.'

'In the baseball-bat video there's a girl in it. Probably about Toni's age. The girl had a tattoo on her shoulder of a leopard. I still don't know who she is, though. There are no reports about her. My guys are still working on searching keywords from all UK police reports and Interpol. They're trying the US now, too, but I think it'll be a waste of time. I'm guessing they're choosing victims who would go unnoticed and unreported if they went missing – homeless people, runaways, drug addicts, prostitutes – people who are vulnerable.'

'Show me the video.'

He clicked on the link. 'Incidentally, there's another error on this page. This video didn't ask for any D-coin payment before viewing it, which must be how Toni managed to access it.'

We fast-forwarded through an hour of footage as the girl tied to the table in the same way as the young guy was beaten to death. From the looks of it, every bone in her body must've been broken.

'Jesus Christ!' I shot to my feet, paced the floor, trying to contain the fury raging through me. 'I've got to catch these bastards.' I stopped pacing. Took some deep breaths. Forced the anger down so I could focus. 'Are all the videos in the same room?'

'All the ones I've seen, yes. There are no identifying marks. I've analysed every inch of it. Nothing to say where it is. It's just tiles and concrete.'

'So we're looking for one location.'

'One location that could be anywhere in the world.'

I ran a hand over my head. 'Shit!'

Lee navigated back to the first page with the black video box that said 'Live Stream Coming Soon!'

'Either they're trolling for the next victim right now, or they're waiting for enough people to pay before they release another live video feed,' Lee said.

I shook my head. 'They already have their next victim. Toni's being held captive by them, I know it. Why kill her already when they can keep her and kill her on a live feed to a paying audience. She's in the red room, I'm sure of it.' I clenched a fist and felt useless. 'If this site is using digital coins, can't you trace them through that?'

'It's complicated. Basically, D-coins and Bitcoins are a cryptocurrency – a form of exchange which is stored electronically and uses encryption techniques to control the creation of monetary units and verify payments. It's a virtual currency – simply a ledger system that maintains a list of addresses and how many units of coins are at those addresses. But you don't really own a coin. What you actually have is a private key that unlocks a particular address. And the keys aren't keys. They're just a string of numbers and letters. I could go into a big, detailed explanation of how it all works, but I can see your eyes glazing over.'

'Just get to the important bit.'

'Unless you have the "key" to someone's D-coin address, it's bloody hard to find someone.' He shook his head with frustration. 'But you have to store your key somewhere, and for most people, there are no good options to securely store cryptocurrencies, so they use an online service that stores the private keys for users. A wallet system that holds the currency like a bank account. Many of the companies that store them have been hacked, but I'd need to try to find *which* company is storing the particular key for this site, which could take months. Also, unless the wallet service they use somehow connects their D-coin address to their *real* names, they could be untraceable. Often, people are using pseudonyms to create their wallet. There are other ways to try to analyse D-coin transactions but that would take too long. And they're most likely using a laundry service to shuffle up payments with other non-related ones.'

I exhaled loudly. 'There must be another way to trace them. I know the Tor network is supposed to be anonymous, but if they found out who Toni was, can't you use the same methods to find them?'

'It's not as simple as that. The Tor network is extremely secure from any kind of traffic analysis I could do and there's no magic way to trace people using it, but the Phantom browser Toni was using has some glitches and *is* vulnerable, and that's what let her down. However, nothing is ever completely anonymous online. I'm just hoping they're lazy with their OPSEC and I can exploit this script error on the webpage, or that it's somehow leaking data. I can also throw data at it, try to analyse network traffic connecting with it, secretly install an application or malware that will send their user data back to me, and various other things.'

'How long will that take?'

'That's the bad bit. Law enforcement have found and taken down some sites from the dark web but it was the result of very long investigations lasting several years. It could take months, years, even. Usually, when law enforcement are trying to track down criminal Tor sites, it's a case of finding some kind of user carelessness – simple mistakes which can expose them another way without having to try to track every digital interaction. They might've slipped up when switching between their real ID and their Tor ID, by logging into their surface email or social media accounts that place cookies which can track them over anything, irrespective of whether they're using Tor or not. Stuff like that. Humans usually err at some point, or become too arrogant to cover their arses.'

I stared at the video box on screen. Before our eyes the 'Live Stream Coming Soon!' text disappeared and was replaced with 'The Next Red Room Will Be Live In . . .' and beneath it was a digital timer.

Lee leaned closer to the screen. 'Fuck.'

'We don't have months to find her,' I said. 'We don't even have days. We need to find where this place is *now*.' I watched the timer clicking down in hours, minutes, and seconds.

16:29:05

16:29:04

16:29:03 . . .

THE MISSING
Chapter 26

I wake suddenly to the sound of screaming. I shoot upwards from lying on the hard floor into a seated position and realise it's not screaming. It's the creaking sound of the wooden door opening. And before I can even question *how* I could fall asleep in this place, in this desperate situation, he's in the room with me.

It's the one who punched me.

He's tall. Wide. Huge. With blonde spiky hair. There's something vacant in his pale-blue eyes, but excitement there, too. I know that look well. It's the same as many of the serial killers and psychopaths I've studied.

He smiles at me. No, not a smile. His lips twist into a curve but it's a sneer. He has crooked teeth.

He carries on sneering as he looks me up and down from the doorway, his gaze crawling over me, chilling me to the core. There's something feral about him that reminds me of a rabid dog.

I shuffle backwards on hands and heels and press myself into the wall furthest from him.

He pushes the door shut without taking his cold eyes off me and stares, the sneer turning into something else, something more menacing. More savage.

My heart threatens to explode. I want to close my eyes and block it out but my eyes have a mind of their own and they're staying open. Wide open.

I refuse, I refuse, I refuse. I will not cry. I will not show I'm scared.

He takes a step towards me.

To block out my fear I recite things in my head about him to tell later. *He's wearing jeans and a white T-shirt. He's got gel in his hair. His right ear's pierced with a gold stud.*

I look down then, away from him, to my feet, and realise, weirdly for the first time, that my trainers are missing. Lost in the van or in the cutting, I don't know.

My trainers are missing. I will not look at you. My trainers are missing. They were black with yellow laces and—

'I think it's time you and me had some fun before the show begins.' His voice stops my thoughts and he laughs loudly, a cackling sound that echoes around the bare room and vibrates through every cell of my body.

I stare at the ground, palms pressed hard against the floor, a lump of concrete digging into the ridges of my spine. Stare until I see a black boot in front of my eyes.

Black lace-up boots. Doctor Martens. There's a scratch on the left toe. And a red stain on the bottom lace. Red stain. Red stain. Blood!

And however brave I'm trying to be, I'm not strong enough to stop the images of the video I saw flooding into my head. The video of the girl with the leopard tattoo. Even though I didn't watch it all the way to the end. Couldn't watch it all. I know she's dead. No one could survive what I saw.

Panic freezes me in its grip. I stiffen, like I'm already a corpse. Already dead, dead, dead, like her.

Then I'm being lifted up in the air as he pulls me by both arms and thrusts them above my head, one of his big hands holding both wrists together. I struggle but I can't move. Even if I wasn't still weak from whatever drug they injected me with, I would never be a match for his strength. His bodyweight pins me against the wall. And I stare the badness I've been researching all these years in the face, because it's the only voluntary movement I can make when he has me trapped, summoning up a little bit of defiance because I refuse.

His breath is on my chin as he smirks and grinds his crotch into me, already hard.

My throat is closed. I can't even swallow. Can't do anything. My lungs forget how to work.

I know he's going to rape me and there's nothing I can do except try to stay alive a little bit longer.

So when his other hand roams over my breasts and squeezes them hard, when his hand goes lower and tugs at the buttons on my jeans, fumbling to undo them, I stare at him and think, *I'm not scared, I'm angry. And anger is just as powerful as fear, but in a different way.* But although my mind thinks these things, my body says something different. All the involuntary things I can't control show otherwise. Sweat beading on my forehead, trickling down between my shoulder blades. My muscles twitching with terror. A gurgling sound in the back of my mouth that says 'No!' My ears ringing with panic.

Although I can't move, there is something I can do after all.

I spit in his face.

He steps back, surprised. He snorts, as if he doesn't know whether to laugh or not. Wipes his cheek. Then he reaches his free hand back, clenching it into a fist. 'You fucking bitch!'

I close my eyes then, waiting for the punch. Waiting for another smash to my nose, or my jaw. My heart races so hard I can hear it pounding in my ears. But the punch doesn't come because the screeching door opens and someone says, 'What the fuck are you doing?'

My eyelids fly open. The pressure on my chest eases up as he twists around to look at the other guy who's just come in. I haven't seen him before.

He speaks with a posh accent, so the swear word sounds at odds with him. He's wearing jeans and a white shirt. He's fat.

'What? I'm just getting her warmed up!' The blonde one chuckles, but he sounds less sure of himself, his voice wavering a little, and I realise that he's not the one in charge here.

'I told you before. Do *not* touch the merchandise before the show!' The fat one points his finger at him. 'They'll pay extra for that if they want. I don't want her damaged before it starts. All the damage starts on screen. How many times do I have to fucking tell you? Didn't you learn anything from the last one escaping?' Fat Man narrows his eyes at him.

The blonde one shrugs, steps back and turns to face him.

I slide to the floor, my legs too liquid to hold me up. I pant hard through my mouth because my nose is still blocked with dried blood. And I look at the half-open door behind the fat one, longing for escape. I can see a sliver of corridor out there. It must lead to the way out. But I know I'd never get past both of them before they grabbed me again.

'Stay the fuck out of here until it's time,' Fat Man snaps, glaring at the blonde one.

He laughs. 'Whatever.' He moves towards Fat Man, then says over his shoulder to me, 'Won't be long now anyway.' He sneers again.

Then they leave, the door screeching again as they pull it shut and lock it with the sound of a bolt sliding into place.

My chin collapses to my chest and the tears fall in a great big, wrenching, painful river, splashing off my jaw and on to my dirty jeans. On to the hard, concrete floor where they sink into the knobbly, pitted, uneven surface, where they're lost forever. Trapped in the dusty cement. Lost, like me. My whole body shudders and shakes, and I don't know if I'll ever be warm again. Only the icy cold depths of death are waiting for me now.

I'm such an idiot! I've already proved I don't know what I'm doing. And that's the stupid, stupid bit. I was on my way to the police station to tell them what I'd found. I'd taken my laptop with me so I could show them what I'd looked at. I'd had the address of the chat room where I'd found the link to the red room written down so I could give it to them. At first, I didn't think it was real. I thought it *had* to be a hoax, because I got on to the site easily, without paying anything like they wanted. I don't know, maybe there was something wrong with the page, but it let me in. Just like that. And I clicked on a video. The girl with the leopard tattoo. The baseball bat. The man dressed head-to-toe in black, his face completely hidden. I still don't know who she is. *Was.* I tried to find out if someone of her description had been reported missing. I tried to research if a red room *really* could exist, but I couldn't find a proper answer. I struggled with myself, the images of the video playing over and over in my head. Fake or not a fake? But in the end, I *had* to go and report it. So what if it turned out to be a hoax and they thought I was just some hysterical, mad girl? Better that than if it was real and I hadn't told the police.

I didn't want to ask the police to come to my house, though. I couldn't think how to explain it all properly on the phone in the first place; it would have to be done in person, to a detective, not a uniformed officer on the beat. Plus, I didn't want Mum to find out what I'd discovered. If she had, she'd never have let me on the Internet again. Never have let me do the criminology course. And if she came home from work for lunch, like she sometimes did, and the police were there, she'd be frantic. Plus, nosey old Bert would've seen them and most likely told her. That's also why, after finding the site the first time, I didn't research it from home and went to the library instead, in case she realised what I'd been looking at. What I'd found. But those men must've been watching me. Must've found out, somehow, who I was. Knew I wasn't like them and all the others who paid to watch what they did. Or maybe they realised there was some problem with the page that was giving away their videos for free and they wanted to trace who'd looked at one. I don't know. I don't understand how the dark web works, especially now, when I thought no one could see what I was doing. *I'm an idiot! Idiot, idiot!*

But then I stop that thought. Push, push, push the scared bits away. I think of Mum at home, frantic, feeling useless. Think of Dad, strong, brave, a fighter, a warrior. I want to be a fighter, too. Even though I've messed everything up so, so terribly, I can still get out of here. I *can*.

I clench and unclench my sweaty hands, working up the anger, rolling it around in my head, poking it with a stick until it blazes.

Then I hear a clicking sound, and I'm expecting the blonde one to open the door again.

I gulp in a breath but the door stays firmly closed. I hear another click. And another. And another. At first I can't work out where it's coming from. But then my gaze drifts upwards. To the plastic box above the door. It's got numbers on it now, illuminated in red LED lights. It's a digital clock, except . . . No, it's not a clock. Not really. It's some kind of timer.

And it's counting down . . .

THE DETECTIVE
Chapter 27

'What's the plan?' Ronnie asked, sliding behind the steering wheel.

'I want you to contact the local intelligence officer for this area. See what you can find out about this Dex guy. We need to pay him a visit. And find out where the local homeless hang-outs are. I'm going to call Becky.'

'All right.' Ronnie got to work on his phone, calling the control room to get a number for the LIO.

I sat next to him, stuck a finger in my free ear so as not to hear Ronnie.

When Becky picked up, the first thing she said was, 'I've got some bad news.'

'What? The whiteboard has put in a complaint about me?'

She laughed. 'That's *notice* board to you. I've just spoken to the forensic technical team and they found nothing of interest on the Jamesons' laptop or Jan's mobile phone. No emails or phone calls or texts to anyone that links to Stevens or a possible accomplice.'

'OK. Is there anything else back from the forensics SOCO took at the scene?'

'No, we're still waiting for the results of the soil samples.'

'I love it when you talk dirty.'

She snorted.

I pictured Tracy Stevens's palm prints recovered from the patio door, thinking it weird that it was only her who'd left easily identifiable evidence of her presence there. Either her accomplice didn't touch anything or they wore gloves. I thought back to Becky saying that they must've been a bad shot because Mike had been shot three times, but I disagreed. The shots were neat and precise, particularly the forehead shot to Mike Jameson. None had missed their target. But then the shot to Jan's neck was messy. Why not shoot her in the head, too? Unless they'd been aiming for her head and she'd moved. No furniture had been disturbed in the lounge and there were no signs of a struggle. No signs of panic after they'd murdered two people in cold blood. Then I thought of the traces of soil left on the carpet. Either it was a highly organised crime scene or it was a complete shambles. I hadn't worked out which yet. 'OK, first thing . . . I want you to circulate Tracy Stevens's details to all ports. She may try and make a run for it out of the country.'

'Got it.'

'Can you also get on to Tracy Stevens's mobile phone provider and see if they can trace a location for her if her phone's switched on.' I gave Becky the number of Tracy's phone. 'And see if they can expedite her call and text logs – see who she was in contact with.'

'Will do.'

'And also look into Tracy's parents' details. There's still a chance she may have gone back to Bristol. If you get an address, can you put a call through to the relevant control room and get them to pay a visit? I don't have time to go up there and check myself. Sorry, I know it's just you on your own there.'

'Don't worry. I thrive under pressure. I've had two chocolate bars and four coffees. I can go all night, if you want me to. And for the benefit of the phone record, that wasn't a sexual reference.' She laughed.

I grinned. 'Good, because I also want CCTV checked for London Road. Tracy was last seen by Alice at about eleven p.m., the night before the Jamesons were killed. Then she seems to have disappeared.'

'All right – oh, and Greene wanted to speak to you as soon as you were free.'

'Oh, goody, could you put me through,' I said.

There was an annoying chime of music while I waited for the call to connect, then Greene picked up and said, 'We just got the post-mortem results back on the Jamesons.'

'I'm listening.'

'Professor Hanley said Mike Jameson's wounds in his chest and leg missed vital organs, but the cause of death was the shot to his forehead, which resulted in severe brain damage and almost instant death. The bullet to Jan Jameson's neck hit the carotid artery, resulting in dramatic blood loss. Death would've occurred in seconds. According to entry wounds, the bullet recovered in the wall, and gunshot residue found, Jan Jameson was shot while the offender was directly in front of the coffee table where the soil prints were most concentrated. The shooter stood in the same spot to kill her husband.'

'Any idea who was shot first?' I asked.

'No. It's impossible to tell but they died within minutes of each other. Time of death has been narrowed only slightly to between eight a.m. and ten a.m.'

I brought up a mental image of the crime scene. The estimated position of the shooter was exactly the same as Emma Bolton had suggested. 'Was there any bruising or injuries on Jan Jameson that indicated she'd been restrained?' I asked.

'No. And no defensive injuries, either.'

'Strange,' I said. 'Why would the accomplice stand so close to Jan if they weren't restraining her?'

'Maybe the intention was to restrain her and it all went wrong too fast.'

'Surely a gun pointed at her or her husband would've been ample threat to an elderly woman, though.'

'They were unorganised and messy because they were drugged up to the eyeballs.'

'On the contrary, I think the bullet wounds Mike suffered look professional. Jan's seems amateur. I think Mike must've been shot first. Either in the chest or leg or both to incapacitate him because he was the bigger threat. Then maybe Jan tried to get away and the shooter fired at her, aiming for her head or chest but hitting her neck as she was moving and killing her anyway. Then they fired one final shot to Mike's forehead to kill him. Were the bullets recovered from Mike's body the same as the one found in the wall?'

'Yes, also nine millimetres. They'll be passed over to firearms for analysis,' Greene carried on. 'That's the crux of it. Have you got any updates for me?'

I told him where I was with things.

'So this Tracy Stevens has done a runner? Hardly surprising after what she did at that house. The press conference appealing for witnesses is due to start in half an hour. I'll get her photo and details out there at the same time.'

I thought again about Tracy's palm prints on the outside of the Jamesons' patio door. Three prints overlapping. 'Why did she leave evidence that could be traced back to her? These days everyone knows about forensic stuff. Why risk her prints being found at a murder scene?' There was something niggling at me about those prints, but I couldn't work out what. Something wasn't sitting right with me. A gut feeling there was more to this than seemed obvious.

'She was a drug addict so anything's possible. If she was high, she could've been acting crazy. And we know she was there. Maybe she pressed her hands to the glass when she was looking into the room, seeing if anyone was inside,' Greene said. 'She was probably out of her head and didn't even know what she was doing. She and her accomplice broke into the Jamesons' with the intent to burgle them. It's most likely they were disturbed and Mr Jameson was shot. While that was going on Mrs Jameson attempted to intercede. A struggle ensued with Stevens and Mrs Jameson was also shot and killed. They panicked then, and fled the scene before they could steal anything.'

'I'm not buying that theory. They didn't search the house for valuables. Didn't take Jan's handbag or jewellery in plain sight. It seems like they just came in, shot the Jamesons and left – what seems like a random act of violence when both Jan and Mike couldn't have been any kind of threat to them because the offenders had a gun,' I said. 'And it's bothering me how a prostitute from Berrisford ended up in a tiny hamlet on the other side of the county in the middle of nowhere, when there would've been hundreds of places to burgle in between, if that was the intention. A place, according to her friend Alice, Tracy had never been to or even heard of. Why pick there? Actually, how could she pick it? She'd have to stumble across it so why go there of all places? There had to have been some kind of connection between her and the Jamesons already, another reason they were both murdered, and I need to find out what it was.'

'I don't want you wasting time on that. I believe it was a random attack. Stevens and her accomplice were driving round the county, high, looking to burgle somewhere, and found the Jamesons' house an easy target. That's what happened. And that's the route we're going down. Now I want every effort put into finding Tracy Stevens.'

But I thought he was wrong. And if I found the connection, it could very well lead me to Tracy Stevens.

THE VIGILANTE

Chapter 28

I spent the drive back to Corinne's house trying to get the images of the snuff videos out of my head and failing miserably. Raging anger coursed through me. I gripped the steering wheel and debated over and over again whether to tell Corinne what I'd seen. I knew what it was like to lose a child. When my son was murdered I spent thirty-one years never knowing what had really happened to him – how he'd spent his last few minutes, seconds, who had been responsible for it. Thirty-one years of torment and guilt and hatred and anger and grief. When I'd finally found my son's murderers I'd thought that some of the heavy guilt I carried on my shoulders would melt away. Yes, watching the people who'd tortured and killed Alex die had been cathartic in a small way. It had helped assuage the guilt to a certain extent. It had certainly made the world a better place without them in it. But it still lived inside me. And taking their lives in exchange for Alex's hadn't made the emotions disappear. They'd lessened now, sure, but they would stay with me always to some degree, like a scab rooted deep within my flesh that I couldn't help picking. I didn't want to inflict the same pain on Corinne. Was it better for Corinne not to know the horrific details? And was that my choice to make?

I'd left Lee working on trying to trace the website or its server, or some other kind of link that would reveal the real IP address of the psychos who ran the red room. He'd thrown jargon at me about other possible ways to crack their identity. I didn't have a clue what he was talking about; it was all computer-speak, and he didn't have time to explain it to me. I would just be a distraction if I stayed at his office, and my expertise lay in a different area to Lee's. I was better off in Bournewood, in case whoever had taken Toni was local. Lee was calling all his guys in to work on analysing that website. All the rest of his jobs would take a backseat until we found her.

But dead or alive? That was the fear burning inside my skull.

It was just gone 4.30 a.m. when I arrived back at Corinne's, and I still didn't have a clue how to tell her.

I parked the truck outside the house, got out and stretched my back, my neck. My eyes were scratchy and raw. I was tired, running on the last of the pent-up anger from what I'd seen in those videos.

I glanced up and down the street. All was quiet. People shut up in their houses, blissfully sleeping, their lives untouched by the horror of the world. Lucky them. I'd seen a lifetime of it. My gaze strayed to Bert's house. The place was in darkness but all the curtains were still open.

I took a last look around the street and then walked up the path. I hoped Corinne was still in bed and Maya would let me in. It would delay the decision I'd have to make about whether to tell her or not. But the door opened before I made it to the front step.

Corinne stood, leaning against the door frame for support, her face full of questions. 'What did you find? Maya told me Lee had discovered something.'

Maya appeared behind Corinne. Our gaze met and she knew it wasn't good news. She could read me well now.

'Let's go inside.' I put my arm around Corinne's shoulder and steered her gently into the kitchen.

'I'll make coffee.' Maya busied herself with filling the kettle.

'I think you should sit down,' I said to Corinne.

'I don't want to fucking sit down! Just tell me what's going on.'

So I did. Because no matter how sick and disgusting and heart-wrenching the truth was, it was the only thing she owned right then.

Not surprisingly, Corinne fell apart before my eyes. A guttural sound escaped her lips and she flopped forward as if she'd been punched in the stomach. Her knees buckled and she slid to the ground as tears, howls of pain, terror, and every emotion I knew so well rose to the surface and exploded, petered out and exploded again. She cried and screamed and shouted as Maya and I both tried to comfort her. But comfort was an obsolete word now. There would be none of it until Toni walked back through that door.

If she ever did.

When Corinne was exhausted with it all, she sat like a ragdoll in Maya's arms staring at some spot on the floor, but I knew she wasn't really seeing it. Instead, she'd be seeing her daughter, held captive in a white-tiled room, waiting to die in the most painful way possible.

'You need some sleep,' Maya said to me. 'You're no good to anyone if you're exhausted. When Lee finds where Toni is, she'll need you. And until then, there's nothing else you can do.'

I acknowledged her words with a twitch of my mouth. I'd said something similar to her in the past. She was right, though. I did need to get my head down. An old rule from my Regiment days was: sleep while you can. Just a few hours' kip to set me up.

I looked at Corinne, broken, distraught. I didn't want to leave her like that, but I could do nothing more until Lee located where that website was transmitting data from.

'We'll be OK. I've had a few hours' sleep. I'll look after Corinne. Get some rest.' Maya nodded.

Slowly, I stood and made my way into the lounge. The pillows and blanket Maya had been using on the sofa were still there.

I lay down, sinking into the soft fabric, adjusted the pillow beneath my head, and closed my eyes, everything floating in my mind.

I blocked it all out. Succumbed to sleep.

Five hours later I bolted off the sofa, wide awake. Because my brain had slotted something I'd seen into place. Something I'd mistaken.

THE DETECTIVE
Chapter 29

'Tracy's dealer, Dex, is dead,' Ronnie said, raising two neatly trimmed eyebrows. 'His real name is Derek Merchant, and he was stabbed the night before Tracy disappeared on the estate he lived in.'

'Anything to suggest Tracy was involved?'

'Nothing, guv. There were witnesses. It was a gang-related drugs turf war gone wrong. An argument with another dealer who's been arrested.'

I leaned my head back against the headrest, fighting exhaustion. It was 3 p.m., I'd had hardly any sleep, and the day wasn't even over yet. 'All right, first, we visit the squat Tracy used to live in. Maybe she went back there.'

Ronnie started the car and drove out of the labyrinth of roads that skirted Kings Tower block and headed to Church Road while I called the local control room to see if they were aware of the squat and could give me the house number. According to the operator I spoke to, they'd had numerous complaints from neighbours about it in the past.

'It's number sixty-three,' the operator told me. 'But the last job we had there was ten months ago, accompanying bailiffs for an eviction order to get the squatters out. Apparently, the house was sold at auction. All of them were evicted.'

'OK, thanks,' I said. 'It's worth a try anyway.'

But it wasn't. When Ronnie and I arrived at number 63 the new owners were in situ, a middle-aged couple who'd renovated the house since it had been a boarded-up mess. Tracy wasn't there and hadn't tried to get in.

Next we tried the main local homeless hang-outs. Under the railway bridge, derelict buildings, park benches, a disused industrial estate. No Tracy Stevens and no one we spoke to had seen her. There were no homeless shelters in Berrisford to try. She could've been sleeping rough anywhere.

'I need something with caffeine in it.' I slapped my cheeks to wake up as I got back into the car. 'Stop at the next shop you see.'

'OK.'

I stared out of the window, thinking. As we drove along a residential street, my mobile rang. It was the conveyancing solicitor dealing with the sale of my house.

'Unfortunately, your buyers have pulled out. They've had problems with getting their mortgage.' He got straight to the point after saying hello. Time was money, and he was probably charging fifty quid just to call me.

'Right,' I said.

'Sorry to be the bearer of bad news.'

I ended the call and thought that maybe it wasn't bad news at all. Maybe it was a sign. I tapped my phone against my lips, wondering if Denise was trying to send me a message. *Don't sell the house. Don't move to London. Don't start the new job.* I felt like going home and just yanking down the For Sale board and taking it off the market.

For Sale board. A thought struck me as I pictured the same board up outside Simms Livery Stables. I clicked my middle finger and thumb together. 'That's what doesn't make sense.'

'What's that, guv?'

'DSU Greene thinks this was a burglary, right? Parker Farm has a lot of security – high walls and gates, even before the owner started putting up barbed wire on top after the Jamesons were killed – so I can understand why that property would seem more trouble than it was worth to break into. But no one was at home at both Bill Graves's farm or the house at Simms Livery Stables, so why didn't they break into either of those empty properties if that was the intention? Depending on which direction they came down the lane from, they would've had to pass one of those to get to the Jamesons'. The house at the stables would've been ideal because there's still plenty of stuff in there worth nicking that Mrs Simms's son hasn't got round to getting rid of yet. Why did they choose the Jamesons' with the Land Rover parked outside it that indicated someone was most likely at home? In broad daylight, too.'

'You can never tell what a druggie's going to do. They're totally unpredictable.'

'Don't you start. You sound like Greene.'

Ronnie blushed. 'Sorry.'

'It wasn't a burglary gone wrong,' I said. 'If they intended to rob the place, why didn't one of them hold the Jamesons at gunpoint while the other ransacked the place? They were an elderly couple who couldn't have posed much of a threat.'

'But Greene said—'

'Greene has been sitting in an office too long. He's a pen-pusher, not a copper.'

'So what's next?'

'I'm going to speak to Paula Eagan and Bill Graves to see if they can shed any light on whether the Jamesons knew Tracy. I want you to come back here with me tonight and we'll go to London Road. Talk to the other sex workers and see if they know anything. We need to find out who Tracy went off with that night, whether anyone saw her again, and if they have any idea where she might be. Becky couldn't find any other known associates of Tracy. And Alice said she didn't have any other friends. But she was with *someone* in that house. How did she get there? There must've been a vehicle involved to get to that remote location. But who was driving it? Was it the person she disappeared with that night?'

'Yes, guv. Anything else you want me to do?'

'You can get the pink stones you collected off to the lab when we get back.'

'Will do.'

'Hey, stop here.' I pointed to a petrol station coming up. 'I'll grab a couple of coffees.'

'Tea for me, please. Peppermint if they have it.' Ronnie checked his mirrors carefully, indicated, and pulled on to the forecourt. 'That salad I had was dodgy.' He rubbed his stomach. 'My irritable bowel's playing up now. I hope I'm not coming down with food poisoning.'

I raised my eyebrows and pulled a face. 'Food poisoning from salad?'

'Actually, bagged salad leaves are renowned for it.'

'Well, you learn something new every day. You're better off with a greasy old burger, then, aren't you? Anyway, mints are meant for sucking not drinking. Do you want me to see if they've got any antacids?'

He pulled a face. 'I don't take them. They play havoc with my IBS, too.'

I got out of the car, entered the garage and came back with a can of iced coffee and a bottle of water. I tossed Ronnie the water. 'No peppermint, I'm afraid.'

We drove back to the nick in silence with the windows down, blasting me with fresh air to keep me awake. I had a feeling it was going to be a long night.

THE VIGILANTE
Chapter 30

I shot off the sofa and strode into the kitchen. There it was, the leaflet discarded where I'd left it on the kitchen worktop after picking it up from the front door mat when I'd first arrived. It was a flyer, touting for business, and I hadn't taken much notice of it at the time. I studied the logo at the top and then read down the page.

> *Your home security is just a step away! Peace of mind anytime, anywhere . . .*

> *The new Pro-Secure family of smart, covert security cameras feature HD video quality, wide angles, live streaming, free cloud recording and alerts. They're wire-free, waterproof, and . . .*

I stopped reading and looked at the logo again. I'd seen it before on an invoice on Bert's table in his hallway.

Maya was washing up cups and glasses at the sink beneath the front window. 'What is it?'

'Where's Corinne?' I asked.

'In her room. She said she wanted to be alone.'

I walked towards Maya, stood next to her and looked through the net curtains at Bert's house opposite. I couldn't see a camera anywhere. His curtains were still wide open, and I spotted the top of his head just above his front window, sitting in his wheelchair, a shadow falling over him. I couldn't see his eyes from that distance but I guessed he was watching the street, as usual, like a sentry.

'What?' Maya said to me, following my gaze.

I was silent for a moment, waiting.

'He lied to me about having CCTV cameras.'

'What?' Maya squinted through the window. 'Why?'

'I think it's because he's not just using it for security. He's always watching everyone and everything going on. Maybe he doesn't like to miss anything so he's recording it all, too, but he doesn't want anyone to know. But hopefully he might've caught something that could help us. If the people who took Toni knew her online identity, they'd have known her address. They might've thought it was too risky to break in to get to her. Corinne could've been in the house. Or a friend. Or a neighbour might spot them. Or someone from the school behind if they went through the rear. All sorts of possible complications. So they did what I would've done. Watched and waited for the right opportunity. They must've been parked up further down the street. Too risky for them to hang around on foot; someone would've seen them. Most likely they were in a white van. Who pays attention to white vans? They're everywhere. We see so many they just become unnoticeable.'

'And they followed her to the cutting,' Maya said. 'Where there was no one around. The perfect opportunity to grab her and throw her in the van. Then they turned her phone off and probably dumped it along with her rucksack, because if they're using anonymous software, then they know about being traceable.'

'And *he* might've recorded a vehicle.' I pointed in Bert's direction, then strode out of the house, across the street. My gaze met Bert's through his window before I banged on his front door.

Bert wheeled himself backwards to accommodate opening the door. 'Good morning.' He looked surprised to see me again. No, more like nervous. And now I knew why I'd got a strange vibe off him. 'Is there any news about Toni?' He gave me a worried frown.

I ignored the question, answering it with one of my own. 'You film people on the street, don't you? You've got cameras somewhere.'

His eyes turned huge behind his glasses. 'Um . . . what . . . Of course I don't!' He tried for indignant and failed. The red, nervous flush creeping up his neck and the quivering of his hands gave him away.

'Spare me the lies. I don't have time for that.' I walked inside and picked up the invoice from his table. It was the same logo. Same company. I read it out to him. 'An invoice for a wide-angled, wireless security camera, two hundred and twenty-five pounds, including installation. Dated four weeks ago.' I waved the invoice at him. 'I asked if you had CCTV and you lied to me. Toni's in serious danger and you might be able to help her. I don't care about you filming the comings and goings of the street, unless you're into children. In which case, you've got a huge problem.'

The flush kept on coming, all the way up to his cheeks. A sheen of sweat broke out on his forehead. 'Definitely not! And I resent that implication.'

'You can resent it all you want. But I need to see what's on the recording. I think whoever took Toni followed her from her house. Where do you store the footage? Laptop or smartphone?'

He didn't answer. Didn't deny it, though.

I stepped past his wheelchair and went into the lounge, looking around. I couldn't see a laptop but his phone was resting on the windowsill.

Bert wheeled himself in behind me. 'How dare you come in here and look at my things! I've a good mind to call the police.'

'So call them. I'm sure they'd love to know what you're doing. Where's the footage?'

His mouth flapped open and closed, trying to think of some excuse or way to get out of the situation. Trying to stop his secret voyeurism being exposed. Then he resigned himself to the fact that there was no getting out of it, and his shoulders sagged. 'On the phone.'

I snatched up the Samsung smartphone and pressed the home button. It asked me for a password. I wiggled it in front of him. 'What's the password?'

'Five, five, four, four,' he said wearily.

I typed it in and the home screen popped up.

'I *don't* look at children. That's disgusting.'

'What, and videoing people without their knowledge isn't?'

'You don't understand.' His voice was quiet now, deflated. 'I can't do anything any more.' He slapped his legs. 'I used to be like everyone else.' He pointed a shaky finger out of the window, towards a man hurrying down the street, carrying a rucksack. 'I used to be able to go anywhere. Now I'm stuck in here and I'm useless. Useless!' His eyes watered. 'So I . . . I film them because I've got no life. And I watch theirs instead. And I imagine that I'm them, walking, running. Going *somewhere*. Being *able* to go somewhere. Having that choice. I record it because I don't like to miss anything. Please don't tell anyone. I'm not doing anything to hurt people. It's not like that.'

Of course I got it. I felt sympathy for him. But I couldn't afford to indulge that in a long spiel about understanding. 'I'm sorry for your situation.' I looked at the phone screen again. 'Was the camera recording when Toni left the house that day?'

'Yes,' he said softly.

I pressed on the security company's icon.

'I wouldn't hurt anyone.' He sobbed out loud.

'Then you'll want to help me, right?'

'Of course.'

'Where's the camera set up?'

'Attached to the satellite dish on the outside wall upstairs. It's really small, you can't notice it.'

Luckily, the videos were listed in date order. I scrolled back through to the date and time Toni went missing, pressed play and watched, my jaw tight with anticipation. The camera had a wide-angle view of the street and crisp definition. The footage had started off filming a thirty-something woman walking past his window. She had high heels on and a short skirt and kept flicking her long hair over her shoulder. After she went out of frame, a sparrow flew down and perched on Bert's wooden bird table in his front garden, pecking at crusts of bread. A little later a mum walked up the street with a pushchair. And then I saw Toni emerging from her front door across the road.

She shut the door and stood on the front step for a moment, hesitating. Then she clamped her lips together and headed down the path. She turned left, in the direction of the cutting. Hurried down the street, her rucksack bouncing against her back as she took long, purposeful strides before disappearing from view.

And that's when a van came into sight. White. Nondescript. No sign writing on it. Nothing to distinguish it from all the other thousands of white vans out there. It was following slowly behind Toni. The driver was blurred by the sunlight reflecting off the vehicle's window, but I could tell he had his head turned away slightly, looking towards the kerb. Towards where Toni would be walking along the footpath. Not even a side profile of him, just the back of his head.

'What is it?' Bert asked meekly.

I waved my hand to silence him. Rewound it. Watched it again. And the more I watched, the more I observed further details I'd missed the first time.

The van had what looked like a patch of speckled rust over the offside rear wheel arch and a dent in the offside front wing in the shape of a V.

And the camera had managed to capture the registration plate.

THE DETECTIVE

Chapter 31

I yawned as I parked the car on the street outside Paula Eagan's small terraced house. I ran my hands over my face and picked up my folder from the passenger seat.

She answered on the second knock. Her eyes were red and swollen from crying.

'Do you have any news? I just saw the press appeal on TV.' She stood awkwardly in front of me, crossing her arms over her chest. 'They showed a photo of that woman. Do you really think she killed Mum and Dad?'

'I don't know if she pulled the trigger, but Tracy Stevens was there. We know that much. Can I come in for a moment?'

'Yes.' She led me into a compact but tidy lounge.

'Is Grant here?'

'Um . . . yes. Upstairs.'

'I need to ask him some questions, too.'

'I'll just go and get him. Have a seat.'

I sat on a sagging velour sofa and heard her footsteps retreat upstairs. Then two pairs of heavy tread on the way back down. Grant came into the room followed by Paula. He was stocky with a beer gut, tattoo sleeves on both arms, and wearing a football shirt. I could understand why the Jamesons had taken a dislike to him. He looked like a thug. He was a drinker and a gambler. They obviously thought their daughter could do better. But everyone made mistakes. Hopefully he would turn his life around now he was getting help for his gambling problem. And looks could always be deceptive.

'Do you have any news?' Grant took hold of Paula's hand and squeezed it. She slumped against his shoulder, as if she needed him for support.

'Not yet, I'm afraid. But I wanted to know if you recognised Tracy Stevens when you saw her on the TV.'

'No. I've never seen her before in my life,' Grant said.

Paula shook her head. 'Never.'

'I have some other pictures of her. Sometimes people look different in different photos.' I reached into my folder and pulled out some more samples, taken from when Tracy was arrested. I handed them to Paula and she flicked through, lips pressed together in a tight line, hatred burning in her eyes, while Grant looked over her shoulder. 'I think it's possible your parents might've known her.'

Slowly she shook her head. 'No. I've never seen her before.'

'Me, neither,' Grant added.

'Anyway, how on earth would my parents have known her? Detective Superintendent Greene said on TV it was a random attempted burglary that went wrong. Mum and Dad surprised them and then they were murdered. He thinks this Tracy Stevens and her accomplice panicked then and ran.'

Grant put his arm around his wife, giving her a look of sympathy. Whatever else he might have been, he looked like a man who genuinely cared about his wife.

'Things aren't always what they seem. I think there had to be some kind of connection between Tracy Stevens and your parents.'

Her jaw fell open. 'You're saying Dad was using a . . . a prostitute?' Anger flashed in her eyes as she walked to the window overlooking the street and turned her back to me. 'That's absolutely ridiculous! They were a happily married couple. And they were always together. He wouldn't have had the time, even if he'd wanted to . . . to . . . shag some whore.'

'I'm not suggesting that at all.'

She swung around to face me, eyes full of hurt. 'Then what *are* you suggesting?'

'I very much doubt Tracy Stevens would've randomly stumbled upon your parents' house, particularly when there were obviously empty properties right next door with plenty of things in them to steal. There must be a reason why they went there.'

She slumped down on the edge of the armchair. Grant stood behind her, hands on her shoulders.

'It could've been your mum that knew Tracy,' I suggested.

'I don't see how that's possible,' she snapped. 'I told you all of Mum and Dad's friends and they're all middle-aged or retired, respectable couples. I'm pretty damn sure she wouldn't have come into contact with a druggie prostitute!'

'Did your parents ever do any volunteer work?'

'No.'

'Did they have any hobbies that took them out of the house? For example, were they members of any clubs, or maybe a gym?' There'd been no monthly payments to any clubs from the Jamesons' bank statements but maybe they'd paid in cash.

'No. They were both homebirds, really. They liked gardening and reading and walks in the country. Sometimes Mum would meet up with her friends for coffee.'

'Tracy Stevens lived and worked in Berrisford. Did either of your parents ever mention going there? Or knowing anyone there?'

'No. As far as I know they've never been there. It's the other side of the county, and they definitely didn't have friends up that way.'

'Did they have any work done recently on their property? Maybe they came into contact with someone who scouted out the house when they were doing jobs for your parents.' I'd found no bills in the collection of documents we'd taken from the house to indicate that but I had to ask.

She shook her head. 'Mum didn't say anything like that, but . . . well, as you know, she might not have done after the argument we had about the money. I doubt it, though. Dad was a dab hand at DIY and maintenance. He used to do everything around the place.'

But Mike had been ill. Maybe there was an urgent plumbing or electrical job that needed seeing to and couldn't wait for Mike to recover.

None the wiser, I left Paula to her grief and got back in the car.

Bill Graves was in the middle of cooking an omelette when I got to his farm. He quickly ushered me into the kitchen and turned off the hob. The smell of fried onion and melted cheese hit my nostrils and my stomach rumbled.

'Sorry to interrupt your dinner. This won't take long,' I said.

'No problem. You're lucky you caught me, actually. I'm just heading down to Brighton for a couple of days after dinner to stay with my sister.' Bill leaned against the kitchen worktop and wiped his hands on a tea towel.

'Did you see the press appeal on TV?' I asked.

'Sorry, I haven't had time to watch the telly.'

I retrieved a photograph of Tracy from my file and showed it to him. 'Do you recognise this woman? Did you ever see her visiting the Jamesons or hanging around the area? I know you didn't see anything on the day of their murder, but before that, maybe?'

Bill took the photo and studied it, concentration etching lines on his forehead. 'No, sorry. I've never seen her before. Is this who you think did it?'

'We have evidence she was at their house.'

Bill shook his head and handed back the photo. 'What could cause a young girl like that to do something so awful?'

I had no answer to that. Yet.

'Did Jan or Mike mention anything about any maintenance people doing work on their property recently?'

Bill scrunched his face up, thinking. 'No. Mike used to do everything like that.'

'But he'd been ill. It's possible someone they came into contact with recently targeted them.'

He shook his head. 'No, they never mentioned any problems. And I'm pretty sure Jan would've just called me to help out until Mike got back on his feet if it was urgent. It's how we've always done things with each other.'

'OK, thanks.'

My next stop was Simms Livery Stables to ask Jenny Fullerton the same questions, but she'd never seen Tracy Stevens before, either.

I drove down the lane, swung a left and headed to Parker Farm.

I pulled to a stop outside the gates enclosing the property. Connor Parker had more security than Fort Knox now. I got out of the car and tried the gates but they were firmly locked. I pressed the bell on the wall several times but there was no response so I called Becky and asked her to see if she could find a phone number for Mr Parker.

After a few minutes of tapping sounds, Becky said, 'He's ex-directory, I'm afraid.'

'OK, thanks. I'll leave a note for him to contact me instead.'

I pulled a business card out of my glove box, wrote on the back, asking him to get in touch, and popped it in his post box attached to the wall. Then I headed back to the nick, knowing that I was missing something; some vital little thread that would make sense of everything, but unsure what the hell it could be.

THE VIGILANTE

Chapter 32

I wasn't holding out much hope that Lee could trace an owner for the van. No one in their right minds would kidnap someone using an identifiable plate number. And these people were organised and clever and knew about anonymity. So the plates were either cloned or the van was stolen. But I had to try.

Lee picked up on the fourth ring. His first words were, 'I'm still searching for some kind of vulnerability I can exploit on the website.'

'I'm not chasing you up. I need something else. Can you check out a number plate for me?' I explained what I'd seen.

'Sure. Go ahead with it.'

I told him and listened to him typing on the other end.

'Email me the video. I'll check CCTV in the area that might've caught the van around the time Toni was taken. And depending on his route, it may have been picked up on Automatic Number Plate Recognition cameras, too.'

'Will do. As soon as I hang up.'

'Got it . . . The owner's registered as a Timothy Clark. He lives in Norwich.' Lee gave me the address. 'There are no reports lost or stolen. The van's got no markers against it. But my guess would be it's cloned.

If it was stolen or on a false plate, it would've been flagged up on any ANPR cameras straight away, and they wouldn't want to risk that with Toni in the van.'

'I think you're right but it's all I've got so I'll take a drive up to the address. It's got a dent in the driver's side front wing and what looks like rust over the wheel arch, but it could be splatters of dirt. If you manage to find any other identifying marks on the van when you sharpen the image, let me know.'

'I'm on it.' Lee ended the call, and I emailed him the video from Bert's phone, which he'd given me without any protest.

I filled a pint glass of water and downed it in one. Grabbed an apple from Corinne's fruit bowl and went to find Maya, who was in the lounge on the sofa, legs tucked up beside her, staring through the French doors at the kids on the school's playing field having a game of hockey, visible over Corinne's boundary fence.

'You OK?' I asked.

She nodded. 'I just feel so bad for Corinne. And I don't think I'm helping her much. When I lost Jamie, I didn't want people around me, watching me, feeling sorry for me, suffocating me. I wanted to be alone.' She sighed. 'I want to comfort her but there's nothing I can do or say. I feel useless, to be honest.'

'You and me both. But sometimes words aren't necessary. Sometimes it's enough just to be there for someone.' I put a hand on her shoulder. 'I have news, though. I've got a lead.' I told her about the van.

Her eyes lit up. 'That's great.' Then she took in the expression on my face and added, 'Isn't it?'

'I think it's a clone, but I'm going to check it out anyway. Who knows? We could get lucky.'

'I'll let Corinne know when she gets up. Hopefully, she'll have managed a few hours' sleep.'

I gave her a hug, grabbed my daysack and got in my pick-up. After setting up the satnav, I drove away.

I was an hour into my two-and-a-half-hour journey when Lee called back with a result. The day before Toni had gone missing, the van had been caught on a CCTV camera outside the public library Toni had visited. They'd obviously been watching her, finding out her movements, doing a recce of the area so they could work out where best to make the snatch. And the cameras had caught the driver in both full-frontal and side shots. Lee was going to run it through various systems and programs to see if he could come up with any kind of facial-recognition match. There were no passengers captured, but I suspected someone else would've been inside the van, hidden from view, ready to snatch Toni when the opportunity arose.

Lee had also enhanced the images from Bert's video and confirmed the discoloured patch over the wheel arch was rust. He'd discovered another identifying mark on the van. A small, round, orange sticker on the corner of the glass panel in the right-hand rear door.

I clutched the steering wheel tight and concentrated on the road ahead, praying we'd found the first intel that would lead me to Toni.

An hour and a half later I was in a residential street of narrow terraced houses. It was just gone 1 p.m., and I was worried that Timothy Clark, if he existed, would be at work. Luckily, a sweep of the road offered me up a prize. The van was outside his address in all its glory. The road was half full of parked cars on either side so I found a parking spot and switched off the engine. I reached for my phone to look at the images of the driver Lee had sent over to me. My first proper glimpse of the man I was certain had taken Toni. Lee had obviously zoomed in the camera shot as it was a close-up. A young guy, maybe mid-twenties. Dark, short hair. Thick eyebrows. A nose that looked like it had been busted a few times. Thin lips.

I ground my jaw, committed his face to memory, then took my Glock from my daysack, slid it into my pancake holster and untucked my shirt to cover it, before getting out of the car.

I approached the van from the rear. And with every footstep that took me closer, my eyes were fixed on the glass panel in the back doors.

No orange sticker.

When I was right up close to it I stood and looked at the driver's side. No V-shaped dent. No rust.

My heart sank.

THE DETECTIVE

Chapter 33

'Cup of coffee, guv?' Ronnie asked from his position in front of the office kettle.

'Yeah, thanks.'

'There's no milk, though. Someone nicked the last lot when Becky popped out.'

'Bastards,' Becky muttered, her head bent over some paperwork on her desk.

I plonked myself on my desk, feeling about a hundred years old. My back ached and my head throbbed. Maybe I should go to the gym. Go on a diet. Stop eating crap. Or maybe I really should retire. Somewhere warm where I could walk on the beach and swim in the sea. Didn't they say the sun was good for old people? Not that I was *that* old, but I felt it these days. 'I'll have my coffee natural-coloured, please,' I said to Ronnie.

'Huh?' He frowned.

'Well, I never know what I'm allowed to bloody say these days.'

'You mean you want it black?' Becky asked.

'Yep.' I sat upright and leaned my elbows on my desk. 'So, what's been going on here?' I asked Becky.

'Tracy Stevens doesn't have a passport, but I've circulated her details to all ports anyway. Her phone's been switched off since 11.31 p.m. on the night she was last seen in London Road. They'll let me know if and when it gets switched back on. I'm awaiting an email from them about her call and text history. They're expediting it so it should be here soon. About the council CCTV in London Road, though . . . Bad news, I'm afraid. There was some kind of major technical problem that night and it was down from the hours of nine p.m. to six a.m.'

I groaned. 'Great. Then we need to contact any businesses or residential properties on that street with private cameras. The businesses will probably all be closed now, but hopefully we can get an out-of-hours number for them and get them to keep hold of it until we can check it out. Are there any bank account details we can go on? Has Tracy used a debit or credit card since she went missing?'

'I'm still working on it, but I can't find any details of Tracy actually having any bank account so far.'

I rubbed my forehead and stifled another yawn. 'OK, good work. Have any sightings of Tracy come in following the press conference?'

'The calls are being fielded to the new helpdesk and not us. Ronnie and I wouldn't be able to cope with all those messages on our own so at least that's something, I suppose.'

The helpdesk had been set up a few months ago to answer all kinds of random and bizarre questions that weren't actually police problems, or that would involve a minimal amount of work finding the answer to. I knew one of the civilians who worked there and she'd given me a hilarious commentary about the kinds of things the public were phoning in about. It seemed crazy to me that police officers and civilians were being hoicked from real departments to answer queries like what to do about a deer wandering around in the garden when we were down to the bare bones of staff investigating a double murder. Modern policing at its finest.

'So far, we've had the usual nutters coming out of the woodwork or questionable sightings. Nothing helpful,' Becky added.

'Are you allowed to say "nutters" now?' I asked.

'Probably not.' She grinned, opening her drawer and peering at her stash of chocolate inside. 'You want a Snickers?' she asked me.

'How come they don't nick the Snickers but they take the milk and my cakes?' I asked incredulously.

Her eyes glinted slyly. 'I keep my drawer locked when I'm not here.'

'A woman after my own heart,' I said. 'I'll give twenty quid to anyone who comes up with a way to lock the fridge door.'

Ronnie stirred my coffee, looking down at the fridge thoughtfully.

Becky threw the Snickers in my direction, then said to Ronnie, 'Want one?'

He rubbed his stomach as he put the mug of coffee on my desk. 'No, thanks. I've got some raw almonds to snack on.'

'Suit yourself.' Becky tore the wrapper off her Snickers as if she hadn't seen food in a week, took a huge bite and chewed quickly.

I did the same with mine and groaned appreciatively. 'I think I'm a little bit in love with you,' I said to Becky.

'Now *that's* sexual harassment.' She pointed her Snickers at me.

'So's pointing a chocolate bar at me in a suggestive manner.'

I was going to miss her when I left. I'd miss Ronnie, too. Even listening to the sometimes graphic descriptions of his delicate intestines. *If* I left. Ellie's words echoed in my ears. *Why don't you have a serious think about what you really want for your future and let me know. But don't leave it too long.* What the hell was I going to do? I pushed the thought away. There were more important things to deal with right now.

Becky put her half-eaten Snickers on her desk and said, 'I finally got the phone and financials back for the Jamesons and Eagans. There's nothing from the Eagans' bank accounts that raises any flags. Other than Paula and Grant's debt problem, which we're already aware of, there's nothing much to tell. Nothing suspicious going on in the Jamesons' bank accounts, either. They lived on a state pension and had a couple of tax-free savings accounts with forty thousand pounds in. There are no strange transactions, no sudden withdrawals or deposits. In fact, they were pretty frugal and predictable in their spending patterns. There's no trail linking them to any criminal activities. Mike didn't have a mobile phone. Jan didn't use hers much, only for texting her friends. There were no calls made from her mobile or the landline at the house the day they were killed and the only ones made in the weeks before their murder were to their GP, to Bill Graves, and to several friends. Paula's phone records are equally innocuous. Nothing to link any of them to Tracy Stevens so far, or to connect the Jamesons to any unsavoury characters. They are what they seem – a respectable, retired couple with no criminal connections.'

'*Were*,' Ronnie corrected.

'Yes, were,' I said, glancing up at the whiteboard with the photos of Mike and Jan tacked to it, frustration and sadness coursing through me at their violent murder. They weren't just a statistic to me, they were real people. Innocent people who didn't deserve to die like that. I tore my gaze away and said, 'OK, maybe the connection isn't with Tracy. Maybe she was just along for the ride. It could be her accomplice that knew the Jamesons. I want you to go through Jan's address book. Ronnie may well have spoken to a lot of their friends listed in it, but see if there are any people unaccounted for that seem suspect. Also find out if anyone the Jamesons knew have connections to Berrisford. They must've known Stevens or her accomplice somehow for them to rock up at that isolated address for whatever reason. There's a link somewhere.'

'Will do.'

'Right, Ronnie, what have you got for me?' I bit into another chunk of chocolate.

'I took the pink stones recovered from Tracy's bedroom to the lab. They had a look while I waited. I used my charm.' He smiled broadly.

'You didn't tell them about your irritable bowel, did you?' I asked.

Becky snorted with laughter and nearly choked on her Snickers.

Ronnie shook his head, taking it on the chin. 'They did confirm the stones and glue appear to be a visual match to the ones found in the Jamesons' lounge, though. They'd need to run more tests to confirm.'

I shrugged. 'It's just ticking boxes. We know Tracy was in both locations so it doesn't move us any further forward.' I threw my chocolate wrapper in the office bin and walked to the whiteboard, staring at the satellite map with the Jamesons' property in the centre. I studied the surrounding area – Simms Livery Stables to the right, Bill Graves's farm on the left, and the country lane in front of them both, the woods at the rear of the Jamesons' land before it led to Parker Farm. The map was crystal clear – you could even see vehicles. No doubt on the Internet you could zoom in and see number plates and street signs. I wondered how often the satellite took photos and beamed them back to earth. George Orwell had got it spot on. Big Brother was watching every move we made, even if we didn't realise it.

I pressed my palms together and rested my fingertips under my chin, my gaze drifting across to the photos of Tracy Stevens and the crime scene photos of the lounge.

I looked at the landline's cordless handset on the coffee table in front of Jan's corpse. Had it really all happened too fast for her to reach for it? I pictured her sitting on the sofa, reading the book that now rested on it, looking up and seeing the offenders at the rear patio doors. One of the offenders opening the unlocked door, the other close behind, suddenly in the room, Jan's jaw dropping open, eyes wide with fear.

My visualisation was interrupted by Becky.

'The email from Tracy's phone company's here.'

I swung around.

'They've got the calls but the texts will take a little longer to come in.' She shoved the last of the chocolate bar in her mouth and clicked a few buttons on her laptop.

I walked to Becky's desk and stood behind her as she opened the email. Attached to it was a paltry one-page document, which she printed out while Ronnie waited patiently by the printer so he could hand it to me when it had finished spewing out its contents.

'Thanks.' I took it and scanned the numbers. Her phone hadn't been used for two days before she'd last been seen. I handed Becky the printout. 'One of those numbers is probably Dex, her dealer. Some of them may be punters who probably won't want to give us anything useful, but still, can you ring them all? See if any of them have heard from Tracy. See if any could be the accomplice she was with.'

Ronnie's phone rang then and he rushed across the room to answer it as I glanced at the clock. It was just gone 10 p.m. and London Road would be coming alive soon.

Ronnie muttered a 'thanks' before hanging up and telling me it had been our counterparts in Bristol, who'd done a house enquiry at Tracy's parents' place. They hadn't seen her since she'd left home at sixteen, and there was still a high degree of animosity directed at their daughter after all these years.

Another dead end.

THE MISSING
Chapter 34

I'm pacing the room. It's seven steps long. Five steps wide. I count the steps in my head over and over again. Back and forth, back and forth I go, trying to get rid of the adrenaline trapped inside. Because I have to be strong when they come back for me. I don't want to be a quivering wreck.

I've thought about what Dad would do. Even though I never knew him, Mum told me stories about what he got up to, and I've read books about the SAS. How they plan things. It doesn't matter that I'm a skinny, short girl and they are huge, powerful men. Strength isn't just about size. It's all about the mental focus, too.

So I focus on the things I know. The red room I saw on the video wasn't this cell-like building. It was bigger, with a camera capturing every vicious thing they did. It was covered from floor to ceiling in white tiles. White tiles that were spattered with . . . No. I'm not going that far ahead. I'm *not* going there. I push away the blood and the girl screaming on the wooden table in the middle of the room with restraints holding her locked in place as she struggled uselessly against them, and the sound of the baseball bat's sickening crack against her body. There was another small table in the corner of that room with other tools that . . . Anyway, not thinking about that part, either.

The point is. The point is . . . it was a different room. So they'll have to move me. Out along that corridor. And when they come for me, when they unlock that door, I can try to escape. The fat one said someone else had escaped. Did they get away? No, they couldn't have, because they would've gone to the police already. They would've led them here. But that won't stop me trying, too.

My gaze darts to the countdown clock.

3:45:23

3:45:22

3:45:21

My death is getting closer.

I swallow back the acid rising in my throat and think again.

Think! Think! Come on!

How? How can I do it when I have no weapon?

I clench my fists. Pace. Picture my dad's face, smiling at me saying, *You can do it, Toni. You can beat them.*

'What would you do?' I say aloud. 'How would you do it?' But my dad was a big man, trained to kill with his hands. He could do a lot more than I ever could.

And then the thought slams into my brain.

The kirby grip in my hair. I can use it.

My hand flies to the top of my head, where I put my fringe up before I left the house to keep it out of my eyes. The grip is brown, like my hair, disguised.

I touch it. It's still there. It didn't fall out when I was punched and grabbed and tossed into the van. It slid further inside my thick hair, towards my scalp, covered over with other hair so that they didn't even notice it.

I slide it out and the front of my hair falls down over my face. I bat it out of the way but it sticks to the slickness on my forehead. I grab it and smooth it away from my eyes then pick off the little plastic nub on the end of the wire grip, designed to prevent you stabbing your scalp with the sharp end of metal. But it's not a grip any more, it's a weapon. And I want that hard, blunt end exposed so I can stick it into an eyeball.

I grip the wire tight between my thumb and forefinger, like a crab's pincer.

Then I hear knocking. And I freeze.

THE VIGILANTE

Chapter 35

I pulled into a layby on the journey back to Corinne's, where a mobile burger van was parked up. I'd had just five hours' sleep the night before and could feel my eyes getting heavy, my mind drifting, not concentrating on the road.

I got out of the pick-up and ran up and down the layby for five minutes to wake myself up, ignoring the curious look from the woman in the van.

Heart rate pumping, a burst of fresh air in my lungs and my muscles woken up, I walked towards her and ordered a monster burger and a bottle of orange juice to get some calories down me while I could.

By the time the bun was fully loaded, Lee was back on the phone. I answered with one hand, tucked the OJ in my pocket and reached out for the Styrofoam container from the woman with the other before heading back to the pick-up. 'What have you got?'

'Still no luck tracing the website. We're doing all we can. Like I said, it's a slow process trying different avenues. *But* I have some good intel for you. ANPR cameras picked up the van on the A1M on the day Toni disappeared. It's definitely the same one, it has the same identifying marks. I hacked into traffic cameras en route and tracked it getting off at junction six, which is the Welwyn turn-off. It's a small village in Hertfordshire. Then it disappeared from any cameras and hasn't been seen since.'

I thought about that as I took a bite of the burger, chewed, swallowed. 'So, three possibilities. Either they swapped vehicles somewhere after that. Or their destination was around that area, out in the country, with no cameras. Or it followed another route after it got off the motorway that managed to avoid any cameras.' I took another bite. 'I don't think they swapped vehicles. They were already using a cloned plate that couldn't be traced to them so it didn't matter if they were caught on cameras because they didn't bank on Bert filming them following Toni. So that leaves the last two choices.'

'I've mapped out the surrounding areas near that junction. There are plenty of back roads with no cameras which lead to many villages along the way. They could've taken her anywhere.'

'I thought you said this was *good* intel.'

'Well, it gets better, because I know who the driver is.'

I detected a triumphant smile in his voice.

'I matched him using facial recognition to the Met Police's databases.'

I quickly swallowed the lump of burger in my mouth before I blurted out, 'Who is he?'

'Jimmy Delaney. He started off with minor vehicle crime – nicking cars and car stereos. Then he moved on to drug offences. Possession of cannabis and barbiturates. He'd been given fines and community service up till that point, until he got involved in an assault. He stabbed a bloke at a petrol station after a road rage incident. He got six years at Her Majesty's pleasure for that, but he got out in three. He's been back on the streets for just over a year.'

'You got an address?' I dumped the burger in the foam container, wiped my hand on a napkin, and reached for a pen and pad in the centre console.

'Last known address was at 198 Balham Place, an estate in south-east London. When he got out, he signed on the dole for six months. At the time he was claiming benefits he told them he was living there. I've checked various databases, and he's not on the voter's register there or anywhere. He doesn't have a vehicle registered to him at that address or any other. According to his tax and national insurance records, he's received no payments from an employer and paid no tax since before he went inside. He's got a bank account and their address for him is still Balham Place. *And* the guy thinks he's clever but he's a fucking idiot.'

'How so?'

'The people who pay to watch or direct the red room footage pay in D-coins, right?'

'Yeah. Which is supposed to be anonymous, I know.'

'Like I said before, it could've taken months to get a trail on the transactions, but his bank actually did me a huge favour. Delaney's been getting payments from the company who holds his D-coin wallet directly into his regular bank account. For a guy who doesn't appear to be working, he's made fifty grand already this year in D-coin payments. He withdraws them in amounts of under ten grand, so it doesn't raise any flags with the bank. All the deposits from his wallet include the same reference number. So I got into the wallet service, traced the reference number back to Delaney's D-coin address and key. Then I made some test payments on the red room site and analysed some D-coin traffic. Long story short . . . Delaney's D-coin address belongs to the red-room site. He's your guy.'

I smiled. 'Are there any other payments from the same wallet service to other people? Delaney can't be doing this on his own. He'd need at least one other guy – someone to work the live feed on the Internet while the other was in the red room. He sounds like the hired muscle to me, rather than the brains behind this.'

'I already checked that out. Delaney's the only one taking money from the website. He regularly withdraws between five and nine grand a time after he takes a payment in D-coins, so I'm guessing he's passing on cash to whoever else is involved. No paper trail.'

'Whoever the others are, they'll be keeping hidden so if anything goes wrong, Jimmy will be the fall guy because the money's gone to his account.'

'I'm going to check out Delaney's known associates now.'

'Good stuff, Lee.'

I grinned and repeated the name Jimmy Delaney over and over in my head.

Got you now, you fucker!

THE DETECTIVE
Chapter 36

Ronnie drove to Berrisford while I got on to the control room, asking for a list of incidents that were logged on that patch during the evening Tracy was last seen. I listened while they ran through a burglary, a road traffic accident, a pub fight, a domestic assault, a shoplifting. All in all, it had been a pretty quiet night.

I stared out of the window as Ronnie said, 'What are you thinking, guv? Why does it matter what was going on that night?'

'Just trying to get a picture of what was happening on the streets. How and why Tracy might've met her accomplice.' I tapped my mobile phone against my lips, thinking. 'OK, this wasn't a burglary, which means they didn't panic because they'd been discovered by the Jamesons in their farmhouse. Jan and Mike had no enemies or criminal connections, so what's the motive for killing them?'

Ronnie looked blank. 'But Greene thinks it *was* a burglary gone—'

'I think he's wrong.'

Ronnie shrugged. 'I can't see a motive other than that. They were a regular, retired couple who led a quiet life.'

I scrunched up my face. The trouble was, neither could I, but there had to be a motive. 'The last time Alice saw Tracy was about eleven p.m.

on Tuesday. The murders were committed the next morning. Where had Tracy been and what had she been doing in the interim period?'

Ronnie shrugged. 'Doing drugs, most probably. Holed up in another druggie's house.'

'Or?'

'I've got no idea.'

'Why was her phone switched off at 11.31 p.m., a short while after Alice saw her, and hasn't been turned on since?'

'Maybe it ran out of battery.'

'Maybe. Maybe not. But I don't think this started when the Jamesons were murdered. Something triggered it.'

'You're not making sense.'

'That happens often. Just ask Greene.'

It was gone 11.30 p.m. when Ronnie parked at one end of London Road. There were about ten girls on the street in various stages of undress and striking a multitude of poses which were intended to be seductive but just looked heartbreakingly sad. I spotted Alice there, too.

'You take that side of the street. I'll take this side,' I said before getting out of the car.

Ronnie nodded and darted across the road.

I approached Alice first. Despite the chill in the air, she wore fishnet tights, a tiny skirt and a skimpy vest top.

She clicked her teeth and rolled her eyes at me. 'What? You gonna nick me for tryin' to earn a livin' now? I told you everyfink I know.'

'I'm not here to nick anyone. We need to find Tracy.'

'Well, she ain't here.' She made a show of looking around, arms wide open.

'And you still haven't heard from her or seen her?'

'No!' She jutted out one hip and looked at a spot over my shoulder.

'Do you know if Tracy charged her mobile phone before you left the house together that night?'

'Huh? What kind of question's that?'

'Think, Alice. Please. It's important.'

She tapped a stilettoed toe on the pavement. 'Actually, yeah, it was charged. We both always make sure it's on full battery at night, just in case. Can't be too careful out here, can ya? Anyway, just before we were leavin' I made some toast. I needed the socket for the toaster and I had to unplug her phone to make it so I checked the battery then. It was full.'

So, had Tracy's phone been purposely switched off on Tuesday night after she'd last been seen on London Road? If she was going on a drugs binge with someone she'd just met it seemed way too pre-meditated because how did she know she'd end up at the Jamesons the next day? The other possibility was that the phone had broken somehow – fallen from her bag and smashed on the pavement, maybe got lost down a drain, or it could've even been stolen. The possibilities were endless.

'Did Tracy have a bank account?'

'Yeah. With Barclays. It was from her Bristol days. She never used it, though. This is strictly a cash business.'

'Do you know if she had much cash on her?'

'Nah. She'd just paid 'er rent to me so she only had a fiver left. She was hoping it would be a busy night.'

'OK, thanks.' I moved away from her and called Becky. Told her to check with Barclays's out-of-hours number to see if Tracy's account had been touched since Tuesday night. Then I moved on to the next girl along the street. She looked in her early twenties but her eyes told a different story. They spoke of a lifetime of seeing things most people couldn't even imagine. She was leaning against a lamp post and pushed herself away from it with a resigned weariness when she saw me heading in her direction, before plastering a fake smile on her face.

'Hey, gorgeous,' she said. 'Looking for some honey tonight?'

'I haven't been called gorgeous in a long time.' I smiled and pulled my warrant card from my pocket. Flashed it at her. 'DS Carter.'

The smile morphed into a scowl. 'Shit. I'm just trying to earn a living here.'

'It's OK. I'm not interested in that. I'm looking for another working girl. Tracy Stevens, do you know her? Know where she might be or who she could be with?' I slid Tracy's photo from my other pocket and held it in front of her.

She swallowed hard. 'Yeah, I know her. She's normally down the end there.' She pointed further down the street, towards a blonde and a redhead. 'I heard you lot are after her, but I haven't seen her for days. Alice is the only one who's mates with her.' She jerked her chin in Alice's direction behind me.

'Can you be more specific which day?'

Her eyes darted from side to side. 'Um . . . would've been Tuesday. Early on in the night, I think.'

'Did you see her with anyone? Or see her leave with someone?'

She shook her head. 'Nah. I was too busy trying to score my own punter.'

'Was there any trouble that night out here?'

She shrugged. 'Trouble's relative, isn't it?' she said wearily, and I understood she was talking about her own situation. 'But no, not that I remember.'

I handed her a card and asked her to call me if she remembered or heard anything else that might help. I also told her the same as Alice, that if she wanted me to put her in touch with some women's projects that could help her, I'd be more than happy to do so. She tucked the card in her tiny handbag and looked down the street, eyes already scanning for a potential customer.

The next girl along was older, with acne scars covered up by a thick layer of foundation. She'd moved to a shop doorway and was smoking with one hand while texting with the other.

She sighed when I introduced myself. 'Oh, great.'

I reiterated I wasn't there to nick anyone for prostitution and her shoulders relaxed.

'I just need information.'

'Yeah, I heard what they say she did, but I can't see it myself.' She took a long drag on her cigarette.

'Why not?'

'Look, I didn't know her well. She kept to herself mostly or hung around with Alice. She was kind of quiet. But you get used to reading people, ya know? Sometimes your instinct is the only thing gonna save you from a dodgy punter who wants to rough you up a bit. Tracy always seemed like the gentle type. Not like some of the hard-nosed bitches on this patch.' She glared at a girl across the road as she said this, her dislike of the other woman obvious from the venom in her voice.

'When did you last see her?'

'I've been thinking about that since I saw her splashed all over the news. It was Tuesday night. She was in her usual spot down there.' She pointed a long, red nail in the same direction as the previous girl. 'Must've been about elevenish?'

'Did you see her with a punter? Or anyone else?'

She ground her cigarette out on the concrete with the toe of her high-heeled boots. 'No. Sorry. I wasn't paying much attention, really. It was a quiet night, and pickings were a bit sparse so I was watching the road for cars.'

'Were there any incidents out here that night? Something Tracy might've seen? Some trouble she might've got into?'

'If there was, I didn't see anything. Like I said, it was quiet.'

'Do you know of any regular punters Tracy had?'

'Nah. Sorry. I didn't know her that well. She was quite closed off. Some of the girls talk to each other. Some of us are friends. I think Tracy only confided in Alice.'

I handed out another business card and offer of help and moved on. Fifteen minutes and four women later, I was back at the car, waiting for Ronnie.

As he slid into the driver's seat, I said, 'Anything?'

'Nothing helpful, guv. A few of the ladies saw Tracy around eleven-nish on Tuesday but don't remember seeing her later on. No one noticed her leaving with anyone. And there was no trouble out here that night.'

Becky called back as Ronnie started the car.

'Tracy's bank account hasn't been touched for a couple of weeks. Seems like she's been saving a bit. Money paid in in dribs and drabs but nothing ever taken out. There's six hundred and fifty-five quid in it.'

'Saving for a better life maybe,' I said. 'So why hasn't she withdrawn any money? If she's in hiding she'd need cash.'

'Yeah, weird, isn't it? The other thing is, I've gone through Jan Jameson's address book and spoken to everyone in it. I can't find any links to Berrisford from people listed.'

I sighed.

'And the one-page phone record for Tracy covered a whole year. She hardly ever used her phone and the only calls she made were to her dealer, Dex, or Alice, or a pizza delivery shop.'

'What about calls *to* Tracy?'

'Again, Dex and Alice were the only ones in contact with her via phone. I just got hold of the text logs and they were only from and to Alice. Just normal chit-chat, nothing suspicious. I called the pizza shop and spoke to the owner. He didn't know Tracy personally, and their regular delivery driver was working during the time the Jamesons were killed so there's no connection.'

I thanked Becky and hung up.

'What now?' Ronnie asked.

'Now we get some sleep. There's not much else we can do tonight. We have no more leads.'

THE VIGILANTE

Chapter 37

Disappointment flooded through me when I found 198 Balham Place. It was a high-rise block of council flats in amongst other tower blocks arranged in a square. It had a sad patch of grass in the middle that housed a children's play area full of broken and vandalised equipment that was currently occupied by some teenagers, sitting on the ground, laughing and passing a can of drink around.

I parked the pick-up next to a small brick building with vented doors that housed an electrical substation. I got out of the truck and glanced about, staring up at the towers, which were run-down and graffitied to death. It was definitely not the kind of place that would have a basement or bunker or outbuilding where the website was being filmed from. The amount of screaming on those videos would've also been heard by neighbours and reported to the police. And it was unlikely they could drag a kidnapped victim into a place like this without being spotted.

There was no point setting up an observation point in a location like that. All I'd see would be a fifth-floor window. It would be useless. And I'd be spotted immediately by all the kids, who were probably runners for the local drug dealers or members of whichever gang operated in this area – stereotypical or not, that was the cold, hard truth of these estates. I couldn't afford to attract attention to myself that might tip Delaney off or slow me down. This wasn't the place Toni was being held, I was sure of that. I could wait and watch and see if Delaney left the building and led me to wherever Toni was, but I didn't have time. I checked the countdown marker on my digital watch that I'd synchronised with the clock on the red room's video box. It was on 3:30:56.

Just three and a half hours to go until the live video feed started.

I made sure my Glock was secure and concealed, and put my taser into my coat pocket, threaded a couple of plasticuffs through my belt loops then jogged into the building. I was worried the pick-up wouldn't be there when I got back, but I'd have to deal with that if and when it happened.

There was a choice of a graffitied lift that stank of piss or graffitied stairs that stank of piss. I ran up the stairs to the fifth floor and found number 198.

The door was grey and battered and looked like it had been kicked a few times. One way in and one way out. Good for me. Bad for Jimmy. If he was in there.

There was no peephole in it for anyone to look through. The element of surprise was all mine.

I glanced up and down the open-air walkway that ran the length of the block. No one was about. A baby cried in a flat further along. A heavy metal rock song pumped out from the flat next door so loud I could hear the lyrics clearly and the drum beat reverberated through the soles of my boots. I put my ear to the front door of number 198 and listened, but the music drowned out any possible sounds from within.

I pulled out my taser and let my arm rest by my thigh. I pivoted a little backwards on my right foot, waiting for the door to open, ready to kick it inwards with my left if needed.

Then I knocked on the door.

THE DETECTIVE
Chapter 38

I tossed and turned in bed as thoughts flitted into my head on a continuous loop – Denise, the collapse of my house sale, Tracy Stevens, Jeremy Wellham and his ex-girlfriend Mandy, what to do about work, Tracy's unknown accomplice, Ellie Nash, the Jamesons.

I huffed to myself as I turned on the light, then picked up the framed photo of Denise on my bedside table and spoke to her, as usual. 'What am I supposed to be doing with my life?' If she was still here she'd kick me up the arse. Talk some sense into me. I was lost without her. Although the depression that had consumed me since her death was slowly starting to lift, now I just seemed to be permanently angry. And I was lonely. Alone. Floating in some kind of limbo. The house was too quiet with just me rattling about in it with the echoes of Denise's laughter round every corner. 'What will make me happy again?' I asked her.

She just stared back at me in all her beautiful glory and a voice in my head said, *You need to start taking responsibility for yourself. You're the only one who can make you happy.*

I sighed, closed my eyes and willed the internal struggle inside my head to bugger off so I could sink into oblivion for a few hours. I was exhausted but, as usual, my mind refused to switch off.

I gave up at 3 a.m., got out of bed and made a cup of tea, thinking about the Jamesons and Stevens again, trying to work out what was niggling at me. Something, just out of reach, was attempting to surface but, again, the more I thought, the more the chatter in my head drowned it out.

It was just gone 7 a.m. when I got to the CID office. I was the first one there. I was about to fill the kettle to make coffee when I noticed some git had stolen that now as well.

I glared at the empty space where the kettle should've been and called Becky to see if she could stop off for supplies on the way in.

'We should put CCTV in our own office,' she said before telling me she'd make a diversion to Costa.

I sat at my desk and opened my laptop, surprised *that* was still there. Then I pulled up all the crime scene photos and videos from the Jamesons' house, studying them all before turning my attention to the paperwork and documents we'd already compiled and carefully reading through them, searching for something I'd missed.

There'd been no sightings of Tracy Stevens overnight and no word from her mobile phone company to say her phone had been switched on so we could trace a location. I was no further forward.

Becky arrived bearing a tray of coffees and a bag of muffins.

Ronnie arrived shortly after, immediately noticed the lack of kettle and let out a little shriek before giving me a horrified look. 'Where's it gone?'

'Nicked,' I said. 'And I haven't got time to scour the station for it.'

'I got you green tea and mint,' Becky said to Ronnie, resting the cardboard tray on my desk. 'Is that all right?'

'I usually have chamomile in the morning,' he said.

Becky shrugged. 'Sorry. That's all they had.' She sat at her desk, opened her laptop and said to me, 'I spoke to the owners of some shops in London Road last night. There are five with CCTV. They'll all be there this morning for someone to go up and look at them.'

'Good,' I said. CCTV was the only possible lead we could check out now. 'Ronnie, you head up there after your tea and check out the recordings.'

Ronnie removed the lid from his tea and sniffed it with a withering look. 'OK.' He put the lid back on the tea and moved it to the far edge of his desk.

'I'm going through this paperwork again. We're missing something here.' I bent over one of the Jamesons' joint bank account statements and read it once more.

Greene appeared in the doorway, muttering a 'Morning all.' He walked over to my desk and said, 'Where are we? I need to tell the Chief Constable something tangible. There's got to be a trace of these killers.'

'We've got nothing. No sightings. Tracy's phone's still switched off,' I said. 'She could be literally anywhere. And there's something not right about—'

Greene held up a hand to silence me before pacing the room for a moment. 'The quickest route from Berrisford to Turpinfield is the A1M before picking up the B roads and country lanes. I want you concentrating on traffic and CCTV cameras along that route. Stevens and her accomplice were intending to burgle the Jamesons so they would've arrived by vehicle.'

'Sir, that's like looking for a needle in a haystack. There are hundreds of routes they could've taken to get to Turpinfield that didn't involve travelling through any towns or using motorways with cameras,' I said, exasperated. 'They could've used any of the back roads and traversed the county on any combination of them. There are too many possible directions of travel.'

'Nevertheless, it's what I want you to do,' he snapped.

'But *what* vehicle?' I said. 'Tracy didn't own a car. She didn't drive. We've found no associates she could be with. And I think it's highly unlikely she met someone out of the blue and suddenly hatched a plan to do a Bonnie and Clyde with them.'

Greene treated me to a frown. 'Check petrol stations between Berrisford and Turpinfield, as well. Maybe they stopped to fill up with fuel and were caught on camera.' He walked towards the Ordinance Survey map pinned to the whiteboard. 'Extend the house-to-house enquiries, as well.' With his fingertip he circled an area around the Jamesons' property of about ten miles, which contained two small villages. 'I want every house in the surrounding villages visited. Someone might've seen this vehicle or Stevens and her accomplice without realising the significance.'

'We've only got three bodies on this! When are we going to have time to visit all those houses in the neighbouring villages and go through all CCTV and check petrol stations? Why waste time doing that? We need to be searching for the connection between the Jamesons and Stevens or her accomplice. That's where we'll find answers. This wasn't a burglary that got out of hand. There's another motive here.'

'There is no connection! You're reading far more into this, as usual. Or are you going to come out with some bizarre *X-Files* theory for this case, too?' He sounded irritated as he referred to my difference of opinion with him about a previous murder, where everyone else had been convinced we had the offender in custody. Still, they'd been wrong about that, too, and I'd been right. A good detective had to look at all possibilities. The first, most obvious answer wasn't necessarily the right one.

'I don't want to hear any more wild theories with absolutely no evidence to back them up,' he said.

I opened my mouth to object but shut it again. I'd just be wasting my breath.

'Is everyone clear on what they're doing?' Greene asked.

Everyone said yes and he left the room.

'It's a waste of time,' I said. 'But still, if that's what he wants, then that's what we'll do.'

Becky raised her eyebrows. 'You're rolling over a bit too easily. You don't normally take any notice of what he says. Are you ill?'

I just grinned at her.

'I know that look,' she said. 'What are you up to?'

'Bollocks to what he says.' I wandered over to the window that overlooked the car park, thinking. 'I'm going to go to London Road to check out the shop's CCTV instead of you, Ronnie. The answer's there, from the last night Tracy was seen before her phone was switched off, I'm sure of it. But Becky, I want you to make a start on going through any CCTV and traffic camera footage for the ridiculous multitude of routes Greene wants us to go through, along with contacting any petrol stations and getting them to set aside their footage for you to look at.'

'I'll be here for a year! Like you said, we don't even know what vehicle we're looking for. And none of the villages around Turpinfield have CCTV.' Becky pulled a face.

'Then it'll just make you look busy until I can work out where we should go from here. At least you both won't get into trouble for not following orders.'

'What shall I do, then?' Ronnie asked.

Down below, I saw Greene striding towards the entrance to the nick. He pressed a button to release the sliding gate and stepped out on to the pavement, looking at his watch, then looking up the main road.

Ronnie was talking but I didn't hear him. I was too busy watching a shiny new BMW pulling up along the main road beside Greene. Watching Greene open the passenger door and climb inside. Watching the vehicle drive away. Whisked off to another stupid time-wasting meeting.

'Guv?' Ronnie prompted me.

I turned around and said to Ronnie, 'You can start on the house-to-house in the villages nearest to Turpinfield.' Then turned to Becky. 'And if Greene asks where I am, say I'm doing the same.'

Ronnie nodded and gathered up a local map book and some photos of Tracy before leaving the office.

A short while later I left Becky tearing her hair out with frustration and drove to London Road.

The five shops that had private cameras were a newsagent, a chemist, a clothes shop, a Tesco Express and a jeweller. It took until the late afternoon for me to go through all the CCTV footage of Tuesday night that their cameras had recorded while they'd been shut. Some of them were only pointing at their own frontage so had no good view of the street. A few had captured Alice and Tracy arriving at 10.46 p.m., walking down the street. I saw them stop outside the chemist and talk for a moment. I saw some of the other girls I'd spoken to on the street milling about nearby. Then Alice hugged Tracy before moseying up to a vehicle that had stopped, the driver winding his window down. Alice got in the car and waved at Tracy, who walked further down the road to her patch at the corner where it met Devon Crescent and disappeared out of view. Then nothing. There were no more sightings of her that night from the angle of the CCTVs.

By the time I left London Road I felt deflated. I arrived back at the Jamesons' house in the early evening to do something I hoped would be much more productive. SOCO had finished there yesterday so the house was empty. I had no clues to go on. No evidence that would point me in a particular direction. I was no further forward, with a brick wall looming in my face. And whenever I got to that stage, I liked to go back to the scene of the crime. I'd missed something. Something important. I had to think like Stevens and her accomplice. Feel like them. Act like they did.

I parked my car and got out, surveying the area – the main house, the driveway that led towards some outbuildings to the left and right of the farmhouse.

No one had come forward about having seen a vehicle that day in the lane and no useful tyre tracks had been found by forensics, but they would've had to have come up the driveway. So why did they go round the back of the house and enter from the rear patio doors? The soil prints indicated the offenders only went as far into the lounge as the coffee table in front of the sofa. They left the same way. Why not just knock on the front door and then force the Jamesons back inside with the gun? Why risk being seen wandering around by the Jamesons, who could've called the police, before they made their move?

I let myself in the front door and the putrid smell of death hit me. The finality of the Jamesons' murder angered me again, reminding me how tenuous our existence was. One minute here, the next, obliterated.

I headed straight into the lounge and stood next to the coffee table, in the area where the shooter had stood and looked around the room.

I extended my hand like I was holding a gun and pointed at where Mike would've been standing when he was shot. Then I swung around and faced the wall to the side of the sofa, pointing to where Jan Jameson's blood was spattered across it.

I kept turning everything over in my mind. Less and less about this case was making sense to me. A prostitute had disappeared on Tuesday night. Her phone had been turned off somehow shortly after and hadn't been used since. She'd ended up fifty-five miles away in a tiny little hamlet she'd never been to before, supposedly to rob the Jamesons, even though there were empty houses nearby. Even though there were thousands of places to break in to closer to Berrisford. Even though she'd never done anything remotely like it before and had no known associates involved in anything similar. And after the Jamesons were shot, Tracy and her accomplice had still not taken Jan's handbag and jewellery or Mike's wallet.

Tracy Stevens had obviously been here. Had she fired the shot and her accomplice was also around five feet tall, the one who'd been standing next to Jan Jameson? Or had her accomplice murdered the couple? I'd quipped to Greene about Bonnie and Clyde, but I thought that was pretty near the mark. *Why* would Tracy suddenly meet up with someone and decide to go on a shooting spree?

I looked at the book left open and face down on the middle of the sofa, as if someone had placed it there intentionally. It hadn't fallen in that position. There was a bookmark on the sofa seat next to it, but it hadn't been used to mark the page. The cover showed a historical romance, and although it was possible Mike had been reading it, I doubted it. Stereotypical or not, it was more likely Jan had been sitting on the sofa, reading it at some point before they were killed. Denise had been a big reader. She'd loved the bonkbusters. She'd also loved paperbacks, the feel of them in her hand, the smell of them. She'd used several bookmarks over the years because she hated folding down the corners of the page to mark her spot. She'd never placed it face down and open like this one was because it made the spine crack and the pages could fall out.

I picked up the novel and flicked through it, finding no turned-down corners, no repeated cracking of the spine that would be obvious if she'd always put her books down that way. So for someone who must've been fastidious about using a bookmark, why hadn't Jan used it? She'd tidied the house before they were murdered; the fresh vacuum marks attested to that. Maybe she'd been sitting on the sofa relaxing for a while with a novel and then she'd been disturbed with no time to slip the bookmark between the pages, so she'd turned it face down instead to mark where she was. And if so, what did that mean? She'd seen Tracy and her accomplice appear at the patio door while she was reading? If she'd felt threatened by strangers in her rear garden, wouldn't her first thought have been to run or call the police? Her landline handset was on the coffee table, which would've been in easy reach if she'd been in the lounge. Surely, she wouldn't have placed the book down neatly first. Unless she hadn't been reading it at all before she was killed and it was completely inconsequential. Or she hadn't felt threatened by them because she knew them.

I picked up the cordless handset, now dusted with fingerprint powder, and pressed the button to make a call. Nothing happened; the battery was dead. Stupid of me not to have checked before. I wondered if it had run out of juice since the Jamesons had been killed or before.

I put the handset back down and glanced around again, pictured Jan putting the book down, seeing Tracy and her accomplice at the door. If Jan didn't know them, she would've been scared. Maybe her first thought was to run out of the lounge to the front door, but they shouted out to her to stop, forced her at gunpoint against the wall. Had Mike come in the room then, alerted by the noise? But if Jan and Mike had cooperated with them, why had Tracy and co. felt the need to shoot them at all? Unless Jan and Mike could easily identify them? And if they could identify them, how the hell did the Jamesons know them?

I blew out a frustrated breath. I was just going round in circles.

I sighed and opened the patio doors, stepped outside on to the terrace. Then I positioned the door at the angle it had been open at when Paula had arrived, using the crime scene photos as a guide.

I moved backwards and stared at the door. Then I got closer and looked at the three palm prints belonging to Tracy Stevens, highlighted with fingerprint powder from the SOCOs.

Greene's opinion was that Tracy had pressed her hands to the glass when she was looking inside to see if the property was empty so she could burgle it. It was now later than the estimated time frame when the Jamesons were killed but even so, the light didn't hit the glass at all, so there was no reflection bouncing back at me. Tracy wouldn't have needed to stand against it and peer inside. They were big doors, so I could see perfectly clearly into the lounge from even ten metres away. And in any case, if that's what Tracy had been doing, surely she would've cupped her hands around her face on the glass to see better, meaning she would've left two edges of palm prints, one for each hand either side of her face. But she hadn't. She'd left three, solid right-hand palm prints, all overlapping each other. She couldn't have been using her hand as leverage to slide the door closed behind her because it was left open, so what had she been doing? She was savvy enough to turn her phone off so no one could trace her location but stupid enough to leave her palm prints here? Didn't make sense.

What was I missing?

Tracy had left traces of grey powder on the ridges of her hand prints. Where had that come from? What was it? Concrete? Dust? Paint? Where had she been in the hours between Tuesday night and the day of the Jamesons' murder? A construction site? A DIY shop? A derelict building?

Tracy had disappeared into thin air from London Road.

Disappeared without a trace.

I clenched my jaw, thinking it was unlikely for Tracy to be able to keep this much of a low profile. She'd need to find cash from somewhere for food and yet her bank account hadn't been touched.

I paced up and down, trying to make things fit.

Jan didn't feel threatened enough to reach for the phone when she saw Tracy. She spotted her at the patio door, put the book down, and what? Opened the door to her? Why?

Jan recognised her.

Or

Jan recognised something or someone.

I stopped pacing and stared again at the palm prints, head tilted.

I stepped closer to the patio door. Pressed my right palm against it. Removed my hand and pressed again, slightly overlapping the first. Then I did it again, mimicking the exact pattern Tracy had left. I stared at it some more, then I repeated the action over again but faster. Three times in quick succession.

And that's when it hit me. The only plausible reason I could think of. What if Tracy had disappeared as in not *missing*. Not *hiding*. What if she'd been *taken*? What if Tracy hadn't been the one to switch her phone off?

Tracy had banged on the door with a flat, open hand because she'd been trying to attract the Jamesons' attention, not because she wanted to rob or hurt them. Jan hadn't reached for the phone because she'd seen a woman at the door who obviously needed help, who was distressed, and Jan hadn't felt threatened at that point. Tracy was fleeing from someone. Someone who'd abducted her on Tuesday night. She came to the rear of the farmhouse because she'd never arrived in a vehicle in the first place. Then Tracy's kidnapper had caught up with her. Tracy wasn't standing next to Jan to restrain her, she was standing there because they were both cowering together from someone who had a gun. It really was random because the Jamesons weren't the target. They had never been the target. They were just in the way. And they were witnesses.

I turned around, my back to the doors, my gaze scanning the area. The woods dead ahead in the distance. The fields to my right that led to the stables. The high rapeseed fields of Bill Graves's land to my left.

But which direction had Tracy come from? How had she ended up here? And where was she now?

THE VIGILANTE

Chapter 39

He was mid-twenties. Dark-haired. But he wasn't Jimmy Delaney.

As he swung the door open lethargically, hair mussed up, yawning, unaware of and completely oblivious to the danger, I shouldered it hard.

He was already stumbling backwards when I tasered him square in the chest. He dropped like a lead weight, the shock rendering him speechless. Two seconds, max, from the time he opened it until the time I was inside, with the door kicked shut behind me.

After the spasms from the taser shock stopped, I flipped him over and plasticuffed his wrists together, then sat him up against the wall.

I drew my Glock and quickly cleared the area. The place was tiny. A minute, open-plan flat with a lounge/kitchen, one bedroom – single bed in the corner, one chest of drawers – and one door that led to a small bathroom, which was empty. I reholstered my weapon and turned my attention to the bloke who was now regaining his senses.

His eyes huge with fear, he panted through his mouth. The smell of ammonia filled my nostrils from where he'd pissed himself.

'Where's Jimmy?' I said.

'What? I . . . I don't . . . know. He doesn't . . . live . . . here, man!' More panting as he struggled to get the words out.

'Where does he live?'

'I . . . don't know!'

'He used this address for his dole money and he uses it for his bank account. So, I'll ask you one more time. Which is pretty generous of me, really. And if I still don't get an answer, I'll shoot you in the head. Where. Is. Jimmy?'

Tears filled his eyes. 'I don't know. He doesn't live here! I let him stay when he got out of lockup, but he ain't lived here for ages. Honestly, man. You have to believe me. I don't know where he is. He just comes and gets his post every now and then.'

I did believe him. My gut told me he wasn't lying. 'Who are you?'

'R . . . Rob.'

'Rob, who?'

'Rob Brown.'

'Right, Rob. You'd better tell me everything you know about Jimmy. And fast.' I drew back my coat showing the Glock in its holster.

His eyes bulged on seeing the weapon. He sucked in a deep breath and nodded manically. 'What do you want to know? I'll tell you anything. Just don't . . . You won't kill me, will you?'

'I don't know. I haven't decided yet. Start talking and I'll make up my mind.'

He gulped in another breath, snivelling with snot, saliva dribbling down his chin. 'He hangs out with the Parkers now. Brett and Connor. Jimmy met Brett when he was inside. They were tight, like, but I haven't seen Jimmy for weeks.'

'You got a phone number for Jimmy?'

'Yeah.' He nodded so fast he was in danger of giving himself a herniated disc in his neck, then jerked his chin towards a phone on the arm of a frayed and stained brown armchair to his left. 'In my phone.'

'OK. Who are the Parkers? Where do they live?'

He groaned, as if he really didn't want to give me more bad news. 'I don't know! I really don't. They've got some farm somewhere. In the middle of nowhere. One of the villages out in the sticks. Don't know where, he never said. I think Jimmy stays with them now, though. I didn't like Brett much. He thought he was better than everyone else. Stuck up his own arse. Brett's a fucking psycho. Jimmy said Brett shanked a guy in the shower once because he sneezed on him accidentally. Didn't know what he was on about half the time. He used to come here to see Jimmy and quote poetry and shit. Really fucking weird.'

A farm in the middle of nowhere would have outbuildings and land and plenty of places to hide what they were doing. Hide the screams I'd heard on those video feeds. It had to be the place. 'What about Connor?'

'He's Brett's cousin. Some kind of computer geek. Jimmy told me he was working with Connor and Brett on something.' He paused, sucked in another breath, stared into my eyes warily.

'Keep talking. What kind of something?'

'Jimmy said they needed an extra man for security.'

'Security? On a farm?'

'I don't know, man! That's what Jimmy said. He told me there was loads of dosh involved. He was gonna be set up.'

'What was Brett inside for?'

'He robbed some geezer and beat the shit out of him.'

'Did Jimmy tell you about a red room?'

'A what?'

It was obvious from the way his forehead pinched into a frown that he'd never heard about it before. 'Did he tell you about kidnapping people?'

'What the fuck? No way, man! Nothing like that. He didn't tell me nothing else. Just he was doing some security work.'

'OK, Rob. You're going to phone Jimmy. Now. Tell him you've got some post for him that looks urgent and he should come and pick it up.' If I could get Jimmy here, I was hoping he'd lead me back to the Parkers and their remote farm when he left again.

I pulled Rob upright, cut the plasticuffs with a heavy-duty penknife from my pocket and stepped back.

Rob slumped a little against the wall. His knees buckled for a second before he recovered. I pulled out the Glock and kept it on him as he walked the few steps towards the armchair.

He picked up his phone, his hand shaking as he scrolled through his address book. 'W . . . what shall I say?'

'Exactly what I just told you to.'

He hesitated for a moment, then pressed a button. He put the phone to his ear, avoiding my steady gaze. A second passed. Two. Three. Then Rob said, 'All right, mate?'

His voice had a tremor to it. He sounded nervous. I just hoped it wasn't a good line and Jimmy couldn't tell.

'Yeah, I . . . um . . . got a letter here for ya. Looks important. You wanna come and get it?' Rob listened for a moment. Then looked at me with wild eyes. He shook his head with a worried expression. 'I don't wanna open it. It's private.' Silence again while Rob listened. 'Nah. I don't wanna do that. Can't you come and get it?' Rob gave me a panicked arm gesture that I took to mean *What shall I do next?* He listened some more. 'Um . . . all right. I'll open it.'

I nodded at Rob. He put his hand over the mouthpiece and I whispered in his ear, 'Tell him it's from his bank. They're going to freeze his account unless he follows the steps in the letter to update his security info.'

'Right. Um . . . it's from your bank, man. They say they're gonna freeze your . . . um . . . account. You gotta do some stuff in the letter. Update your . . . um . . . security.' Rob listened again, his legs trembling now. 'Can't you—' A pause while Jimmy cut in. 'Yeah. OK. See ya.' Rob turned to me, his whole body shaking now. 'I tried. You saw me! But he says he's busy. He's gonna come and get it another day. I tried!' Rob's gaze drifted to the gun in my outstretched hand. 'Don't kill me. Please don't kill me.'

'Give me his phone number.'

Rob held out his phone, displaying Jimmy's number. I programmed it into my own, ready to pass it on to Lee. It would be a pay-as-you-go SIM card, but Lee could hopefully find cell-site or GPS data to locate where it was being used from.

'If you tell Jimmy I was here asking questions, I'll come back and kill you. If you mention I was here to *anyone*, I'll come back and kill you. If I find out you're involved, I'll come back and kill you. You got that?'

'Yeah. Yeah. Course. I ain't gonna say nothing. And I ain't done nothing. I promise.' He held his palms up in surrender.

I left Rob there with a new wet patch spreading down the legs of his jogging bottoms.

As I walked back to the pick-up at the edge of the car park I saw a group of youths milling around it, looking inside the windows, probably working out if there was anything worth nicking.

There were four of them, all dressed in a uniform of low-slung jeans and hoodies. One spotty, one with greasy hair, one with a skinhead, and one with his ear pierced probably more times than he knew how to count up to.

'Let's jack it. Smash the window,' Spotty said to Skinhead. 'That stereo's worth a fuckin' fortune.'

'What else he got in there?' Pierced said. 'Somethin' in a bag.'

They were so intent on looking through the windows they didn't hear me approach.

I got to within two metres of them and coughed.

They spun around. Three of them glanced at Skinhead, as if asking what to do next.

Skinhead took a step closer to me, eyes narrowed, a sneer on his face. 'Give us ya fuckin' money if you wanna get outta here in one piece.'

I looked him up and down. He was maybe eighteen. Stocky build. Probably weighed about eleven stone. A tattoo snaked up the side of his neck.

'And who are you?' I asked.

He scowled at me. 'What? What the fuck it matter who I am! This is my ends, and I'm the manz that fuckin' run it.'

'Look, lads, I'm in a hurry. Get out of my way and I'll get out of yours.' I smiled, trying to be nice and polite about it. 'Get off your arses and get a job if you want money, instead of trying to rob people.'

Skinhead clicked his teeth with his tongue, looking round at the others who'd gathered behind him, testosterone oozing off him. 'Ooooh,' he mocked. 'Or what, Granddad? What you gonna do?' He snorted and started laughing.

The others took that as their cue to laugh in support.

'So, you're the big, hard man here, are you?' I raised an eyebrow.

'You better watch. Don't mess wiv me, man. Shut the fuck up and just give us ya money!' Skinhead reached his right arm behind him, pulled out a gun tucked down the waistband of his jeans, and pointed it at me.

My Glock was in my pancake holster at my waist, hidden under my shirt. I seriously considered just whipping it out and shooting him straight away. A leg shot to disable him. Before he knew what had happened he would be on the deck. In agony. Bleeding. It would teach him a lesson. Put him out of action for a while and stop him terrorising the residents around here. But he was still just a kid, even though he had a deadly weapon in his hand. And I couldn't shoot a kid.

The gun was a Baikal. Designed in Russia; originally used to fire tear gas pellets but now being modified en masse to fire real 9 mm bullets. Black. Compact. Cheap. Reliable. Accurate. Lightweight to fit comfortably in the palm of a teenager's hand. No wonder it had become the new weapon of choice for gangs all over the UK. This one had a suppressor on the end.

Skinhead's scowl was supposed to look menacing, but that didn't stop his hand shaking slightly as he held the pistol out in front of him about ten inches away from my forehead.

'You're going to shoot me in front of all these potential witnesses?' I pointed up and around to the tower blocks looming above us.

'They ain't gonna say nothing. Told ya, *I* run this yard, innit?'

'Stupid,' I said, shaking my head.

'Yeah, you fuckin' are *stupid*, dissin' me! Now I'm the hard guy with the *gun* so gimme your fuckin' money, old man,' Skinhead snarled.

The others stood closer to each other behind him, shoulder to shoulder, his little gang of soldiers, watching with a feral excitement.

'I didn't mean me. I meant you,' I said.

OK, I'd tried polite and it hadn't worked.

I shot my left hand out, grabbed the barrel of the gun and twisted it across to the right and down, away from my body. At the same time my right hand punched him in the face. As he staggered backwards, shocked, disorientated, my left hand still on the barrel, I cupped the underside of the pistol with my right hand, twisting it out of his grip before he landed on his arse on the ground.

One and a half seconds, maybe, in real time from start to finish.

He stared up at me, mouth hanging open, his jaw probably throbbing where my fist had connected with it. His three crew members took a few steps backwards, staring, mouths open. I guessed everyone else they'd pulled this on so far had just given in when threatened with a gun and handed over their belongings.

Greasy Hair turned and ran across the patch of grass towards one of the tower blocks. Pierced shouted, 'This is on top!' before doing the same. He was quickly followed by Spotty.

'Just you and me, then.' I smiled. 'So how hard are you now?'

He still couldn't quite let go of the sneer. 'What? You gonna shoot me in front of all these witnesses?' He threw my words back at me.

'I've got a good feeling that no one would see a thing if it meant an end to you and your gang bullying them and stealing from them.'

He scrabbled backwards, using his hands and heels, until he hit the wall of the electric station and had nowhere else to go.

'You don't know the meaning of the word hard,' I said. 'Try living in a city being bombed by repeated airstrikes every day. Where you hear the screams of your friends and family as they're blown apart right in front of your eyes. Where your parents are trapped in a collapsed building that's just been hit, dying slowly because people can't get to them under twenty storeys of rubble. Where your sister is raped and murdered. Where you're tortured.' I narrowed my eyes. 'Try starving because the food and water has run out and no aid can get through because it's too dangerous. Try breathing in dust and chemicals until your lungs crackle and burn and you can't breathe. Try running over extreme terrain in horrendous weather conditions to get to a refugee camp. And then try living in tents with nothing but the ragged, torn clothes you're wearing, packed in like sardines in the blistering heat.' I leaned closer and he pressed himself against the wall, squeezing his eyes shut. '*That's* hard. But you . . . You don't know how lucky you really are. And you rock around here thinking you're the toughest guy in the world but there's always someone tougher than you. Look at me when I'm talking to you!'

His eyelids snapped open.

'So you're either going to die out here, playing soldier wannabes. Or kill someone else and take an innocent life with you. Or you can sort your life out. And you can give me all the shit you want about disadvantaged youth, living in poverty, learned behaviour, blah, blah, blah. But we all make choices. And if I come back here and find out you and your crew are still trying to control this estate, then next time, I'll shoot you in the head. And I'll bring *my* mates with me.' I winked at him. 'Got that? Or do you want me to repeat it?'

He nodded manically. 'G . . . got it.'

'Good.' I got in the pick-up and watched Skinhead running away towards the same tower block his mates had disappeared inside.

THE DETECTIVE
Chapter 40

The sky was turning into a patch of reddy-grey dusk as I stood in the Jamesons' rear garden. I pulled out my phone and tried to call Becky but there was no signal.

'Shit,' I muttered, walking further towards the woods at the end of the garden with the phone outstretched in front of me. I didn't even get one bar. And I'd left my police radio in the office.

I locked up the house and walked up the long driveway between the rapeseed fields, which rustled in the breeze. When I hit the entrance to the country lane, I got two bars.

'Where are you?' Becky asked when she picked up.

'At the Jamesons' house. Can you do a background check on two of their neighbours for me? Connor Parker and also Emily Simms's son, Roger.' Roger was supposed to have been in Hong Kong for the last two weeks but he could've lied to me. Bill Graves's background check hadn't revealed anything suspicious before, but still, he was in Brighton at his sister's so I could have a nose around the property while he was gone, just in case.

'Sure. But why? Do you think they're involved?'

'I don't know. But it's worth checking out.'

'I've been trying to call you for a while.'

'There's a patchy signal out here.'

'Emma from SOCO tried to call you but she couldn't get through so she called me. The results on the soil samples from the Jamesons' lounge carpet have come back and there are traces of manure in it.'

'Manure,' I repeated. So Tracy had come from the direction of Simms Livery Stables.

'The grey powder found on Tracy's palm prints is concrete.'

'Right.'

'And something else. When they finished analysing the tread patterns of soil and manure from the lounge they found a few partial footprints.'

'Footprints? Not shoe prints? As in, someone was barefoot?'

'Exactly. Size five.'

'That confirms it for me,' I said, more to myself than Becky.

'Confirms what?'

I thought about telling her my theory. In the past Becky had been my ally and confidante, even when I'd been on suspension. I knew she could keep a secret, but I didn't want to chance anything getting back to Greene in case he put the kibosh on me digging further. Until I had proof, he'd just shoot me down in flames and have me pounding pavements doing pointless inquiries. 'Nothing,' I said and changed the subject. 'How's Ronnie getting on with the house-to-house?'

'No results so far, I'm afraid.'

'OK. I might be a while. I'm just going to poke about up here and see if I can find anything else. SOCO didn't get to check the surrounding area because Greene was too worried about the budget. I'll see you 1—' The call dropped out. I looked at my screen and the signal bars had disappeared.

223

I pocketed my phone and skirted around the side of the house that led to the back garden. I started at the patio and kept my head bent, looking at the ground as I walked through the fields towards the stables in the distance, eyes peeled for some kind of trace evidence that might help. The light was fading fast. I didn't have long left and there was a lot of acreage to cover. You could be out here for weeks and not find any additional evidence the killer might've left behind.

Ten minutes later, I reached the post-and-rail fence that signalled the border where the Jamesons' property met Simms Livery Stables. In the far distance, I could see several horses in the fields.

I shuddered. How fast could a horse gallop over to me? Pretty damn quick, I should think. I took a deep breath and climbed over the fence into the grassy field, sweat breaking out over my forehead.

I walked as quietly as I could so as not to disturb the four-legged fiends, until I came to the dusty path at the back of the Simms's house and hopped over the fence that enclosed the field. I hadn't seen any obvious signs of a break-in when I'd visited the house previously, but if someone had abducted Tracy on Tuesday night, then a perfect place to keep her would be inside an empty house. I approached the back door to the property. It was single-glazed, the wooden frame rotten in places, with an old-fashioned lock that would be easy to pick. But judging by the rot and woodworm, you could've just shouldered it and it would've opened easily.

I pulled the cuff of my shirt over my hand to avoid contamination and tried the handle. It was locked.

I looked inside the windows. No sign of life. I inspected the outside of the house, walking in a loop. I tried the front door but again, it was locked. No windows so far were insecure, either. I was debating whether to force an entry and see if Tracy Stevens was inside when my phone vibrated in my pocket, signalling a text message.

I pulled it out and stared at the screen; the signal bar was wavering on and off. I opened the text from Becky and read it:

Can't get hold of you by phone so hoping this gets through. One of the sex workers Ronnie talked to last night just called back. She's remembered Tracy getting in a white van about 11 p.m. She didn't get a licence plate no. None of the Jamesons' neighbours are known to us.

I read the text again. Just to be sure.

White van. White van. White van.

Something clicked in my memory.

I still wasn't sure about the *why* but I thought I knew the *how, where* and *who* now. I'd seen a white van on the satellite area map I'd put up on the board in the office. And it was too much of a coincidence not to be related.

I thought about the new barbed wire Connor Parker had been erecting above the walls when I'd arrived the day after the Jamesons had been shot, and I was certain then I knew where Tracy had been after she'd disappeared from London Road.

Parker hadn't been putting up barbed wire to keep burglars out. He'd been doing it to keep people in.

THE VIGILANTE
Chapter 41

I dialled Lee and put the phone on loudspeaker as I drove away from Balham Place. After passing on every bit of intel that Rob had told me, I said, 'I need you to try and trace Jimmy's location from his phone.' I rattled off his number.

'Will do. And I'll look into this farm of the Parkers. I was checking out Delaney's known associates but nothing interesting flagged up so far.'

'Delaney met Brett Parker when he was banged up, so it's likely the police's intel databases don't show it. I'm heading down towards Welwyn. The place must be somewhere around that area. By the time I get there, hopefully you'll have a target address.' I hung up and dialled Corinne's number.

Corinne answered on the second ring. Breathless. Anxious. 'Have you found her?'

'Not yet. But I'm close.' I filled her in. 'This farm has to be the place.'

'I want to come. I want to be there.'

'I can't put you in danger. I don't know how many guys they've got there, and I'm not going to risk you getting hurt in the process.'

'But you're on your own. I want to help get Toni back. I can be a lookout or something, just, *please*, I want to come with you.'

'It's not safe. Corinne, this is what I'm trained to do. If she's there I'll bring her home. I promise.'

Corinne let out a wail full of pain but there were no further objections. I told her I'd call as soon as I had news. Pictured her pacing up and down, crying with anguish, Maya trying to comfort her.

I pressed my foot down on the accelerator.

By the time I hit the Hertfordshire county line, Lee was back on the phone.

'I've got it,' he said. 'According to GPS data, Jimmy's phone is currently at a place called Parker Farm in Turpinfield. It's a small settlement of four properties.' He gave me directions, which I noted. 'The farm's owned by Connor Parker. It used to be a farm, growing wheat, but it hasn't been a working farm for three years. It was left to Connor when his parents died. He's twenty-nine. Some kind of freelance web designer, according to his tax returns.'

'Designing sick red rooms. But he pays taxes to make it look like he's doing something legit?' A wolf hiding in sheep's clothing. I seethed inside.

'Yeah. On the surface he looks like a regular, respectable guy.' Lee snorted with disgust. 'Brett's a different story. He's only twenty-three, but he's got a criminal record for multiple assaults and violent behaviour.'

'So Connor's the brain and Brett and Jimmy are the brawn,' I said. 'But not for long.'

'Do you want me to carry on digging into their backgrounds?'

'Yeah, thanks.'

'I've looked at satellite images of the farm, which I'm sending over now. The best place for access is going to be at the rear, where the property is separated from its neighbours' fields by woodland, which should give you some good ground cover.'

'Cheers.' I hung up and drove along the A1M until I reached the Welwyn exit, then turned off the motorway and headed down some country lanes towards Turpinfield, looking for an unobserved location to stop.

I pulled off the lane, drove down a bumpy track that led to a disused and derelict water tower, and stopped the pick-up.

I reached for my phone and brought up the images Lee had sent. First I looked at the photos of Brett and Connor Parker that he'd included. Studied their faces, committed them to memory. Then I turned my attention to screenshots of the satellite map.

Parker Farm was set in around twenty acres of land. The fields, which were once used for growing wheat, were now just scrubland. The front of the farm was accessed by a country lane with no immediate neighbours. A high wall with gates separated it from the road. A long driveway led straight up to the red-brick farmhouse. At the rear of the main house were two large outbuildings. Behind them, Parker Farm butted up to a semi-circular patch of woodland, which separated it from the nearest neighbours, Turpinfield Farm, Beech Lodge and Simms Livery Stables.

In an ideal world, I'd have liked time to set up an observation post, watch them for a few days, see how many guys they had up there, learn their routines, work out which building they were holding Toni in. But this wasn't an ideal world. It was one full of psychopaths who inflicted torture and death for money.

I looked at the countdown marker on my watch. Thirty-five minutes left until the live feed started. No time to prepare.

The sun was setting as I took my daysack out of the pick-up and placed it on the bonnet. I retrieved a camouflage sniper suit and swapped it for my black clothes. I unrolled my camo balaclava and put it on my head like a beanie hat. Pulled on some ultra-lightweight gloves that fitted like a second skin. Then changed the number plates on the truck for false ones.

I checked my Glock, extra ammo, wire-cutters, taser, ASP baton and other items. Then I turned my attention to the Baikal and conducted mechanical safety checks, which confirmed that it was in working order. I fired a test shot. It was dead accurate. The suppressor silenced the noise adequately.

With the business end all sorted, I got back in the truck.

All dressed up with some place to go.

PART TWO

Dying is a wild night and a new road

Emily Dickinson

PART TWO

THE VIGILANTE
Chapter 42

Half a mile away from Parker Farm I pulled off the road again and drove down a bumpy track that led to a small copse of trees. Somewhere quiet and unseen where I could tuck the pick-up away. I doubted this remote rural location would get much passing traffic. I hadn't seen a single car en route from the water tower. Dusk was settling now, too, so it was unlikely there'd be anyone around who might stumble across it and start asking questions. I found a suitable gap between a couple of trees and reversed in, ready to bug out quickly if necessary.

At the edge of the trees was a hedgerow that separated it from the outer field belonging to Turpinfield Farm. I set off at a tactical pace, scanning my front and keeping to the cover of the hedgerow, my day-sack on my back, my Glock keeping me company in my holster.

I reached the semi-circular patch of woods that surrounded the rear of Parker Farm and then trekked through the dense trees and bushes, searching for a good vantage point. Most of the foliage was in full bloom and far too thick for useful visual. I carried on until I found an area of sparser trees and greenery along the edge of another field belonging to Simms Livery Stables, separated from the woods by a post-and-rail fence.

The field contained some horses munching on grass. They were the last thing I needed. Livestock in fields were a pain in the arse. Their inquisitive nature had compromised many a soldier's covert OPs in the paddy fields over the water, and I didn't need half a dozen horses sticking their heads into my position when I was on target.

In the far distance, I could see the shadow of a house and a stable block but no lights were on. I made my way slowly and cautiously, parallelling the edge of the fence, using natural cover and the undulating ground, until I identified a good spot to establish a night-standing OP. It was a natural dip, with dead ground behind it and some frontal camouflage with a few bushes and a thicket of nettles. It wasn't as close as I would have liked to be but the fields of observation were good and I had an excellent panoramic view of the whole rear of Parker Farm.

I lay down in the dip, slowly slipped my daysack off and placed it in front of me so I could put my binos on top, an ideal observation aid. I pulled my balaclava down, took the Baikal from my daysack and placed it on the ground next to my Glock as I observed my arcs.

I checked the timer on my phone, synced to the countdown clock on the video box.

Twenty-five minutes to go.

It wasn't dark enough yet to use my night-vision goggles so I started to scan the target area to my front with my binos.

The farm was enclosed by barbed wire fencing. All was quiet. The only sound was the occasional snort from the horses in the field behind me.

I observed the target area and took in the detail. There was no one wandering around in the grounds of Parker Farm. The main house was about fifty metres away to my front. A light was on downstairs in what I could see was a kitchen but I spotted no one in the room. Another light was on at an upstairs window. I wondered if the house had a cellar, accessed from the inside. Was the red room in the house, underground? Or in one of the outbuildings?

To the right side of the main farmhouse building was a large wooden barn with a corrugated iron roof. It was in a state of disrepair; some of the wood on the walls had splintered away and had darker patches that I suspected were rot. It had a huge sliding door, big enough to allow entry for a lorry. A storage facility, perhaps, from when this was a working farm. The door was open, and from this angle I could see the rear end of the white van used to abduct Toni but couldn't see anything else inside. It was doubtful that was the place. It would have better security, for starters. They wouldn't want anyone innocently visiting the property – the postman, for example – to stumble upon what they were doing. The red room was a concrete structure, which meant it would either have to be built inside the barn, or underneath it, and why go to that trouble but not maintain the outer part?

So I turned my attention to the left of the farmhouse, where the other outbuilding stood at the end of a long driveway that ran up the side of the house. It was about the size of a treble garage. Flat-roofed. There were no windows I could see because my position only afforded me a diagonal view of one side and part of the rear.

But it was made of concrete. Old, crumbling, moss-covered concrete. It was most likely the place but I couldn't be sure. I'd have to sit it out and wait a little longer. If someone made their move towards it I'd have confirmation. But the prevailing thought twisting my gut was that one of them could already be in that red room right now with Toni, getting everything ready for the torture show they were about to put on, or maybe having their warped idea of pre-show fun with her.

A movement at the periphery of my vision caught my eye. I panned across with my binos, and there was Jimmy Delaney, exiting the back door of the farmhouse, lighting up a cigarette as he talked on his phone, laughing.

Fucking laughing!

Raging blackness rose inside.

I picked up my Glock and aimed it at his centre mass.

I had a clear shot, but I couldn't take it. Not from this far away. The Glock was short-barrelled, designed for close-quarter combat. And I couldn't afford to shoot and miss. Not when Connor and Brett could still be in the house. I'd give up any element of surprise. I couldn't use the Baikal, either, even though it had a suppressor to mask the sound. When I'd test-fired it, the accuracy on the Baikal was only good for short distance. My only option was to move closer and engage him.

I scanned the area, looking for some sort of covered approach. It was crucial that he didn't see me until I was able to neutralise him quickly without him raising the alarm. Speed, aggression, surprise: the old SAS maxim.

My heart rate quickened. Adrenaline pumped through me.

Delaney walked towards the barn to my right, getting closer. He was still talking but I couldn't make out his words. I was waiting for him to get inside it before I made my move. Take him out under cover of the barn and I wouldn't be spotted by prying eyes from the house.

I took a deep breath, watching carefully. Delaney stopped, turned back the way he'd come, still chatting casually. And then—

Something clicked in my head like a switch being fired, and I was no longer in a dip in the ground in rural Hertfordshire. I was in the compound in West Africa. Eighteen years in the past.

Explosions from the flashbangs roared. Gunshots. People shouting. Running. Hostages screaming. Everything playing out in double-speed. It drowned out the sound of the horses in the field nearby and my pulse hammering in my ears.

In my mind, I was standing over the rebel lying on the ground. I shouted 'Clear!' Turned away. Then everything slowed down as I saw the rebel's rounds catch Tony in the back. Saw Tony jerk forward as they hit his body armour. The fatal round hitting the base of his neck, its upward trajectory taking the 7.62 mm short round through his head. The kinetic shock causing massive head trauma. I watched Tony die again right in front of me before he hit the ground.

I blinked rapidly. Tried to slow my ragged breath. Tried to focus. My head swam, my brain tuning in and out. Past. Present. Flashes of memories from Africa mixing with the here and now, like I was under water in a storm, breaking the surface before being dragged down again into its unforgiving depths.

And then I heard a sound that snapped me out of the flashback. Less than a second later, before I could react to what my subconscious and ingrained self-preservation already perceived was some kind of threat, a heavy weight landed on top of me, knocking the Glock from my hand and into the dip.

My first thought was that a horse had jumped the fence and fallen in on top of me. But I managed to scramble around on to my back and dislodge the weight a little. Every synapse was alive with energy as I tried to work out what the fuck had just happened.

I came face to face with a man. Literally nose to nose as he was half on top of me.

Thoughts fired quickly through my head.

One: He was part of the gang who'd kidnapped Toni and he was their lookout.

Two: He was a dead man.

THE DETECTIVE

Chapter 43

It was almost dark and I had two choices. One, I could go back towards the country lane, get a better phone signal and call Greene with my suspicions. Or two, I could go and check out the back of Parker Farm myself and see if the van was there or find any sign of Tracy Stevens. I knew what Greene would say: that Connor Parker had no criminal record and wasn't known to us, that there wasn't enough for a search warrant, and that he didn't believe my theory anyway.

Looked like it was choice number two, then.

There was no evidence that Tracy had been shot at the Jamesons' house, which meant she could still be alive, and I didn't have time to waste on trying to convince Greene I was right. A woman's life could be at stake.

I climbed over the post-and-rail fence that separated the Simms's house from the field of horses. They were still at the far end to my right, thank God. The woods were just a blur of dark shadows in front of me as I walked forward slowly and silently so as not to attract the horses' attention.

I held my breath, alternating between trying to watch my footing and keeping one eye on the equine monsters. They were still at the opposite end.

So far so good.

I thought about turning the torch app from my phone on but there was a slight possibility it would be visible through the woods and I didn't want to take the chance of alerting Connor Parker I was nosing about.

I heard the horses now, blowing out air and neighing. One of them lifted its head and watched my trek across the field. Another one did the same. I couldn't see their eyes but I knew they were staring at me.

I swallowed and stopped walking for a moment, rigidly standing there, making sure they didn't move.

One horse separated away from the others and began to walk in a wide circle around to the back of my position. One more followed it.

Then another.

Sweat broke out on my forehead as two more horses circled around. They were still to my right but almost behind me.

I swallowed hard.

One of them started cantering in my direction.

That was when my fight-or-flight instinct took over and I ran towards the woods in front of me and the fence that separated it from the field.

I didn't dare look behind me as my legs pumped forward, but I could hear the horses' hooves chasing, closing in.

I tried to climb over the fence, but panic made me clumsy, arms and legs moving at once, scrabbling to get over.

I slipped.

And then I was flying through the air.

It all happened in a split second. One minute I was falling, and the next, I'd landed on top of some kind of hard lump.

I didn't have time to register surprise. Or the air being expelled from my lungs as the landing force hit me square in the chest. Or the wrenching pain in my stomach and shoulder. Because I was being flipped over on to my back by a man, and our positions were reversed.

He pinned me down, his forearm digging into my throat.

I struggled for air, trying to gulp in breaths and failing. Fear squeezing my throat.

Then there was a gun digging into my forehead as I stared into a face covered with a balaclava, two shadowy dark eyes the only features visible. My heart beat erratically. My vision swam with the lack of oxygen.

Two thoughts rushed into my head.

One: I'd found the bastard who'd killed the Jamesons.

Two: I was going to die.

THE VIGILANTE
Chapter 44

While my left forearm was digging into the bastard's neck, reducing his oxygen intake, my right was scrabbling around in the dip. My Glock had fallen from my hands when he landed on top of me but the Baikal was still resting next to my daysack.

My fingertips touched the Baikal's cold metal and then it was in my grasp and pointed at his temple, anger blasting through me because I'd missed an opportunity to take out Delaney. I wanted to lift my head out of the dip and check if he was still out there, but I had to deal with this problem now, and it would help if I had as much intel about their positions as I could get.

'Do not make a noise. Answer quietly only when I ask you something,' I whispered.

The guy looked like he was about to have a heart attack, clammy forehead, gulping for breath, his eyes frozen in terror. He nodded he understood.

'How many other guys are in there?' I asked.

'I . . . I don't know.'

'I'm not pissing about here.' I ground the muzzle harder into his temple to add emphasis. 'How many?'

He squeezed his eyes shut. 'I don't know!'

'Don't bullshit me. How many of your gang are inside?'

'I honestly don't know! I'm not working with them. I'm a police officer!' he whispered back to me and gulped in a breath.

I frowned. Lifting my forearm just a little, allowing him to breathe easier. *What the fuck?* 'You got proof of that?'

He opened his eyes, panted in and out. 'In my . . . pocket . . . warrant card.'

I released my forearm, keeping my gun in the ready position until I was sure, and patted his trousers down. Left-hand side. A mobile phone. Right-hand side. Something flat.

I slid my hand into his pocket and pulled out a wallet. Flipped the cover open. The light was dim and I brought it closer to my eyes, seeing a card in a clear pocket section that read: *DS Warren Carter. CID. Hertfordshire Constabulary.*

'Shit.' I leaned back, lifted the Baikal away from him but kept it rested on my thigh. I beckoned him to slide down further into the OP. 'What are you doing here? You need to start talking quickly. I don't have time to mess about. A girl's life is in danger.'

He sat half crumpled up, still trying to regain proper control of his breathing, forehead one creased line. 'Tracy Stevens? You're looking for her, too?'

'Who?'

'You don't know her? Who are you looking for, then?'

'You first. Talk quickly.'

He took a big gulp of breath. 'I'm investigating a double murder. The Jamesons – an elderly couple who lived behind here. Tracy Stevens was a suspect, but I think she was abducted by Parker and held at his farm. I think she managed to escape and went to the Jamesons for help, but he chased her and killed them because they were witnesses. I take it you're *not* working for Connor Parker, then, if you're asking who's in there? So who *are* you?'

'Let's just say I'm a keeper of justice, too. The people in that house kidnapped my goddaughter.' I lifted my head out of the dip. There was no sign of Jimmy Delaney and I couldn't hear him talking on the phone. 'Fuck!' I hit the ground with a flat palm. 'They're going to torture and kill her, like they've done to many other people. And they'll film it and stream it live to other barbaric fuckers who want to watch.' I glanced at my watch. 'I've got ten minutes left before they start.'

'What? *That's* what this is all about?'

'Look, I don't have to time to explain anything else. She's in there somewhere. There are at least three guys involved but I have no idea who else is there with them.'

DS Carter adjusted his position, peering over the rim of the dip, looking through the barbed wire fencing towards the house. 'Tracy Stevens could also be in there. After they shot the Jamesons, they must've taken her back here.'

I thought of the last video streamed on the red-room website. 'Did she have long dark hair, a leopard tattoo on her shoulder?'

'Yes.'

'I hate to tell you this, but she's already dead.'

'How do you know?'

'Like I said, they film it. I saw it. They beat her to death over an hour of footage.'

'Jesus.' He gasped and shook his head with disgust.

'What did they use in the shooting?'

'A handgun. Nine-millimetre rounds.'

I clamped my jaw tight and carried on watching the farm. 'I'm bringing my goddaughter out of there alive. Whatever it takes. I can't have you hindering me. Can't have you on the phone to your firearms unit and storming the place before I get her out. She might be dead by the time they arrive.' I didn't mention that I wasn't intending to leave Brett, Connor, Delaney, and whoever else was in there alive, either, and I didn't need a witness. A copper in the mix was a nightmare, but I had few choices now. I wouldn't shoot him, and I couldn't think that far ahead. I'd deal with that problem later. 'I need to restrain you and take your phone while I get in and out.'

I pointed the Baikal at him again as I slid some plasticuffs from the belt loops on my trousers.

THE MISSING
Chapter 45

I listen hard, straining my ears to work out what the knocking noise is that's started up again. It's faint, coming from behind one of the walls.

I step closer. Press my ear against the cold concrete, the hair grip still clutched in my hand. I wonder if the walls have some kind of soundproofing because it's a muffled sound.

And then it stops.

I take deep breaths to counteract the rising panic filling my chest, expanding with pressure, up, up, to my throat, to my head.

Then someone bangs on the door, and I jump so hard my shoulder knocks into the wall and the grip falls from my hand on to the ground.

'Just a few last-minute adjustments for the themed live stream!' the blonde one shouts from behind the door to me. Then he cackles with laughter again – a deep, ugly, blood-curdling sound that rakes through me.

The door unlocks.

I crouch down on the ground, facing the blonde one whose eyes are crazy. My trembling fingers slide over the floor behind me, desperately searching out the grip, trying to connect with the tiny bit of wire that's my only hope.

He steps towards me, a crooked smile on his face.

My hand scrabbles over the gritty, dusty surface, my chest about to explode with fear.

Where is it? Where is it?

He takes a step closer, and I let out a silent scream, my mouth open but my vocal chords frozen.

My hands work frantically but it's not there.

It's not there!

Then he towers over me and yanks me to my feet and pulls both arms roughly behind me.

I twist and stagger in his grip.

He pulls tighter, so my arms are at an unnatural angle, high up behind my shoulder blades, tugging at my muscles and soft tissue.

He laughs and says, 'Go on, struggle. I like it when they struggle. Better when they scream, though. And you'll be screaming your head off soon.' The weight of him pushes me forwards, towards the open door.

I try to dig in my heels, but I have no shoes and there's no traction to keep me holding on to firm ground. The rough concrete scrapes across my soles, and then I'm being pushed through the doorway along a narrow, dimly lit corridor. My gaze darts around manically, looking for escape.

A little further along is another wooden door, which must be the red room. At the end of the corridor are some steps leading upwards – they seem miles away. If I can run towards them . . . if I can get out of his clutches, they will lead me out of here towards freedom.

I grunt hard with effort as I twist my body towards the steps, trying with everything I have to wriggle from his grasp.

But there will be no freedom, no escape, because suddenly my arms drop down behind me and his heavy forearm circles around the top of my chest, pressing me backwards into him tightly. Squeezing, squeezing. And he has a knife in his other hand now.

'You ain't going nowhere.' He presses the blade to my throat and whispers in my ear, 'Do you know what this film will be called? Death by a thousand cuts.'

I freeze again, not wanting to risk the blade sliding in, cutting through skin and muscle and tendons. One nick to my carotid artery and it's all over. I don't want to bleed to death. *I don't want to die!*

But then suddenly I *do* want to die. Because having my throat slit will be a quick death. Not slow, agonising torture like I witnessed on that video.

So I press my throat harder against the blade. Feel the top of it digging into my skin. Feel a twinge of burning pain.

'Do it . . . now . . . then,' I manage to rasp out. 'Go on, just . . . kill me. Right . . . here.'

'Nah. Too quick. No audience. You're worth a fucking fortune.' He pushes at the back of my head, driving me forwards, towards the other wooden door. 'Besides, the big boss is coming up specially to do you.' He cackles.

My feet stumble. I try again to twist out of his grip, to struggle, but it's no use.

He pushes me through the doorway into the red room. Then he picks me up by my waist as if I'm not seven stone of living, breathing skin and bone. As if I'm nothing. I kick out, but my bare feet barely connect and do no damage.

He body-slams me on to the long wooden table in the centre of the room and leans his torso over my chest, his weight crushing me as he reaches for the restraints. They're thick leather, connected to the table with some kind of metal bracket. I try to move my arm. His grip on my wrist is too tight and he snaps the leather around my right wrist, tightens the buckle.

He reaches for the next restraint to tether my other wrist.

I bring my knees towards my chest. My kneecaps connect with his ribs as he leans over me, but it's not hard enough to hurt. So I try to buck my hips up to throw him off, but again, he's too heavy, too strong, and the weight of him is making it hard to breathe. The edges of my vision swim in and out of focus.

The cuff snaps around my left wrist. I tug against them but my arms barely move. They're locked in tight.

He eases off a little to twist around so he can restrain my feet in identical cuffs. I pull up my knees again and catch him with a kneecap to his cheek.

An eruption of pain flashes in my knee but the blow barely registers on him.

He laughs. Grips my right ankle and cuffs it to the table.

I try to kick at his head with my left heel, the only unrestrained body part I have left to use, but I have to bend my knee at a twisted, awkward angle and it only glances off his forearm.

My eyes bulge. My muscles strain as I push and pull and try to move.

Then the final cuff is snapped around my ankle and he stands back, stares down at me, his forehead sweaty, his eyes demented, a twisted smile on his face.

He leans over me, and I press my back against the table but there's nowhere to go from here.

His tongue licks along the side of my jaw, right up to my temple.

I clench my teeth tight, squeeze my eyes shut, and tremble as if hundreds of spiders are crawling around under my skin.

Then I feel a cold wetness on my face as he moves backwards and the air hits his saliva on my cheek.

I open my eyes and turn my head towards the door that leads to freedom and Mum and my house and memories of Dad. I want to tell Mum I'm sorry. I should've told her what was going on. It could've saved my life. I finally allow myself to cry, the tears pooling at the edges of my eyes before they snake down my cheeks.

He pauses for a moment, glancing up at another countdown timer high up on the wall.

Then he steps towards me.

THE DETECTIVE
Chapter 46

I didn't know the full story yet, but I'd been a copper for more than a quarter of a century, and like the sex worker I'd spoken to on the street had said, you learned to rely on your instincts. It had helped me solve a multitude of crimes, even if it had pissed off my bosses.

This guy could've been telling a pack of lies, but my gut was shouting loudly at me that he was telling the truth. I didn't know which one of those bastards had killed the Jamesons in cold blood – Connor or one of his accomplices – but the trail led here, and I was certain one of them had abducted Tracy and held her here. According to Balaclava Man, Tracy was already dead, and the death toll was a lot higher. Torture and murder on a live stream for people to pay to watch? I thought I'd seen and heard the worst of what people could do to each other in my long career but this was unthinkable. If this guy's goddaughter was in there, she was also in grave danger.

Although he didn't say it out loud, *Whatever it takes* spoke volumes to me. He had a gun and he looked like he knew what he was doing – ex-military, without a doubt. One of the Parker gang had already used their weapon on the Jamesons and it wasn't rocket science to figure out there could be a potential firefight or hostage situation if Balaclava Man went in there.

I had to call it in. Somehow. But even if I could get my phone out of my pocket without him seeing, it was likely there was no mobile signal.

What would happen to me in the meantime? I was a witness to a vigilante with a gun. A vigilante who obviously wouldn't hesitate to kill the offenders to get his goddaughter out of there. Would he kill me, too?

As he looked back through the barbed wire fence at the house, I eased my left hand into my pocket. My fingertips touched my phone.

I slid it out on to the soil next to me, my body hiding it from his view. I glanced down at it without moving my head, without giving myself away.

I could press 999 but even if there was a signal, the operator wouldn't know it was me calling. I could tap out a text to Becky but the light from the screen would show up as soon as I hit a key. I could press redial to call her, but again the screen would illuminate in the darkness, giving me away.

But then he pointed the gun at me again and the quandary was out of my hands.

THE VIGILANTE
Chapter 47

'Give me your phone,' I said.

'You don't need to do that,' Carter said, watching the gun carefully. 'My phone has no signal here anyway.'

'Pass it over.' I held out my free hand.

Reluctantly, he gave me his mobile. I put it in my pocket.

'Lie on your stomach with your hands behind you,' I said. Ideally, I would've restrained him against a tree, but I couldn't risk one of those bastards seeing him.

'Look, really. You don't have to do—'

'It's non-negotiable. On your stomach.'

He glanced nervously at my gun again and did what he was told, shuffling on to his stomach awkwardly.

I'd just plasticuffed his wrists together behind him when a noise jerked my head in the direction of the farmhouse.

The kitchen door swung open and Brett appeared, dressed in black overalls. The same kind of overalls I'd seen on the videos. He strode towards the concrete outbuilding with a smirk on his face, a balaclava in his hand.

Fuck. I'd wanted to plasticuff Carter's ankles and duct tape his mouth, too, but there was no time now. They were about to start streaming soon. But by the time he managed to get to his feet and get away and call his colleagues I'd be in and out and gone.

Hopefully.

'As soon as I do the extraction I'll come back and let you go,' I whispered. 'That's a promise. I have no fight with you. Stay down and stay quiet and you'll be fine.'

I watched Brett disappear into the outbuilding before picking up my Glock from the ground and tucking it into my pancake holster. With the Baikal still in hand, I leaped out of the dip and moved along the edge of the woods so I would emerge directly behind the concrete structure and be shielded from view of Connor and Jimmy and whoever else was inside the house, controlling the video stream.

I made my way up to the fence and quickly used my wire-cutters to open up the barbed wire fencing and climbed through the gap. Once on the other side I pushed forward to some cover at the back of the outbuilding. I edged along against the wall hidden from view, and when I came to the corner, I poked my head around, looking at the farmhouse.

No one was at the windows watching.

So far so good.

There were two large wooden doors at the front of the outbuilding but they weren't locked. One second later, I'd pulled one open, slipped inside, and closed it behind me.

THE DETECTIVE

Chapter 48

Shit! Fuck! Shit!

I rocked from side to side on my stomach, my shoulders groaning in protest at being hoicked up behind my back. I tried to pull my arms outwards, attempting to rip the cuffs, but it was no use. Of course not. The police used the same kind of plasticuffs, and I knew how strong they were. Unless I wanted to gnaw off a hand, there was no way I could get out of them.

I tried to think calmly, rationally. Tried to slow my breathing down. Panicking would most likely get me killed.

Think!

There was no point trying to struggle, I was just wasting energy and would probably have a heart attack in the process. If I managed to stand up, I could still run. Get away. Call it in.

I rolled on to my left side and tried to sit up, but my centre of gravity was all off and I flopped around like a beached whale.

I stopped. Took a deep breath.

Come on, Carter.

I pulled my knees in towards my stomach and pressed my left arm against the ground, attempting to sit up and failing.

Once. Twice. Three times. I was too old and inflexible for this shit. *Just do it!*

I dug my elbow into the ground and pressed upwards. Then I was in a twisted seated position with my feet tucked behind and to my side. All I had to do now was stand up. Easier said than done.

I rocked my hips. My core muscles were sadly lacking. If I ever got out of this, I'd take up Pilates.

I rocked a few more times, not lifting up more than a few inches. Something clicked in my shoulder and an almighty burning sensation stopped me cold.

I panted in and out, waiting for the pain to subside. My palms were slick with sweat. It trickled from my forehead into my eyes and I blinked rapidly, the salt stinging.

I pressed my knees into the ground, ignoring the pain in my shoulder as I pushed down with my hands at the same time, giving me some leverage. The movement wrenched my shoulder again and a loud gasp escaped.

I braced my stomach muscles and gave one almighty push.

Then I was on my knees, pushing upwards with my feet and, finally, I hobbled to standing, my limbs trembling with effort.

As I climbed out of the dip, I leaned my torso forwards, head down, like a charging bull, to counterbalance the lack of arm movement. My shoes slipped on the soil a few times, the unnatural angle throwing me out of whack, but then I was out and hurrying awkwardly to the post-and-rail fence of the Simms's house, suddenly with no fear of the horses that had now retreated back to the other side.

I hoisted myself on to the fence backwards, using my hands to lift me up before swinging one leg over and sitting astride it. I flipped my second leg around, felt a crunch in my hip bone as I did so, and jumped down. Actually, more like tumbled down, landing on my knees so hard my teeth smashed together, gasping through the pain behind my kneecaps. The only good bit of news was that it was easier for me to get to my feet again from that position, and after another round of huffing and puffing I was up again, running in the direction of my car, wobbling all over the place. Bizarrely, the catchphrase for the seventies kids' toy called Weebles came into my head . . . *Weebles wobble but they don't fall down.*

Adrenaline was making me lose the plot. *But you won't fall down, Carter. Keep going.*

I pumped my legs wildly, my pulse hammering in my ears.

I twisted over on one ankle. Sucked in a breath. Righted myself. Kept on going.

Eventually I came to the fence separating the stables from the Jamesons' farm. I repeated the weird backwards manoeuvre to climb over and ran to my car. Luckily, Balaclava Guy had forgotten to take my car fob, and I had a seatbelt cutter inside, designed to be used in an emergency if you were involved in an accident and couldn't release it manually. Never did I think it would be put to use for this kind of scenario.

I leaned against the car bonnet for a minute, overcome with giddiness. I bent over, my heartbeat so erratic I felt dizzy. A stitch had formed in my side but I tried to block out the stabbing pain and the throbbing in my ankle. When I'd caught my breath again I stood up and slid my hands across my back to my right-hand jacket pocket. I reached in and pulled out the remote-control fob.

My hands were so slippery with sweat that as I fumbled with it to press the button and release the central locking, it fell to the ground.

'No! No no no! Shit.'

I closed my eyes for a moment and tilted my head to the sky, allowing myself only a moment's self-pity before doing what had to be done.

I dropped to my knees on the ground in front of the fob. Scrabbled around with my fingertips behind me. Touched it.

Then it was in my hand and I pressed the unlock button.

I'm not afraid to admit that there was a tear of relief in my eyes. Or maybe it was just sweat.

I shuffled on my knees towards the driver's door, a stone digging painfully into my shin, then turned with my back towards it. I steadied myself against the car and slid upwards into a crouch so I could grab the door handle with one hand.

I popped it open and crouch-shuffled forwards, opening the door. Then I positioned myself so I could reach into the driver's side door pocket.

My fingers touched a CD case, a map, an empty crisp packet, and finally – finally! – the seatbelt cutter.

It was shaped like a miniature hammer with a groove down the handle that housed a very sharp blade.

I clutched the hammer end and tried to slide the plasticuffs into the groove. Missed. Tried again. The cuffs just slid along the smooth plastic and didn't catch.

I tried again.

Yes!

The plasticuffs slotted into the groove and I rubbed against the blade vigorously. It only took a few seconds before the cuffs were off and had fallen to the floor.

I wiped away the sweat on my forehead with the back of my hand. My throat craved water but there was no time to search for something to quench my thirst. More important things to do. The Jamesons' landline phone was out of battery, I didn't want to risk trying Emily Simms's house for a phone in case Roger had cut off the utilities after Emily'd moved out, so the nearest phone was at Bill Graves's house. I'd just have to smash a window and break in, but it would be quicker to drive there than run across the acres of fields.

I circled my arms around, getting back the circulation into my shoulders. The pain had subsided now but something was definitely clicking in my right joint. Then I got in the car and started the engine before roaring up the Jamesons' driveway towards the lane.

I was just pulling out when a sudden flash of headlights was upon me and a car blared its horn to warn me of its approach.

I stamped on my brakes and a BMW whizzed past; instinct made me turn my head and clock the number plate, even though it was going too fast for me to see who was driving.

It was a car I'd seen outside the police station car park. A car that belonged to whoever had been giving Greene a lift that day.

What the hell was it doing here? In the middle of nowhere?

It couldn't be coincidence.

Then everything clicked into place. Detective Superintendent Greene had repeatedly tried to ram down everyone's throat that the Jamesons' murder was a burglary gone wrong, despite no evidence to support that. He'd restricted the collection of forensic evidence, blaming it on budget cuts. He'd had us all running around on a wild goose chase, searching for impossible sightings of an unknown vehicle we were never going to find. Tied us up doing pointless house-to-house enquiries. Searching for a suspect who we'd never locate because she was already dead, if what Balaclava Man said was right, and how would he have known about her tattoo if he hadn't seen the footage he'd described?

Had Greene been got at? Pressured from above? It wouldn't be the first time. I thought of Lord Mackenzie's massive insurance fraud again. Greene had said the order to quash the inquiry had come from above, but what if it had all been Greene's doing?

Red, boiling anger rose. I'd thought Greene was just a useless copper, rusty from years in an office, blinded by bureaucracy, succumbing to pressure from the top to toe the line because he wanted to keep his cushy job and his nice, fat pension, but what if it was more than that? Was Greene corrupt? Or at least malleable by the corrupt?

The BMW driver I'd just seen must be involved in this red room. The live streaming of a snuff film was about to start soon. Where else would he be going?

I had a responsibility to uphold the law, but if I called in a firearms team there would be protocols and risk assessments that would take time. A hostage negotiator would probably be called out from God knows where. It was also possible there would be delays due to Greene stalling them so this man and the Parker gang could get away with everything. Other higher-ups in the brass could be involved for all I knew.

I also thought about Jeremy Wellham, the latest criminal to get away with his crimes. Thought about justice being eroded over the years. Yes, I was old school, but maybe that was the whole point. Before political correctness, paper-pushing, number-crunching and corruption got involved in the mix, the law was about protecting people and putting criminals away. And that vigilante with the gun was doing what the law couldn't, or wouldn't, do any longer. He was protecting his goddaughter, a victim of a kidnapping. A victim who was about to be brutally murdered like the Jamesons and Tracy Stevens. Knowing what I knew now, if my goddaughter was in there, I'd do the same.

The bottom line was a young girl was being held against her will, about to be killed. I couldn't just play by the rules now and let her die. By the time I called for reinforcements, it could be too late. And Greene and the BMW driver had already proved the rules didn't apply to them.

I knew then I was about to cross the line from good cop to vigilante.

THE VIGILANTE
Chapter 49

The outbuilding was filled with vehicles, pallets and junk. An old, rusty scrambler motorbike, a collection of dusty fire extinguishers, a chainsaw and baseball bat, metal toolboxes, an old armchair, tins of paint, vats of fertiliser, a JCB digger. The stench of musty dampness, engine oil, and something far more abhorrent hit me.

At the far wall were steps leading down under the ground. Light seeped upwards, partially illuminating the space.

I stealthily moved towards the steps, eyes scanning the shadows of junk, the Baikal outstretched in my hand.

Silently, I descended the stairs into a basement. There were two doors, both closed, but I could tell which one Toni was being held captive behind. Her desperate screams gave her away. I knew the layout of the red room from the video so I wasn't going in completely blind.

I kicked open the door and registered two things in quick succession.

One: Toni strapped to a table, eyes squeezed shut, whimpering now.

Two: Brett Parker leaning over her, touching her breasts.

Brett jerked upwards, away from Toni, but by the time his eyes could process the threat, he was wearing another one straight through the centre of his forehead.

His body went slack as the bullet lodged in his brain, killing him outright. Dead even before his knees collapsed and he fell to the floor.

Toni screamed.

'I need you to be quiet,' I said. 'I'm going to get you out of here.'

I turned and kicked the state-of-the-art video camera and tripod over, sending it smashing to the floor. Pulled out wires from the wall to stop any transmission. Registered the countdown timer on the wall still had six minutes to go. Prayed that no one in the farmhouse was monitoring a live feed yet which would compromise me.

I rolled my balaclava up so Toni could see my face.

Her eyes widened, mouth gaping open.

'I'm Mitchell, a friend of your dad's. I'm going to get you back home safely.'

She nodded blankly, clearly in shock. Then said, 'I know who you are. I've seen photos.'

I released the leather restraints one by one. 'Are you OK?'

'Uh . . . I . . . mostly.' She sat up and swung her legs over the edge of the table. She rubbed at her wrists with shaking fingers.

'Can you stand?'

'Yes.'

I took her hand. She stumbled off the table on wobbly legs and I led her up the corridor.

When we reached the top of the steps, I poked my head up and back down again. A split-second recce of the junk area.

No one was there. I heard no sounds from outside.

'It's clear. Stay behind me, OK?' I trained the Baikal on the wooden doors as we moved towards them.

I pushed the left one open an inch. From here I had a diagonal view to the kitchen door of the farmhouse. No one was rushing out to greet us.

I pushed the door open further.

And that's when it all started to go wrong.

THE DETECTIVE

Chapter 50

I gunned the engine and followed the BMW. I was a couple of minutes behind him, and by the time I'd driven down the lane to Connor Parker's house, his tail lights were disappearing through the electric gates.

I pulled to a stop along the verge, turned off the engine and ran towards the entrance, praying no one would see me.

The electric gates were closing now. There was a gap of about one metre.

Half a metre.

I ran faster and slipped inside just as the BMW pulled to a stop further up the driveway that ran along the side of the house and led to the concrete outbuilding.

I pressed myself against the wall. There was no security lighting there and I was hidden in shadows.

Connor Parker emerged from the front door of the house and strode up the drive to the BMW.

The driver got out of the car but he had his back to me and I couldn't see his face.

'You're cutting it a bit fine. We're almost ready to start,' Connor said, shaking the driver's hand.

I watched the intricate hand movement and gritted my teeth. I'd seen it before, many times in my career. A lot of coppers were Freemasons. The secret society that also included royalty, judges, top military brass and religious leaders. The powerful and influential. Was Greene a member of their lodge, too? Is this what his involvement was about? Protecting a fellow mason? Or was there more to it?

'What took you so long?' Connor snapped.

'Less of your cheek, sonny.' The driver got closer to Connor and poked his forefinger in his chest. 'Don't forget it's me who keeps you and our enterprise protected.'

I still couldn't see the BMW driver's face, he had his back to me, but I'd heard that voice before. It was distinctive. I knew who he was. And his presence here confirmed to me that my suspicions about Greene were correct, and this wasn't the first time Greene had well and truly crossed the thin blue line to protect someone.

Connor looked at his watch. 'You've got two minutes to get in there and suited up before the stream starts.'

'Well, stop wasting my time chatting, then! I'm ready to torture this bitch.'

They walked towards the outbuilding doors dead ahead of them.

I crouch-ran towards the corner of the house and pressed myself against it, watching.

The outbuilding door opened and I glimpsed Balaclava Man inside, the stricken face of a young girl behind him.

Connor stopped. 'What the fuck?'

The BMW driver froze.

Connor reached to the small of his back and pulled out a handgun which had been tucked down the waistband of his jeans.

Balaclava Man fired at Connor.

Connor darted out of the way and fired back.

The wooden door slammed shut.

The BMW driver shouted, 'What the hell's going on here?'

'We've got company, Jimmy! Get out here,' Connor yelled towards the farmhouse. And then he fired repeatedly at the door.

THE VIGILANTE
Chapter 51

I pulled the door closed and slid the interior bolt across. I'd wanted to get in and out quickly, unseen, but the last thing I'd expected was a vehicle pulling up outside.

'We're going to die, aren't we?' Toni whispered, her voice shuddering through the air in the semi-darkness.

I couldn't risk Toni being shot and killed in the crossfire. I'd made a promise to Corinne I'd bring her home safely, and that's what I'd do. I pressed the Baikal into her hand. 'Here. Take this. Go back down the stairs out of sight. Hold the gun as firmly as possible in both hands. If anyone comes, aim for the middle of their chest and keep squeezing the trigger.'

Her whole body trembled in front of me as her eyes pleaded with mine. *You have to get me out of here.*

More shots fired at the doors, splintering the wood. I dragged her backwards, further into the room and pushed her towards the steps. 'Go!'

She stumbled back down into the basement as panic took hold of me.

*I can't fail. I have to get her out of here. But we're fucking trapped now.
I need to clear the area. Clear it!*

The image of me shouting 'Clear!' to Tony in West Africa rammed
into my skull again. No way would I let that happen a second time. I
wouldn't let another innocent person be killed because of a mistake I
made. This time I had to make sure they were all dead before I brought
Toni out alive.

I drew my Glock from its holster and scanned the room, my gaze
hitting the JCB digger. I'd driven one before, a long time ago, but it
looked old, rusted. I had no idea how long it had been in here or if it
would even start.

I jumped up into the cab and saw the keys in the ignition. I turned
them and it made a tiny click but the engine didn't fire.

'Come on!' I turned the keys again.

Click.

More shots fired at the doors.

I twisted the keys and the diesel engine sputtered and sprang to life.

The JCB was parked too close to the doors to get a decent momen-
tum going. I turned off the handbrake, pushed down a lever arm
attached to the steering wheel to reverse and depressed the foot pedal.

The machine moved backwards, pushing the motorbike out of the
way and on to its side with a scrape of metal against the concrete floor,
crushing some rotting pallets against the rear wall.

When I'd retreated as far as I could go, I pulled on the joystick to
raise the digger bucket up so it was in front of the glass cab, protecting
me from Connor who'd been shooting from the driveway.

I pulled up the lever arm to move forwards. Gave it some throttle.

The wooden doors creaked and splintered outwards as I emerged
from the outbuilding.

A shot hit the bucket. Closely followed by another.

I moved the beast forward in a straight line, heading for Connor's
last position on the driveway.

More shots started from my diagonal right. Jimmy Delaney stood outside the kitchen door with a handgun, firing repeatedly into the side of the cab.

I fired back. Missed.

A shot fired from Connor.

Delaney shot at me again.

And hit me.

THE DETECTIVE

Chapter 52

I edged my way along the perimeter brick wall in the opposite direction to the driveway. I needed a weapon and the only chance of finding one out here unseen would be in the barn at the rear.

Shots fired out. A noisy engine started from somewhere behind the house that I couldn't see from my current position.

I jogged up the side of the farmhouse and the barn came into view.

When I came to the back corner, I poked my head round it. I could no longer see Connor or the BMW driver from this angle, but I saw another guy standing in front of the kitchen door, his back to me, a handgun angled towards the outbuilding doors, firing rapidly.

I ran into the open-ended barn and frantically looked around for something to use.

Steel barrel drums, the white van they must've used to kidnap Tracy, old agricultural equipment, dirty and neglected.

Next to a pile of chopped logs was an axe embedded in a chopping block.

I yanked it out and gripped it tight.

I moved to the entrance of the barn. The guy by the kitchen door still had his back to me.

There was an almighty crunching sound as a JCB exploded through the outbuilding doors.

The guy in my sight fired into the side of the JCB's cab.

I couldn't see Connor from here, but a gun fired from the direction of where I'd seen him on the driveway. The bullets bounced off the metal bucket raised in front of the cab.

Balaclava Man fired back at my guy.

I sneaked towards him, but I couldn't get too close because I'd get caught in the crossfire. My best bet would be to run back down the side of the house, enter through the front door and then come out of the kitchen door behind him and surprise him.

Just as I was running to the corner wall of the house, my guy fired again and hit Balaclava Man.

Balaclava Man slumped slightly and his head disappeared from view.

Change of plan. I sneaked up behind my guy, the sound of the JCB's engine masking my footsteps on the grass.

I swung the axe backwards and brought it down in an arc on top of his head.

He dropped to his knees, then fell face forward on to the ground.

I looked up at the JCB still continuing forwards. Locked eyes with Balaclava Man who'd sat up again.

Then I heard a loud scream.

THE VIGILANTE
Chapter 53

The Glock fell from my hand on to the floor of the cab. I ignored the burning pain tearing through my upper arm and leaned down, my hand scrabbling around to find my gun.

I grabbed it. Sat up and heard a loud, agonising scream over the engine noise.

The JCB had metal teeth on the end of the bucket. Designed for excavating and scooping up heavy loads. And impaling Connor Parker through the neck.

By the time I stopped the vehicle and jumped out, his screaming had stopped.

Connor was wedged between the front of the BMW and the JCB and very, very dead.

I ran towards the other bastard who had bolted back down the driveway and was trying to push a button on the side of the electric gates to open them.

He pressed and pressed repeatedly but nothing happened.

The irony wasn't lost on me. The very security Parker had designed to keep his captives in this compound of death was the same thing that kept this guy from escaping.

I slowed down and closed the gap between us.

He turned around, squirming his back against the brick wall, eyes bugged out with fear. 'I've got nothing to do with this! I'm just an innocent bystander.' He held his palms up, the standard *Don't shoot me* gesture. 'I . . . I was having car trouble, and I pulled in here to see if they could help.'

I grinned. 'Don't waste your breath. You don't have much left.'

I lifted my Glock, aimed it at his centre mass.

Then I heard a sound from behind. Before I could turn my head, Toni had run around me and stood side-on to the man, the Baikal in her hand, a crazed expression on her tear-streaked face.

'Please help me!' the man pleaded with her. 'Make him see sense. He's a mad man!'

'I *heard* you talking!' she hissed, her top lip curled. 'You wanted to torture me!'

'No . . . no, you've got it wrong. You misheard what I—'

He didn't get to finish the rest of his sentence because Toni aimed the gun at his leg and fired.

She was an excellent shot, too.

It hit him in the side of his right thigh. His knee buckled. He clutched his hands around the bullet wound and looked down at his leg, aghast.

Toni pointed at him again, her lips pressed together in a tight line. Her eyes hardened with fury. She was Tony's daughter all right.

'Please . . . don't!' the man gasped out between trembling lips.

'Toni, no,' I said. 'It's under control.'

She looked at me but didn't alter her stance. 'Why should I stop? I want him to suffer. What do you think he was going to do to me? We have to stop him doing it again.'

'Not like this,' I said.

She looked at him, bit her lip. Then finally lowered her gun arm so it was down by her thigh.

She needed this. She needed revenge. I got that. Torturing him was one thing. He deserved it. It was karma in a way. But I had no idea how far she planned on going, and even though we were in a rural location, someone could've already heard the shots and called the police. We needed to get out of there. And killing a person wasn't as easy as the movies made it out to be. Killing a person could haunt you. It would change you irreparably. I hoped, eventually, Toni would get over the horrific experience she'd been through so far, but I didn't want her to wake up in cold sweats in the middle of the night from a nightmare. Didn't want her suffering flashbacks and post-traumatic stress. Didn't want her to become me.

She stepped closer to the man and lifted her gun hand again, pointing it at him. 'You kidnapped me. You kidnapped all those people! And you murdered and tortured them in terrible ways.' Tears streamed down her cheeks but her voice was hard and unwavering.

'Toni, no,' I said, more forcefully. 'You don't want a death on your conscience. Believe me, I know.'

'He deserves to feel some of the pain his victims did.' She shot him again, this time in his right arm. If the circumstances of Toni being here weren't so tragic, it would've been comical because he didn't know which wound to clutch.

'Stop!' I placed a hand on her shoulder.

Toni snapped her gaze to me, then back to the man. She adjusted her weight, first one foot then the other. Gripped the Baikal tight in both hands, aim steady.

'It's not just me here,' I said, jerking my head backwards to where I could hear DS Carter's heavy footsteps coming up behind us. 'There's a witness. A copper. You don't want to do this. I can't let your life be ruined.'

I watched her thinking, fighting against my words in her brain. 'It's already ruined,' she said.

Then I pulled the trigger and shot the guy straight through the heart.

When the worst happened, I'd take the fall for her.

THE DETECTIVE

Chapter 54

I froze in place, apart from my chest heaving up and down and my heart clanging erratically beneath my ribs, and stared at the vigilante and the girl and Lord Mackenzie, the driver of the BMW. The man with friends in high places who'd got away with millions of pounds in his classic car scam. The man Greene had protected then and protected still.

I'd just killed a man with an axe. Watched his head splinter like a pumpkin. Felt the crack of metal slice open bone. Part of me was horrified. Part of me felt numb. But the bigger part of me knew it was justified.

I couldn't stop the girl shooting Mackenzie even if I'd wanted to. They both had guns and I had an axe. But I didn't want to. He deserved it. They all deserved it. For what they'd done to the girl. To the Jamesons to keep them quiet. To Tracy Stevens and the others I knew I'd find evidence about in the days that would follow. Maybe I was in shock, but I felt a sudden clarity for the first time in a long time. A picture of Jeremy Wellham's ex-girlfriend, Mandy, swam into my head. All those hours I'd spent with her in the interview room while she bravely recounted her brutal rape at his hands, even though she wanted to never relive it, never retell it. Her life ruined. Smashed to smithereens. The intrusive forensic examination that violated her all over again. The relentless questions asked of her.

I wouldn't put this girl through the same thing – a long investigation, countless interviews, a lengthy, stressful court case where their lawyers exploited the system. Courts weren't even interested in the truth. It all came down to who told the better story. If Mackenzie was allowed to live, no doubt he'd use his influence and connections to get away with his part in this horrific crime, too, just like he'd done before. I had no idea how deep the seed of corruption went. Did it go higher than Greene? With the kind of connections the Freemasons had, I doubted it would even get to court. Justice would never be served. The only way to end this thing and stop any other innocent people being murdered was if there was no one left to talk about it. With Mackenzie still alive, it was even likely he'd get someone to kill the girl. As a witness against someone who was so powerful they would want her silenced, and the vigilante couldn't be with her all the time. Or Mackenzie could do it all over again, with a new set of accomplices.

'It's not just me here,' Balaclava Man said to the girl. 'There's a witness. A copper. You don't want to do this. I can't let your life be ruined.'

'It's already ruined,' she whispered.

I closed my eyes, fighting the exhaustion and the emotion that pricked behind my lids.

Then a shot rang out that made me jump, but I didn't see a thing. I didn't really want to. Just knew that it *had* to be.

When I opened my eyes again Balaclava Man was bending over Mackenzie, rifling through his pocket.

'His name's Lord Mackenzie,' I said wearily. 'I think he was being protected by my boss. Maybe other top brass, too.'

The vigilante nodded as he pulled out Mackenzie's wallet and flipped through it, a tight frown on his face as he studied the contents. His balaclava had been removed now but I didn't want to look into his face. Didn't really want to remember who he was, even though I knew I'd never forget.

I looked at the girl. Blood was smeared over her face, her cheeks streaked with dirt and tears. There was a haunted look in her eyes that would probably never go away now. 'Are you OK?' I asked her, which was a stupid question, but my mind was wobbling all over the place. My hands trembled. I was definitely in shock.

She glanced at Balaclava Man. Back to me. He returned Mackenzie's wallet to his pocket then wrapped an arm around her shoulder, hugging her tight towards him.

She rested her head against him. 'Maybe I will be.' She paused then said to me, 'Thank you. For helping get me out of there.' She looked up at Balaclava Man. 'Both of you. If it wasn't for you, I'd be dead now.'

Then I laughed. Tension releasing. A pressure cooker of adrenaline exploding, dissipating. 'How the hell am I going to explain this crime scene?' I scrubbed my hands over my face. My prints would be on the axe that killed a man. *No. Killed a murdering, torturing bastard.* His DNA would be on my clothes, which would transfer to my car from the blood and brain matter that sprayed on me. My own DNA and fibres could potentially be all over the place.

'You don't have to explain it.' Balaclava Man dumped his backpack on the floor and crouched down in front of it, pulling things out – an all-in-one camouflage jumpsuit, an industrial bin liner, some plastic shoe covers, latex gloves. He handed them to me. 'Change of clothes so you don't transfer evidence to your vehicle. Put the axe in the bag and dispose of it. Then go home and wait for someone to report it.'

I looked at the girl. 'Your fingerprints will be in there.' Then looked at him and jerked my head towards the JCB. 'And your blood from the gunshot.' Blood seeped through his clothes now, glistening silky wet.

'Don't you worry about that,' he said. 'We'll clean up before we leave, but we all need to work quickly. Someone could've reported the shots.'

'The nearest village is six miles away. The only neighbour is out all night. Even if someone did call it in, the control room would most likely think he was rabbit-shooting again.'

But we all hurried, just in case. I took the items, not asking him how he was going to clean up. Then stripped down to my boxers, dumping my blood- and brain-matter-soaked clothing inside the bin liner. I pulled on the suit and gloves and picked up the axe to deposit it in the liner as well.

When I finally opened the gates and got in my car, I felt as if I'd aged thirty years. I wasn't just exhausted. I was weary right down to my soul.

THE VIGILANTE
Chapter 55

After it was done, I led Toni back through the woods and retraced the route which took us back to my cached pick-up truck in the laying-up point.

As I helped her into the vehicle, she stared at my arm. 'It looks bad. Is there a bullet still inside?'

I lifted my shoulder and inspected the ripped material of my sniper suit. 'No, it just grazed me. I've had worse injuries.'

Her eyes watered but she blinked the tears back, pressed her trembling lips together and nodded.

I looked into her eyes. Tony's eyes. 'You're OK now. You're safe.' I shrugged off my daysack and handed it to her as I got in. 'My mobile phone's in the side pocket. Wait ten minutes from leaving this location until you turn it on and call Corinne.' I shut her passenger door and climbed in behind the wheel.

'Safe,' she repeated, pulling the mobile phone out and clutching it in her hand. Then she turned her head to look out of the window into the darkness.

'There's water and food in a bag on the rear seat.' I started the engine and drove away.

'I'm not hungry. I just want to go home.'

'Don't worry, we'll be there soon.'

When we hit the A1M Toni dialled the number.

'Mum!' she cried. 'Oh my God, I didn't think I'd hear your voice again. I'm safe, Mum. I'm coming home!'

Corinne's cry of relief was loud enough for me to hear in the space between us.

I pressed down on the accelerator and allowed myself a smile. The battle was over.

THE DETECTIVE

Chapter 56

On the afternoon after the girl was rescued, I received an email to my private Gmail address. It came from an account made up of numbers and contained a link to a website. A website I couldn't access on Google. There was a brief message, telling me the site was on the dark web. But I couldn't access it. Not then. If my laptop was ever seized they'd want to know how I knew about it before the police had ever received a phone call about the massacre at Parker Farm. There were also screenshots of the website attached. Images that made my blood boil and my heart sink.

At the end of the email was one sentence that read: *I'm sorry I didn't thank you. If you ever need anything, call this number . . .*

Balaclava Man knew who I was, but I didn't know who he was. I'd seen his face at the end, but I had no intention of looking for him.

It took two days until the phone call came. Two days of lying to Becky and Ronnie. Two days of going through the motions, carrying out house-to-house enquiries in the villages surrounding Turpinfield, looking for Tracy Stevens, a woman I knew was already dead. Two days of trying to be civil to Greene when all I wanted to do was throw him up against a wall and pummel him. My acting skills were put to the ultimate test.

In my spare time, I'd been busy searching for proof of the connection between Lord Mackenzie and Detective Superintendent Greene and anyone else. I'd been going over the old case files from when Lord Mackenzie had staged the burglary and theft of his classic car collection, searching through his financial and phone records gathered at the time for something I might've missed before, but I found nothing. There was no way I could put in a request to investigate Greene's bank accounts or phone records. Not without a warrant authorised by someone higher up. And I had no proof yet to justify such a move.

I'd finally made a decision about my future but I had to wait to put it into action. I needed to be the detective on scene at Parker Farm as part of the investigation into what happened that night in case I'd missed any of my DNA. Then I'd have a legitimate reason for cross-contamination of any evidence left behind.

It was 10.16 a.m., and I was trudging back down the driveway of another house I'd just visited, asking if they'd seen Tracy, when the control room got hold of me.

'We've had a report from a postman delivering letters to Parker Farm who noticed a strange smell coming from somewhere behind the wall,' the operator told me. 'We despatched a unit and they've confirmed it seems suspicious, but they wanted to let you know before they forced an entry. Given the recent murder at Beech Lodge, they thought it might be connected.'

'Really?' I said, faking surprise. 'Thanks. I'll make my way over now. ETA ten minutes. Tell uniform not to do anything until I get there.'

'Received.'

I clenched my jaw as I got in the car. Inhaled deeply. Exhaled. Clutched the steering wheel.

You can do this.

When I arrived at Parker Farm, the same two uniformed officers who'd been first on scene at the Jamesons' murder were waiting outside for me.

'Morning, sarge,' the female said as I got out of the car.

'Sarge.' The male nodded at me.

'Morning.'

'I hope it's not another murder,' the female said. 'You still haven't caught Stevens and her accomplice, have you?'

I shook my head.

'We thought you should be called first. Could be another potential crime scene,' she said.

'Can you smell it?' The male officer scrunched up his face.

I took a step closer to the air and made a show of sniffing. The unmistakable stench of death that I'd come across far too often filled my nostrils. 'Yes.' I stared at the heavy metal gates. 'Have you tried them?' I asked, even though I already knew they would be locked from the inside.

'Yes,' the male said. 'They're electric. Can't shift them.'

'OK, let's get an Enforcer up here. Can you call the control room and get a unit up here with one?'

The male spoke into his radio, asking for the battering ram to be brought up so we could effect an entry.

It took an hour before an officer trained to use the Enforcer was located and made their way to us. Good job it wasn't an emergency. In that time I called Ronnie and asked him to come to the scene.

As Ronnie pulled up behind my vehicle, the gates were being bashed open.

'Gosh, that doesn't smell good,' Ronnie shouted over the noise, pinching his nostrils closed.

The gates exploded inwards. I stepped over the threshold, instructing the others to stay on the outside. I glanced up the drive. Saw the JCB with Connor Parker still impaled on it against the bonnet of the

BMW. I turned my head in the direction of the smell, towards Lord Mackenzie lying against the wall.

'Call out SOCO and the Home Office pathologist,' I said over my shoulder to Ronnie, stepping backwards. 'We've got another murder scene.'

By the time I'd retrieved a forensic coverall from the back of my car and was suited and booted, Ronnie was off the phone.

'I want you to start a scene log,' I said to him.

Ronnie headed back to his car to collect the paperwork needed to record everyone coming in and going out of the crime scene. When he came back, I looked at my watch, gave him the time and he wrote down my entry to Parker Farm.

I walked up the driveway slowly, in case anyone was watching me. It had to look authentic. I expected to feel self-loathing and disgust but I didn't feel much at all except a sense of justice.

The JCB had been set on fire – its shell now a burned-out wreck. Any of Balaclava Guy's blood spatters from his shoulder wound would've gone up in smoke.

I made my way to the concrete outbuilding, through the burst-open doors the JCB had smashed through. As I stepped inside, I instantly smelled something I'd come across many times before at the scene of fires. Fire extinguisher foam.

I smiled as I made my way down the steps to a basement. Everything was covered with the brilliant white foam, obliterating any evidence that the girl had ever been there. It clung to the walls of the red room and the holding cell, like the first fall of snow. Like fresh new beginnings.

Like light expunging darkness.

Balaclava Man hadn't wanted any DNA or prints left from the girl to be found in case they could identify her – most likely because he didn't want her to have to relive the ordeal. And also in case she could lead them back to him. It didn't matter that the red room had been obliterated, though, because in the days that followed, we found evidence too sick and twisted to comprehend. Multiple recordings of the numerous live-streamed torture and murders they'd carried out, partially dissolved bodies of the victims found inside steel barrel drums that contained sulphuric acid. Nine women, four men, two children. Some had been reduced to just bits of skin, hair and bone. Only Tracy Stevens's body was still in one piece, wrapped in plastic sheeting, no doubt to be dumped in a convenient location, thus ending the search for her and relegating the investigation of the Jamesons' murder to a cold case. With no links to any accomplice, the Jameson/Stevens file would gather dust in a pile in a storeroom. I pondered briefly why Connor Parker hadn't just taken the Jamesons' bodies and disposed of them in the same way as the other victims, but that would've sparked off a high-profile missing persons case and we'd have come sniffing around his farm, looking for the elderly couple, searching outbuildings and land, and he couldn't have that.

At that moment, I did feel something. I wanted to kill Greene myself. He'd miraculously gone off sick with a bad back when the news of Parker Farm broke. No doubt he was panicking, trying to cover his tracks, doing some damage limitation.

I went through the motions, gathering evidence. The full accounting would take months, but we'd begun to find a D-coin trail that led to some of the people who'd watched or ordered the torture of the captives. It would be a mammoth task to bring about prosecutions for all those who'd participated in the murders by ordering such abuse online. We also found digital communication links between Connor Parker and Lord Mackenzie but no money trail as yet. In the end, that didn't matter to me. They were all dead so none of them would be prosecuted. I was more interested in Greene, but I still had nothing to link him to any of it and there would be no authorisation to investigate him through official channels purely on a hunch.

I needed help, because I wouldn't let it rest.

I left Ronnie and Becky examining more paper trails and slipped out of the office on the pretext of getting sandwiches for them. I waited until I was out of the building and walking down the road before I called the number from the email.

Balaclava Guy picked up on the fifth ring.

'Does that offer of help still stand?' I asked.

THE DETECTIVE

Chapter 57

Three days later, I slid my key in the lock of my front door, craving a drink. I shut the door, loosened my tie and went into the kitchen.

I froze when I saw it.

As I stood and listened to the house for noises, I knew Balaclava Guy wouldn't still be there.

I picked up the thick brown envelope he'd left me and emptied the contents on to the table. Then I grabbed a beer from the fridge, opened it and took a huge swig before slowly reading through the documents. Some of it I already knew, some of it I didn't.

This is how the story went . . .

Lord Mackenzie was an old Etonian peer whose parents died in a car accident. At the age of thirty-three, he was left the ancestral estate, which comprised a Grade 1-listed stately home, a golf course, an island in the Caribbean, plus many financial portfolios. But he was a classic playboy, and his millionaire lifestyle slowly ate away at his inheritance. Last year, when he realised he was facing bankruptcy, he'd staged the theft of his classic car collection while he was conveniently at a charity dinner in London with bigwig politicians and royalty.

Enter Detective Superintendent Greene. After I'd investigated the case of the missing cars, I was getting too close to revealing Mackenzie's own involvement when I discovered a classic car salesman who met with Mackenzie in the weeks before the burglary to set up the fake theft. Then Greene had suddenly quashed the investigation on supposed orders from higher up due to what he'd said was lack of evidence, the salesman suddenly disappeared, and Greene threatened me with suspension if I didn't stop looking into it.

After Mackenzie collected on the fifty-million-pound insurance, he'd stashed some coffers away in an offshore account in the Cayman Islands. A bank I'd had no knowledge of. A bank where Greene also happened to have an account. Mackenzie had deposited a cool two million in Greene's account shortly after the insurance company had paid up.

There was the evidence of Greene's corruption in black and white, but how did they know each other? I'd found nothing to link the two of them during my own investigation into Mackenzie.

It was the final documents that revealed the answer. And I had no idea how Balaclava Guy had got hold of them. Photos of Lord Mackenzie, Greene and Connor Parker at their Freemason Lodge events, dressed up to the nines in tuxedos, wearing decorated aprons and collars and white gloves, arms around each other with beatific smiles on their faces.

I sat back in the chair, staring at the photos, a smile of my own forming as I reached for my mobile.

It was five thirty but a receptionist was still there, fielding calls.

'Professional Standards Department, how can I help you?' she asked.

'I'd like to make an appointment with someone from the Anti-Corruption Team, please.'

With a date and time set for the following day, I wondered for a brief moment if I was a hypocrite. I shook the thought away, though.

Yes, there was blood on my hands, but at least I'd done it for a good reason. I wasn't squeaky clean but I wasn't dirty. I wasn't corrupt. Sometimes the right thing to do is wrong. There were different kinds of justice.

I tapped my fingertips against the evidence on the table and thought about another call I needed to make.

I took a final swig of beer, set the bottle down and dialled Ellie. I wouldn't be joining her unit after all. I'd finally made my decision to retire. I needed a break. I wasn't just disillusioned any more, I was bone-tired of the ways people wanted to hurt each other, and I was done with policing.

I'd be leaving a shitstorm in my wake, but it would no longer be my job to untangle it all. And at least I was going out in style.

THE MISSING
Chapter 58

There are days when I wake up in a cold sweat, the nightmare so real that I'm back there, in that room, waiting to die. And other days when I feel like Supergirl. I cling on to the fact that I survived. I'm strong.

I'm not giving up. Not going to lock myself away in fear of everyone, every look, every sound behind me, even though Mum would prefer me chained to the house these days. I get it. I understand her worries. But I'm not living in another prison. I had enough of it in the time spent in that cell to last a lifetime. They didn't break me. They couldn't. Only *I* can choose to be broken or not, and I'm choosing Supergirl.

The papers and TV have been full of the sensational story. *Bloodbath Farm!* they've called it in their gleefully macabre reports. The body count is up to twenty-one now. Twenty-one people lost their lives and I'm the only one around to tell the tale. Except I won't be telling anyone. The perpetrators are all dead. The police corruption probe into Detective Superintendent Greene is still ongoing, but he's suspended, pending further investigation. That detective who helped saved me is also helping the Anti-Corruption Team with their enquiries. They don't need me. And now is a time to heal.

I know I'm lucky in many ways. There's more of my dad in me than I realised. We're all the sum of our experiences, and there's no rule that says mine have to shatter me. They will teach me to be a better victim advocate instead.

Talking with Maya has helped, too. Helped both of us deal with trauma, I think. She's a Supergirl as well, but I'm not sure she realises that yet.

Mitchell is spending more time with Mum. It's a slow process but I think there's something special there between them. Something that could last, if they're prepared to give it the chance.

The psychology and criminology course is going so well. My grades are high. I volunteer with a victims' support agency in my spare time. It's my vocation. My life's purpose, and I will not let my experience take that away.

You see, I refuse to be a slave to fear. I'm not afraid of the darkness, because stars can never shine without it. Evil can't be driven out by evil. Only light can conquer it. The only way to stamp out fear is to trample it beneath your feet and dance on its grave. That's the real power.

And maybe, just maybe, you can only truly understand light from the wisdom of darkness.

A NOTE FROM THE AUTHOR

Although all events and characters in this book are entirely fictional, *Into the Darkness* was inspired by the horrific real-life investigation into Peter Scully's red room in the Philippines. After an international manhunt, thankfully, Scully is now in prison, although he did escape the death penalty. For anyone familiar with Hertfordshire and Buckinghamshire, most of the locations in this novel are a figment of my imagination or a mix of places I know. If you're interested in reading more from Mitchell and Maya, you can find them in my thriller *Untouchable*. DS Carter is also featured in *Duplicity*.

Firstly, I'd like to say a huge thanks to my readers from the bottom of my heart for choosing my books! I really hope you enjoyed *Into the Darkness*. If you did, I would be so grateful if you could leave a review or recommend it to family and friends. I always love to hear from readers so please keep your emails and Facebook messages coming (contact details are on my website: www.sibelhodge.com). They make my day!

A massive thanks goes out to my husband Brad for supporting me, being my chief beta reader, fleshing out ideas with me, and putting up with me ignoring you when you're trying to talk and my brain's overloaded with plot noise.

Thanks SO much to JY again for all your SAS advice and input, and for bringing Mitchell's and Lee's military background to life. You know who you are!

Big thanks to D. P. Lyle, MD, for all your information on gunshot wounds. And for all the amazing advice you freely give to authors from your blog and books.

Huge thank you to Jenny Parrott for all of her editing suggestions, and to Gillian Holmes and Ian Critchley for catching all the things I didn't.

Big thanks to Emilie Marneur for all of her help, advice and support over the last few years, along with Laura, Sammia, Sana, Hatty, and the rest of the Thomas & Mercer team. It's very much appreciated.

And finally, a loud shout out and hugs to all the peeps in The Book Club on Facebook, and to all the amazing book bloggers and book reviewers out there who enthusiastically support us authors with their passion for reading.

Sibel xx

ABOUT THE AUTHOR

Sibel Hodge is the author of the #1 Bestsellers *Look Behind You*, *Untouchable* and *Duplicity*. Her books have sold over one million copies and are international bestsellers in the UK, USA, Australia, France, Canada and Germany. She writes in an eclectic mix of genres, and is a passionate human and animal rights advocate. Her work has been nominated and shortlisted for numerous prizes, including the Harry Bowling Prize, the Yeovil Literary Prize, the Chapter One Promotions Novel Competition, The Romance Reviews' Prize for Best Novel with Romantic Elements, and Indie Book Bargains' Best Indie Book of 2012 in two categories. She was the winner of Best Children's Book in the 2013 eFestival of Words; nominated for the 2015 BigAl's Books and Pals Young Adult Readers' Choice Award; winner of the Crime, Thrillers & Mystery Book from a Series Award in the SpaSpa Book Awards 2013; winner of the Readers' Favorite Young Adult (Coming of Age) Honorable Award in 2015; a New Adult finalist in the

Oklahoma Romance Writers of America's International Digital Awards 2015, and 2017 International Thriller Writers Award finalist for Best E-book Original Novel. Her novella *Trafficked: The Diary of a Sex Slave* has been listed as one of the top forty books about human rights by Accredited Online Colleges.

For Sibel's latest book releases, giveaways and gossip, sign up to her newsletter at: www.sibelhodge.com.